A SHOP IN THE HIGH STREET

Edward Jenkins has long dreamt of opening a shop in the small Welsh town of Pendragon Island. So, when his parents die, leaving the Montague Court Hotel to their two children, he glimpses the possibility of his dream being realised. Edward, though, lacks the will of those around him. His sister, Margaret, has her own plans for their inheritance and she, unlike Edward, has the determination to see them through. Can he, for the first time, stand up to her? Elsewhere on the island, the battle between the philandering Lewis Lewis and his long-suffering wife Dora continues to rage . . .

The latest instalment of the Pendragon Island saga.

Books by Grace Thompson
Published by The House of Ulverscroft:

A WELCOME IN THE VALLEY
VALLEY AFFAIRS
THE BOY SARAH
VALLEY IN BLOOM
FAMILY PRIDE
THE HOMECOMING

THE PENDRAGON ISLAND SERIES:
CORNER OF A SMALL TOWN
THE WESTON WOMEN
SUMMER OF SECRETS
UNLOCKING THE PAST
MAISIE'S WAY

Grace Thompson was born in Barry, South Wales. She is a widow with a son and daughter, four grandsons and one granddaughter. After her children grew up, she qualified as a nursery nurse and worked with children in care and schools. Then, following six years in Berkshire watching her grandchildren grow up, she moved back to South Wales, and now spends her mornings writing and afternoons walking the cliffs and beaches of Mumbles and Gower with her Welsh collie.

GRACE THOMPSON

A SHOP IN THE HIGH STREET

Complete and Unabridged

ULVERSCROFT
Leicester

First published in Great Britain in 1999 by
Severn House Publishers Limited
Surrey

First Large Print Edition
published 2000
by arrangement with
Severn House Publishers Limited
Surrey

British Library CIP Data

Thompson, Grace
 A shop in the High Street.—Large print ed.—
 Ulverscroft large print series: general fiction
 1. Pendragon Island (Imaginary place)—Fiction
 2. Domestic fiction
 3. Large type books
 I. Title
 823.9′14 [F]

 ISBN 0–7089–4236–9

Published by
F. A. Thorpe (Publishing)
Anstey, Leicestershire

Set by Words & Graphics Ltd.
Anstey, Leicestershire
Printed and bound in Great Britain by
T. J. International Ltd., Padstow, Cornwall

This book is printed on acid-free paper

1

Edward Jenkins of Montague Court Hotel and Restaurant stood in the pouring rain on an April evening, staring through the grimy window of an empty shop. It wasn't much on which to build a dream, but he envisaged the window clean, freshly painted, and filled with a display of sports equipment such as the small Welsh seaside town of Pendragon Island had never seen.

Until recently, when his parents had died leaving him a half share of Montague Court, he had pushed the dream of owning and running a sports shop far from his mind. With his commitment to the family business, and his sister Margaret determined he would never forget his responsibilities, he had given up all hope. Now, everything had changed. *He* had changed and the idea was no longer a fanciful dream, but a possibility. This tatty-looking shop was the chrysalis from which the butterfly of his future life would emerge.

He smiled at the well-worn metaphor, his thin schoolboyish features softening, the mouth relaxing from its usual tautness. He was a tall man, wearing a riding mac over a well-cut suit, a trilby protected from the downpour by an ancient umbrella. Like his conventional clothing, Edward had formal attitudes and an accent that clearly showed his background and schooling had been expensive.

Until very recently he had done everything expected of him: supported the family in their efforts to hold back the tide of progress; doing his duty and hating it. Then he had suddenly rebelled — stepped aside from a family entrenched in the traditions of monied background — and told his sister he would uphold the family business no longer.

It was exhilarating, but also frightening, to be completely alone, belonging nowhere and with no one.

Edward brought his thoughts back to the present and stared at the dilapidated shop in front of him, the appearance of which was worsened by the dark, wet, dreary evening. The name above the rain-spattered window was faded but he could still make out the words: William Jones, Draper.

The weather over the years had taken its toll, and mildew had added its camouflage colours. Water had made its relentless way through rotten wood and lay in an ever widening pool on the floor inside. The confidence that had spurted long enough for him to outsmart his strong-minded sister Margaret had quickly faded. As he stood there, hardly aware of the rainwater running down the large black umbrella and dripping onto the bottom of his trousers, seeping into his socks and the expensive leather shoes, he felt the last dregs of it fading away.

He was so alone. If only he'd found someone to share it, to be his partner, but, he admitted sadly, he wasn't that good at making friends. Once, a long time ago there had been Rachel, but Margaret had made sure she hadn't been waiting for him on his return from Egypt when he left the RAF. More recently there had been a rather foolish involvement with a woman called Maisie but she had left him too.

How could he consider running a business when he had no one to help or even with whom he could discuss his plans? It was hopeless. *He* was hopeless.

He heard someone running towards him and began to move away. But, as the approaching footsteps slowed to a walk, he turned back for one last look at the mess that was to have been the beginning of his splendid new life. He had been a fool to think he could do it.

The footsteps drew nearer then stopped

and he heard a woman's voice mutter, 'Damnation!' He turned to face the woman, now wildly waving her umbrella as she hopped about on one foot, trying to deal with a problem shoe.

'Can I help?' he asked hesitantly. Even from the single word he'd had the impression this was no helpless female desperate for a man to offer assistance. Then, as both umbrellas were tilted back to reveal the two people to each other, he recognised Megan Weston, once wealthy, spoilt and very confident, and wished he hadn't spoken. Megan Fowler-Weston was certainly no helpless female; in fact, with her overbearing, dogmatic personality, she was someone who unnerved him completely.

'Miss Weston. Have you hurt your foot?' he asked.

'Broken the blasted heel!'

Edward wanted to run away, make some excuse about an important appointment, but he couldn't. Unwillingly, he offered his arm. 'I'll be pleased to help you to a phone box,' he suggested, 'or, if you don't mind accepting a lift from me, my car is not far.'

'Your car,' she said peremptorily. 'And why should I mind?'

He didn't reply.

She walked on one foot and one toe tip as

they made their way around the corner to where he had parked his Morris Minor. He almost apologised for the smallness of it, remembering that her grandfather had once owned a Jaguar. Then he reminded himself that Arfon Weston — in fact all the Westons, Megan included — had since come down in the world and he now drove a more modest vehicle.

With the engine humming, she settled into the passenger seat, threw her sodden umbrella behind the back of the seat and kicked off both her shoes before offering a belated, 'Thanks.'

'Where would you like to be taken?' he asked as he took a cloth and wiped the misty windscreen.

'Somewhere miles from Pendragon Island, from choice!'

He hesitated, his hand on the indicator. 'North? South? East or west?' he smiled.

Edward was rewarded with a rueful smile. 'Sorry, I'm fed up with doting families if you must know. Drive me home, will you?' He was given directions to Glebe Lane where Megan lived with her parents, and set off through the heavy rain, which had emptied the streets of traffic.

He wanted to ask her what was wrong, but didn't know how to begin. He knew she was

5

expecting a baby out of wedlock, of course. That had been the source of gossip in the kitchens of Montague Court for weeks.

His sister Margaret Jenkins was having an affair with Megan's Uncle Islwyn, which was another source of kitchen gossip, but only when his sister was not around.

Groping around for a safe subject he dared to ask, 'When is the baby due?' then wished he hadn't.

'August,' she answered easily. 'It seems a long way off. Too far off to start worrying about it yet, but my mother and Grandmothers Weston and Fowler are fussing as if I were the first person ever to produce without the supporting arm of a husband.'

'You don't want to marry my cousin?'

'Edward! You've just gone up in my estimation!'

'Why? What have I said?'

'Everyone presumes that it was I who was 'left in the lurch', whatever that means. No one has considered that I did not want to marry Terrence. You are the first to suggest it. Thank you!'

Embarrassed, Edward said, 'To be perfectly truthful, I can't imagine anyone wanting to marry Terrence. He's far from my favourite person. I'd hate to think you married him for the sake of giving the baby a name.'

'What were you doing staring into an empty shop, Edward?' she asked a moment later.

'Oh, I was just, I was — '

'It's all right. You don't have to tell me. Just because I unburdened my soul to you, doesn't mean you're obliged to reciprocate!' Her loud, confident voice made her sound irritable even when she wasn't. This time she took the sting out of her sharpness with a smile.

'All right, if you want to know, I want to open the depressing-looking place as a sports shop. There, aren't you going to tell me how stupid I am? That the town doesn't have the need of one? That I'll fail because I'm not friendly enough? That I'll end up destitute, having lost all my money?'

'I think it's a brilliant idea. If it weren't for The Lump,' she patted her slightly extended stomach, 'I'd offer to help!'

'My turn to say thanks,' he grinned.

Megan was surprised by the difference the smile made to his bland face. He normally wore a sombre, slightly nervous expression and appeared ready to apologise the moment someone approached him. Now this unexpected encounter seemed to have relaxed him. His eyes glinted in the darkness and his teeth showed even and white. She realised

7

that he was much younger than she had previously thought.

'To take over the old draper's shop and transform it will be costly,' she coaxed and waited for his reply. She watched him in the gloom of the evening, guessing from his slight frown that vanished the smile without trace, that he was undecided whether or not to continue to discuss it. 'Starting from nothing — in fact, less than nothing, seeing the awful state of the place.' Still no response. 'You'll need an awful lot of capital to buy the property, clean it up and stock it sufficiently to attract buyers. It isn't an impossible dream though.'

She knew she had said the right thing; his frown lifted and he turned to her and asked, 'Megan, will you come with me tomorrow and look at it?' Then, regretting the impulse he quickly added, 'but there, I don't suppose you have the time, a busy young woman like you. Sorry I mentioned it.'

'Why me?' she enquired, ignoring his retreat.

'I shouldn't have asked you, but I need a second eye on the place. I don't think I see clearly because I want it so much.'

'What fun!' she smiled. 'Shall we say two o'clock? I have a ghastly visit to the doctor in the morning, to make sure The Lump is making good progress.'

'You'll come?'

'Try and stop me!'

Edward watched her walk away, limping up the path on her broken shoe to her front door and letting herself inside, while he idled the car engine and held back from letting in the clutch. He felt slightly embarrassed, wondering what the forthright Miss Megan Fowler-Weston would think of the almost derelict property. It looked even worse inside. He sighed, accepting the inevitable, that he would walk away after their two o'clock appointment convinced that he would never succeed in creating his own little empire. He could almost hear his sister Margaret's laughter at his failed and costly efforts.

He drove back to Montague Court in time to clear the last of the dishes and set the tables for breakfast, wishing he were miles away from the seaside town of Pendragon Island. But where he would like to be, he had no idea. A ship without a rudder, that's me, he sighed.

★ ★ ★

Megan was waiting for him when he reached the old draper's shop the following day. Edward was tense, having had an argument with Margaret about his refusal to finish his lunchtime duties and, seeing an offended frown on Megan's face — probably because he'd had the audacity to keep her waiting — he showed less than his usual politeness as he said, 'Don't start. I was unavoidably held up.' He felt a frisson of excitement as she opened her mouth to speak, then closed it again without uttering a word. For a moment he wanted to apologise but held it back. The next few minutes would give her plenty of chances to get her own back!

To his surprise she didn't react unfavourably at once, but walked around the double-fronted premises in silence. She followed him into the back room where the draper had once kept his stock but which was now a mess of broken shelves and unrecognisable clutter.

A door which squealed its protest on the red and black tiles was opened to reveal a kitchen which, in turn, led down rickety steps to a small, completely overgrown garden.

'Hard to imagine, Edward,' Megan said then, 'but this faces almost due south and would be a sunny and a pleasant place to sit.'

'I always feel there's something sad about an abandoned garden, although heaven knows why I think so. I've never so much as cut a blade of grass, and I wouldn't know which way up to plant anything. I can't even name these trees.'

'You have bramble, nettles, some optimistic ash and sycamore trees and the ubiquitous buddleia,' she said with authority.

They left the tangle of vegetation and went back inside. 'Pretty hopeless, eh?' Edward said with a shrug, feeding her with words.

'D'you think so? I was imagining it once someone like Mrs Collins — Victoria's mother — had had a few days here. It really wants little more than a good clean. Then there's the Griffithses. Good at odd jobs they are. Get them to clear out all the rubbish first, then get them back to do some painting and you'd have a place burgeoning with possibilities.'

'I thought you'd tell me to forget it.'

'Well if you're that defeatist you might as well,' she said, the sharpness returning to her voice.

'You're right. I expect to fail. It's time I changed all that, isn't it?'

'I should say so.' She looked at him, staring in a way that made him edgy, like a pupil before a headmistress's accusations. 'I can't do anything really useful, Edward, because of The Lump, but I'm bored and I'd enjoy helping with the planning. In fact, if you decide to go ahead, I'll go with you to see

Frank Griffiths and get him to agree to the cleaning-up process. Phone me when you decide.'

'We haven't sold Montague Court yet. There have been viewers but I suspect most of them have been local people curious to see inside what was once a manor house and is now in the reduced circumstance of a restaurant and hotel. I also suspect,' he added slowly, 'that my sister is discouraging those who do show interest.'

'Then be there yourself. You can find out from the agent when to expect prospective buyers if Margaret is devious.'

'Yes, of course. That's what I'll do. And there are ways of getting started without waiting for a sale. The agent explained it all to me.'

'So?' Megan said with a touch of impatience, 'So will you continue to think about it? Think and think until the opportunity is gone?'

'I have decided,' he said and it was as though he was listening to someone else talking. 'I am going to do it.'

She didn't enthuse or even show surprise, she just said, 'We'll go and see Frank and Ernie Griffiths this evening. Call for me at seven.'

Going back to the estate agent, Edward

explained that he wanted to buy the shop but until the estate was settled he wasn't able to commit himself, and after long negotiations with the owner, a contract was drawn up for one year's rental during which time he had the opportunity to buy. He went home feeling more drunk than sober even though he hadn't touched a drop. He left the office trembling with that now familiar mixture of fear and excitement.

★ ★ ★

The rain had stopped and a weak moon showed itself as Edward knocked on the door at seven o'clock. Megan didn't invite him in, she was waiting for him and came out immediately.

'We'll walk, it isn't far and I feel the need to stretch my legs after a day of rain.'

He locked the car and they set off together, chatting easily about the work needed and the sequence in which it should be done. He had some letters to post and they were passing her grandparents' house on the way to the main post office, when they heard shouts. A man ran out of Arfon and Gladys Weston's gate and pushed past them. Edward steadied Megan before seeing her grandfather shouting and gesturing for him to chase the man.

He ran a short distance down the road and amazingly caught up with the man, who was of equal height as himself and about the same weight.

'Get off me you damned fool,' the man muttered, his voice surprising Edward by its well modulated tone. He grabbed the man's shoulder and tried to swing him around; he wore a mask, and as Edward made an attempt to remove it, he lost his grip. The man wriggled violently and made his escape.

'Sorry, but he got away,' he apologised. 'But I heard him speak and he didn't sound like a working-class chancer. He was educated and from the way he struggled, very fit.'

Arfon was hugging Megan and he said gruffly, 'Are you all right my dear? Not hurt? You'd better come in.' Arfon peered at the man now standing beside his granddaughter and added, 'Edward Jenkins isn't it? You'd better come in too. Hurry Megan, I need to call the police and you can help settle your grandmother.'

'Police? Grandfather! For goodness sake tell me what happened?'

'Someone tried to rob us that's what, but we're all right. No one harmed. What cheek! At this time of an evening too!'

Going into the large, well-furnished house

overlooking the docks, Edward felt uneasy. This wasn't his affair, and it would be best if he left. He began to excuse himself from staying, but Megan insisted he waited until the police arrived, so he went into the kitchen and made tea while Megan comforted Gladys and Arfon who were complaining loudly.

*　*　*

The thief stopped not far from where he had lost sight of Edward and took a breath. Then he walked slowly and casually through the streets back to the house he shared with Barbara Wheel and their two daughters. The accent had been a sudden improvisation and it had given him an idea. Tomorrow he would go into Cardiff and buy himself a really smart suit, shirt and some shoes. The police investigating the robberies wouldn't be looking for someone like Percy Flemming, assistant gardener, would they? Not if the intruder had been described as well dressed and with a 'posh' accent.

*　*　*

The police arrived and Arfon went into what Gladys called his public speaking mode, and in a pompous voice described how he and Gladys heard something and went to investigate and saw a man in the hall. Arfon made much of the way he chased the intruder; Gladys cried a little and Megan and Edward added what they knew, before they abandoned their intention to visit the Griffithses and Edward took Megan home.

When they had gone, Gladys looked at Arfon with disapproval on her face. 'What is our granddaughter doing with Edward Jenkins, Arfon? I don't think he's a suitable companion, do you?'

'Nonsense, dear. He's pleasant enough. Good family and all that.'

'I suppose so, although with that cousin of his seducing Megan and leaving her in the lurch, causing us all such trouble, and his sister Margaret stealing Sian's husband, they're hardly a good family any more.' She frowned. 'But if Megan likes him, shall I invite him to tea?'

'Oh that'll be fine, won't it! Shall you invite his sister Margaret as well? His sister and Islwyn? Our Sian's husband who she ran off with?'

Gladys shook her head. 'Best not, dear.'

★ ★ ★

16

Dora Lewis sat in her living room filling in the details of the day's takings at the Rose Tree Café. Every time she completed a column of figures she was aware of the silence. The house had once rattled with the noise of a lively family: herself, Lewis Lewis her husband, and their three children. Now she was separated from Lewis and he was living across the road with their daughter and her family.

After a brief attempt at reconciliation with Lewis, soon after their daughter's marriage, she was on her own once more. Lewis had slipped quietly into her bedroom a few nights after his return to number seven Sophie Street and although she wanted him so much that her love and need of him was a continual ache, she had sent him away. Pride, or fear of being let down again when he found another woman, had been too much for her to bear.

With their son Lewis-boy dead and his widow remarried to one of the Griffithses, and their other son Viv married to Megan's sister Joan, she had hoped that her daughter Rhiannon would stay, at least for a while, until she accustomed herself to the emptiness.

But now Rhiannon was married to Charlie Bevan and living across the road. They were all gone and seven Sophie Street felt like a barn.

Dora reached over and picked up a wedding photograph of Rhiannon and Charlie with Charlie's son Gwyn. Newly wed and burdened with Lewis sharing their home. It wasn't right. And here she was, sitting alone in the family home with empty rooms mocking her.

She wanted Lewis back so badly. But, afraid he would let her down again, she ignored his pleading eyes and showed no one how much she still loved him. The fact that her errant husband was sharing his daughter's house just yards away and wanted to come back, was like a forbidden treat, a reward unearned and ungiven.

She hadn't believed him when he had told her he was moving in with the young newly-weds across the road. But today the car had been parked outside her house while Lewis had carried a rather bedraggled assortment of clothes into Rhiannon and Charlie Bevan's home.

It was blackmail, she was aware of that. Rhiannon and Charlie were just married and needed time to themselves; Charlie's son, Gwyn, wanted to be with his father and his new stepmother without interference from anyone, let alone Rhiannon's father, who had resented Charlie Bevan from the moment he had seen his daughter talking to the man whom he still referred to as 'that jailbird'.

She should offer Lewis a room here, in the home they had once shared, but she had been hurt so much she couldn't face it. Rhiannon understood and Charlie understood, but that didn't make Lewis living there a good thing.

Dora pushed the photograph away from her and stared into the fire. The silence of seven Sophie Street settled around her and she felt chilly draughts she had never before been aware of, and felt the expanse of emptiness reminiscent of hiding in vacant, soulless houses as a child, waiting for a friend to find her and shout with glee.

Just how long she could cope with the silence, the hollowness, the realisation that she was unneeded, she didn't know. Thank goodness she and Sian Fowler-Weston had their café.

Both women had been left by their husbands: Lewis to live with Nia Williams who had since died, and Sian's husband Islwyn to live with Margaret Jenkins at Montague Court. For both of them, the Rose Tree Café, near the boating lake, was their sheet anchor. Coming home, to the empty unwelcoming house, was like being stranded by the outgoing tide.

Lewis Lewis, Dora's estranged husband, finished taking his belongings into Charlie and Rhiannon's spare room. He stood at the window and stared across at number seven, where a light shone bleakly through closed curtains. He imagined Dora sitting there and wished he was with her. He had treated her badly, leaving her for Nia Williams who had died in a tragic accident leaving him bereft. Now he no longer had a place in his family, no place to live, and no one to hurry home to. Rhiannon had accepted him here under sufferance, and he knew he would be expected to stay in his room rather than share the evenings with them. Lewis Lewis was not good at being alone.

He ran down the stairs and called, 'Rhiannon, love, I think I'll just go to The Railwayman for an hour, perhaps see Viv there.' Swallowing his unwillingness he added, 'Fancy coming, Charlie?'

'No thanks, we're going to see the Griffithses. Rumour has it they've got some baby goats and Gwyn would love to see them.'

'Right then.' He patted his pocket. 'I've got a key, so I'll see you later.' He went out, walking up the road aware of disappointment, wishing Charlie and Rhiannon had invited him to join them for their walk to the Griffiths' house, but knowing he could expect nothing more.

He stopped on the corner and looked at the sweet shop called Temptations. Nia Williams, the woman for whom he had left Dora, had owned it and his daughter, Rhiannon, had been working there for a couple of years. With Nia dead, it was now owned by Nia's son Barry. There was a light in the flat above the shop and he wondered idly whether it had been rented out, and to whom.

Since his son Viv had married Joan Fowler-Weston, he was no longer a regular visitor to The Railwayman, so it was with pleasure that Lewis recognised him sitting in a corner with Frank and Ernie Griffiths and Jack Weston. They were deep in discussion about something and he hesitated to join them, going instead to the bar to order a pint. He glanced across and pretended to have just noticed them when Viv raised a hand and beckoned him over.

'Want a job, Mr Lewis?' Frank said, a lugubrious expression on his long face.

'Not unless it's well paid, with a car and plenty of perks. Why, what's up?'

'That Edward Jenkins bloke from Montague Court came to see me this afternoon. Seems he's buying old Jones the Draper's shop and wants me and our Ernie to clean it up a bit.'

'A bit?' Lewis groaned theatrically. 'It was a mess before the old man closed down. More rats than customers was what I heard. And spiders as big as a man's hands and cockroaches to fill a man's shoe.'

'Thanks! That's cheered me up no end.'

'He isn't going to be a draper is he? A bit too posh for anything like that I'd have thought,' Lewis said, taking a chair from another table and sitting down.

'Sports shop I believe.'

Lewis joined in the discussion as the viability of the business was considered, but his mood was melancholy and he edged away from it and stared around the room, hoping to find more interesting company. Molly Bondo came in and caught his eye, but he didn't react. If he were seen talking to the local prostitute he'd never be allowed back into number seven Sophie Street! Somehow he had to behave himself for as long as it took for Dora to forgive him, or take pity on him, whichever came first.

* * *

22

Edward's sister Margaret was in a dilemma. She had begun arrangements for the house to be extended and a swimming pool added, before Edward had dropped his bombshell, telling her he wanted the house sold to release his half of the value. With Islwyn Heath-Weston, who shared her worries and her bed, she was going through the accounts trying to find a way to continue with her plan without Edward's money. It all seemed hopeless.

'There are two separate prospective buyers coming this afternoon,' Islwyn said, handing her the diary.

'I don't want to sell,' she said despairingly.

'There isn't an alternative, my dear. Edward saw to that.'

'My stupid brother. Why can't he see what he's throwing away? With the improvements we'd planned, Montague Court would be a real money-spinner. People are thinking more and more about holidays, and offering them a stay in an impressive house like Montague Court, a place with such a history, and treating them like high-class ladies and gentlemen, it would have had strong appeal, I know it would.'

'We should have brought him into the discussions sooner.'

'It wouldn't have made any difference, Issy.

23

My brother isn't a reasonable man.'

The first of the viewers were shown around by Islwyn, who pretended to work for the family. Offering warnings as asides throughout his tour of the beautiful old building, he managed to convince them that it had every kind of rot and most insect infestations.

'We can't always be that lucky,' he sighed as Mr and Mrs Threedling walked away.

Islwyn was just setting out with the second of that day's viewers when to his disappointment, Edward returned.

'Thank you, Mr Heath-Weston, but I will attend to Mr and Mrs Grant.' For a moment Edward thought Islwyn was going to argue but Edward snatched the notepad from him and smiled politely at the prospects and invited them to follow him.

Annie Grant was a small, neatly dressed woman in her forties and when she spoke her voice was gentle. Leigh Grant was louder in dress as well as voice, wearing a rather bold check jacket and grey trousers, and a shirt and a discordant tie. He appeared the more confident, yet it was to his wife he looked when queries were raised and it was she who asked the most pertinent questions.

Edward explained that Montague Court had been their family home for more than three hundred years.

24

'Death duties and repairs forced our parents to sell the estate, including woodlands and a couple of farms, eight smallholdings, and a sawmill. For the last few years we have managed the house as an hotel and restaurant to keep it in the family. But that is no longer possible.'

'You'll regret selling it?' Leigh Grant asked.

'Not really. It's my sister Margaret who has strong historic fervour. I want a life free from worries about the roof and the prospect of damp and woodworm and the rest.' He smiled then, guessing what would be Mrs Grant's next question. 'It has been treated for those things and so far as I know there aren't any serious problems about to emerge. But you'll check everything of course?'

'We'd need to have a survey,' Mr Grant said. He turned to his wife and asked, 'What d'you think of it Annie? Would you be happy here?'

Edward slowly guided them around the spacious, beautifully proportioned rooms, entertaining them with an occasional anecdote about how they had been used in his grandmother's time and he knew they were impressed.

When Mrs Grant asked whether the curtains and carpets would be available to buy, Edward felt a surge of hope. He wrote

25

the name of his solicitor on the notepad and handed it to them.

'You have our telephone number, but I'll write it down again for you. Please will you speak to me when you have a query, or if you would like a second look? My sister gets so upset you see,' he explained. After the reminder from Megan, he knew he didn't want Islwyn or Margaret talking to, and discouraging, them. 'It's important you deal with me over this.' He hoped they wouldn't give Margaret and Islwyn a chance to intervene. He needed to be free of the place as soon as possible so he could concentrate on the sports shop.

* * *

When Islwyn and Ryan had married Arfon and Gladys Weston's twin daughters, they had been given a life of comparative luxury. Neither worked very hard, leaving the running of the Weston's Wallpaper and Paint Stores to a succession of managers, the most recent being Dora and Lewis's son Viv.

While idling their time and digging into the till when they needed extra money, the business had failed. Then a series of disasters had hit the family and Arfon had sacked them both. To their further fury, Viv Lewis had been given the position of manager.

Sian's husband, Islwyn, had found work in a fish and chip shop, an occupation chosen mainly to embarrass Old Man Arfon into giving him his job and salary back. To his disbelief, Arfon had refused and had allowed Viv Lewis not only to stay, but had given him a partnership. His long-time affair with Margaret Jenkins had provided him with an escape and when his wife, Sian, sold their home to give the money to Arfon and Gladys, he had left her to live with Margaret at Montague Court.

Ryan, who was married to Sally, hadn't worked at all. He had just sat idly watching as Sally rearranged her life and took in paying guests to provide them with an income. For a while he found it amusing, but gradually the thought that his wife was managing to keep their home, providing for himself and their daughter Megan by her efforts, was making him more and more tense.

Old Man Arfon showed no sign of relenting and, to add to his unhappiness, his brother-in-law Islwyn seemed to have found himself a very comfortable life at Montague Court, and his daughter Megan was expecting an illegitimate child.

The hardest part was their openness about their misbehaviour. Islwyn made no pretence of the fact he was living with Margaret Jenkins, sharing her bed, and unrepentant about Sian's humiliation, and Megan seemed inordinately proud of her predicament, flaunting her disgrace instead of hiding away and making plans to dispose of the baby. She was out and about without a moment's embarrassment and telling everyone that she was keeping the child. He rose out of his chair and hurried from the house. It was all too much.

* * *

Islwyn had a visitor that afternoon. To see his brother-in-law, Ryan, walking along the drive of Montague Court was a surprise. Since he had walked out on Sian, no one in the family had spoken to him. He hadn't even seen any of them except his schoolteacher son, Jack, who had begged him to go home. Seeing his brother-in-law approaching and obviously in a bad mood, he presumed Ryan was intent on making the same request.

'Ryan. What a surprise. Come to tell me to go back to my grieving wife, have you?'

'No I haven't,' Ryan said glumly. 'Why should you when you've landed yourself with all this?' He waved an arm around the house and its gardens.

28

'It isn't as good as it looks,' Islwyn said, getting into step with Ryan and edging away from the house. 'Margaret is having to sell. That stupid Edward is being uncooperative.'

'Stupid? He's managed to scupper your plans rather neatly!'

'Not yet he hasn't.'

'You're still better off than if you'd stayed with your wife, sharing that rabbit-hutch of a house in Trellis Street. Especially with her out all day working at that damned Rose Tree Café with Dora Lewis. You'd have been reminded every day what a failure you are.' Ryan sighed. 'What a mess eh? My having to keep out of the way in my own home, as Sally entertains strangers and gives them the attention she should be giving me, and you — ' he tilted his head and smiled sarcastically, ' — poor you, suffering all the discomforts of living in a mansion with a wealthy woman.'

'If Edward had cooperated it would have been wonderful, but it's falling apart.'

'Poor you.' Ryan said again, and the sarcastic grin remained.

'You can sneer, but it isn't as good as we'd hoped, although we are in it together — I'm not alone. I don't have to sit back feeling sorry for myself, and wait for my wife to feed me! I'll never regret leaving Sian for

Margaret, whether things turn out good or bad. It's an exciting new start. What have *you* got to look forward to? More of the same, while you get older and older and more and more sorry for yourself? Pathetic you are Ryan, and you always were!'

'Thief!'

'Loser!'

Ryan was seething as he walked back to Glebe Lane. The house was impressively large and he knew it was still theirs solely because of Sally's efforts. He had been unlucky. The Westons losing their money had been a disaster for him. Until then he had been working at the Weston's Wallpaper and Paint Stores, and receiving a good salary, while having Viv Lewis do all the work. Islwyn was right, he was sitting around waiting for Sally to spare him a moment between fussing over her guests. Resentment, slowly simmering over the past weeks, began to build.

He went through to the kitchen, where Sally was preparing vegetables for the evening meal she provided for her guests.

'Fetch me some tea,' he said as he brushed past her.

'Make it will you, Ryan? I have to finish these before I go to the shops. Megan will be home soon. She'll be glad of a cup too.'

'Me make it? For you and that disgusting

daughter of yours? You're my wife. You make it. I'll be in the lounge with the morning papers — if your boarders haven't ruined them!'

Sally turned to him, her face flushed, an uneasy defiance in her eyes. 'I don't have time.'

Ryan turned on his heel and hit her.

2

After Ryan had hit Sally with a vicious left-handed cuff across her face, they stared at each other in disbelief. Sally didn't feel the pain immediately and her eyes were wide with shock. Ryan watched as a small straight weal appeared and darkened to deep reddish-blue on her left cheekbone. He registered vaguely that it had been caused by his wedding ring.

'Ryan,' Sally whispered, when the truth of it finally reached her brain, 'you hit me!'

Ryan's more frightening thought was how badly he wanted to hit her again. He hurried from the house, unaware of where his feet were taking him. Walking fast, occasionally breaking into a run, he didn't stop until he was breathless. And still he was filled with a desire to hit her, again and again, to make up for the frustrations of the past months. It was her fault. She should have insisted on her father helping them out, not succumbed to the pathetic need to show everyone how brave she was, an example of how well the Weston women coped.

Bitter thoughts swelled in his head until he thought his skull would crack with the fury of them. Who would have guessed he'd be reduced to this? A wife who gloried in her self-righteousness, reminding him every day of how he had failed them, and a daughter who had let them down in the most sordid way.

It wasn't as though the failure was his. Old Man Arfon had promised him a job for life, and now, deprived of the bounty of his father-in-law's generosity, he was a nothing, a nobody. And it was all Arfon's fault and Sally's for giving in and not demanding his continued help.

Ryan had long ago covered up the truth that it was really his and Islwyn's fault that Weston's business had failed. Remorse and painful guilt had quickly changed to more acceptable resentment, with Arfon a convenient scapegoat.

Ryan had come to believe that if Sally had supported him, pleaded his case with her father, they wouldn't have had to take in lodgers, or boarders, as Sally preferred to call them.

Since the disaster, he hadn't even looked for work. While Sally dealt with the running of the house, the shopping and cleaning and was there smiling to welcome the travelling salesmen and the higher-class reps that called every few weeks to be fussed over and fed, he sat around, read the newspaper and seethed at the unfairness of it all. So when his wife had hinted he might help a little, all the frustration had culminated in his outburst today.

Besides the trauma of losing the comfortable and well-paid position at Weston's Wallpaper and Paint, there were other things to cause him anger. The way his twin daughters had turned out after years of expensive education and pampering. Joan had married Viv Lewis, that common little upstart who had usurped him, and Megan was expecting a child and absolutely refusing to marry the father. What a mess. He hadn't spoken to Megan since being told the news of her condition and had no intention of doing so in the forseeable future.

In the aftermath of the explosion of anger, he muttered to himself, 'Sally's fault, Megan's fault, Arfon's fault. Those who should have supported me have let me down.'

Ryan started to walk again, heading towards Trellis Street, where Islwyn's wife lived. When the financial crash came, Islwyn's wife had insisted Islwyn and she move from the large house they had owned, to live in a tiny terrace house in Trellis Street. With one of the common Griffithses for a neighbour. No wonder Islwyn had opted for Margaret

Jenkins and Montague Court!

At least he and Sally hadn't done that. They still lived in Glebe Lane, a rather smart area of the town. That it was due solely to his wife's efforts didn't worry him at all. After all, he reasoned childishly, it was her family who had taken away their high standard of living.

He was still tense with unreleased anger and he walked through the narrow streets of neat, well-built stone houses trying to settle his mind. He had a vague plan of visiting Sian in Trellis Street but circled around, trying to calm himself first. He didn't want Sally's sister to see him while he was so stressed. In fact, he thought he would call and behave at his most charming.

He passed Temptations sweet shop on the corner of Sophie Street which was run by Viv Lewis's sister. Up Brown Street to where his nephew Jack lived with his wife, a girl who used to clean for Gladys and Arfon. What had happened to the once proud Weston family?

A sandwich and a cup of tea would be welcome, Ryan thought, as he approached forty-four Trellis Street. He was about to knock the door when he remembered that his sister-in-law Sian wouldn't be at home. She would be at that stupid Rose Tree Café with Dora Lewis! Anger revived, he turned around and set off back to Montague Court. There should be a cup of tea there without an argument about who would make it!

He walked through the gardens of the large house, where birds were singing and the trees were beginning to show their new green leaves. Daffodils nodded in the gentle breeze, wallflowers were already beginning to hint at the display to come, and there was the fresh scent of newly cut grass. Ryan was aware of none of these things as he walked along the gravel path and in through the kitchen door.

The room was empty. Clean coffee cups were stacked on a small table with a few plates still covered with biscuits. Vegetables were simmering on the large cooker. From the oven the rich aroma of roasting meat reached him.

It was frustrating to find no one there. God help him, a cup of tea was all he wanted! Anger that had just gone off the boil returned and he slammed back the door leading into the dining room and called.

'Islwyn? You there?'

Islwyn appeared through a doorway at the end of the large room and recognising his visitor hurried towards him.

'What's wrong?' he asked.

'Wrong? Nothing's wrong!'

'You look as if you're bursting with bad

36

news. You haven't been offered a job, have you?' he joked.

'Had a bit of a row with Sally if you must know,' Ryan said, immediately regretting his words. 'Nothing serious. I get a bit fed up hanging around without a job to go to.'

'You should have done what I did, take any old job, the lowlier the better just to rub it in to Old Man Arfon how he let us down. When I told him and Gladys I was working in a chip shop I thought they'd explode.'

'Not working in a chip shop now, are you? Fixed up nicely at Montague Court with the mistress — if you'll pardon the word — of the house. Very nice.'

'I tried to explain before, it sounds better than it is,' Islwyn assured him. 'Margaret and I had great plans for this place, but her brother Edward is insisting on taking his share of the inheritance and that doesn't leave us enough to keep the place going. We'll have to sell, unless a miracle happens. And they don't come along very often.'

' 'We'll have to sell',' Ryan mimicked sarcastically. 'There's a pity. You'll only have several thousand pounds to spend on something almost as grand. Poor old you!'

'Margaret was born here and her ancestors built it. She wants to stay.'

'Well, yes, I can sympathise with that, but

37

you must admit you made a soft landing when you left Sian and moved out of Trellis Street.'

'Margaret and I have known each other for a long time. To be honest, I'd wanted to leave Sian before, but I waited until Jack was safely home after the war; then it seemed best to wait until he was married. The loss of my job with Westons was the end of more than working for father-in-law. It was a suitable time to end my marriage to Sian too.'

'Lucky sod.'

'Why? You and Sally are all right. She works hard and doesn't seem to mind being the breadwinner.'

'But I *do*!' Suddenly the anger was back and Ryan hurried out.

'Come back, Ryan. What's the matter with you? Stay for a cup of tea,' Islwyn called, but his brother-in-law was running along the path, sliding on the gravel as if escaping. But from what he couldn't imagine. What had he said to turn his mood so dramatically?

'Something's wrong,' he told Margaret later, 'but I can't work out what it is. We thought he might crack up when all the trouble with Weston's came out, but he seemed to get over it.'

'He's lazy and self-centred and he's just

38

realised he doesn't like himself,' was Margaret's diagnosis.

'Perhaps Sally's turned like the proverbial worm, and thrown him out. He hasn't bothered to seek me out twice in one day before!'

'We don't take him in, Issy,' she warned.

'We most certainly do not,' he agreed. 'Miserable old sod.'

★ ★ ★

Sally didn't move for a long time after Ryan had run out of the house. The pain in her face grew stronger and stronger until she began to sob. Still she remained standing, staring at the door through which Ryan had fled. Tears ran unchecked down her face; her cheek where he had struck her felt enormous. Her legs began to weaken and she realised her arms were trembling. Sinking down into a chair she held her arms against her body, trying in vain to still them.

What should she do? Although she was a grown woman with twin daughters and a grandchild on the way, she desperately wanted to run to her mother, tell her how she had been treated and feel Gladys's arms around her. But she couldn't. This was something she had to deal with herself, and in private. Like her husband, who was walking without purpose, she was aware of a foolish longing for someone to make her a cup of tea.

A knock at the door brought her back to her senses. Carefully drying her face with the tea cloth she was holding, she went to the front window to see who was there. Seeing the baker, she asked for three loaves and managed to hide her cheek from him by pretending to be wiping the windows. When he had gone she went slowly upstairs to look at her face. When she saw it she cried again.

Ryan's keys were on the dressing table with some small change and a half empty tube of peppermint sweets. She picked up the keys feeling them cold against her palm. What should she do, throw them away and refuse to let him in? That wasn't a solution; there would be a scene and she couldn't bear to have others knowing he had hit her. She dropped them back into the glass dish and went slowly down the stairs. Her decision wasn't made but there was lunch to get for Megan and herself, and the dinner to prepare for the five boarders for seven-thirty. Ignoring the throbbing in her cheek, she went back to her preparations.

When the phone rang she hesitated to

answer it. If it were Ryan, what would she say? To her relief it was her daughter Megan, calling to tell her she wouldn't be home for lunch. A reprieve, she thought with renewed sobbing, and a chance to perfect her story about what caused the bruising.

★　★　★

Megan was with Edward Jenkins and Frank Griffiths, in the old draper's shop.

'Don't know whether it'll look any better with the rubbish moved out, Mr Jenkins,' Frank was saying sadly. 'Show up the mess the walls and floors are in, won't it?'

'Perhaps I shouldn't have — '

'Are you saying you don't want the job?' Megan asked sharply as Edward began to apologise. 'Because we'll soon find someone else.'

'No, no. I'll do it, like, I was just saying that I hope you won't expect it to look spick and span once I've finished.'

'We don't expect to open the doors for business the following day. Which reminds me, Mr Jenkins will be looking for someone to do the decorating once it's all cleaned out. Are you interested in quoting for that?'

'I might be. If I can get our Ernie to give a hand.'

41

'When can you start emptying the rubbish?' Edward thought he'd better add something to the conversation, although he was happy to step back and leave the negotiations to his companion. 'Tomorrow?' he added boldly and Frank nodded his solemn head.

'First off we'll get the garden cleared, give us some room to work, right?'

'Better than taking all the rubbish through the shop,' Edward agreed. 'We can take down some fencing and use the lane as access.'

'Right then,' Frank said. 'Tomorrow, nine o'clock sharp it is.'

'Either Mr Jenkins or I will be here to make sure of it,' Megan added, smiling at Edward.

When Frank had sloped off to The Railwayman for his lunchtime pint, Edward bought fish and chips and they sat on the bottom stair, thinking about the sequence of the work in front of them.

'If you wish, Edward,' Megan suggested, 'we can call on my sister and Viv at Weston's Wallpaper and Paint and order cleaning materials and some of the paint.'

'Good idea. I thought of having blue and green for a colour scheme. What d'you think?'

'Add a sandy sort of tan and it will be a seascape theme. Ideal I'd have thought. Well done Edward, I was so afraid that after years

42

of being under Margaret's influence you'd have chosen dark brown and cream!' They were laughing as they walked down the road towards the large shop owned by her grandparents.

Crossing the road, Edward said, 'Isn't that your father?' He pointed to where Ryan was hurrying along, head bent, his tie crooked and without his trilby.

Megan called to him but although he looked up briefly, he didn't acknowledge his daughter. She smiled grimly. 'Daddy hasn't spoken to me since I told him about The Lump,' she said.

They watched as Ryan impatiently pushed his way through the afternoon crowd, and turned down the hill towards the railway station.

* * *

Ryan was going into Cardiff, to the pictures probably, he thought. Seeing Megan he knew he couldn't talk to her about what had happened. Or anyone else. A trip into Cardiff was a way of getting out of the town, avoiding people he knew, killing time until he could decide whether or not to go home that night.

He wanted to go home; after all, what alternative did he have? But was afraid that

43

the scene from which he had run away, might be repeated. A vision of Sally's shocked face was never far from his mind and instead of shaming him, he felt an excitement that was almost sexual. Yet that side of their marriage had faded away when he had left the family business and he didn't want it to restart. He wanted out of it all: his marriage, the shame and disappointment of his daughters, the awful in-laws. A fresh start. But where would he go without money and without a job?

* * *

Walking into Weston's shop, Megan began at once to reach for colour charts and carpet samples, waving vaguely towards her brother-in-law, Viv, who was attending to a customer.

Viv greeted Megan with a kiss on the cheek and Edward Jenkins with a handshake. On being told the reason for their visit, he called to his wife.

'Joan, love, your sister is here.'

From the office high above the shop floor, a face appeared in the window that oversaw the customer area, and with a shout of delight, Joan ran down the steps to greet her twin.

'Are you all right? Is The Lump behaving itself?' she asked.

'The Lump is fine and so am I. It's Edward who needs help.'

While Viv and Edward discussed the project of the old shop, Joan and Megan went up to the office to sit and chatter. Viv had gestured to one of the staff to make tea, and when the tray arrived, the two girls came down again to join them. Before they left, it had been arranged that all four of them would go to the old draper's shop and discuss the best way of restoring the place into a magnificent showroom for displaying sports goods for sale.

★ ★ ★

There were several empty shops in the row in which the draper's shop was situated, some in a seriously dilapidated state. Dusk was falling after a rainy day had brought evening in early, when, behind one of the buildings, a man was carefully removing some silver items from their hiding place. He arranged them about his person in padded pockets made in the lining of his loose-fitting overcoat, moving experimentally to make sure they didn't make a noise. Once he was satisfied, he left the property, making his way carefully through the gardens behind the shops, including the one taken by Edward. A short drive to a public house near Newport where he was to meet his fence and the money would be in his pocket.

He planned six more robberies and then he was finished with it all for good. A couple of narrow escapes recently had made him face the fact that, even disguising himself as well as he could, his luck wouldn't last forever.

Percy Flemming was tall, thin and with the kind of looks people found difficult to describe. Nondescript, he'd been called at school and nothing he'd done since had altered that nonentity impression. His clothes were ordinary, he walked with his head down, his shoulders bowed and rarely spoke to anyone he met. Considered surly by most, that pleased him. It was what he wanted.

He rarely went into The Railwayman, apparently content to spend his evening at home with Barbara and their girls. Very little was known about him except that he was considered a bit of a bore. Only Ernie and Frank Griffiths knew otherwise, as he had once involved them in a daring raid on a factory — something he would never do again. He was a loner — depending on no one but himself was safer.

He was employed as an assistant gardener in a local hospital, but with his other activities he had gathered together enough money to buy a house in a pleasant area of Cardiff, where no one would know him. There he could begin a new life, open out a bit and enjoy a few social activities, no longer having the need to stay out of sight and concentrate on being ignored.

Barbara Wheel, his common-law wife, was still refusing to marry him but he hoped that when they had made the move and were settled with their two daughters, he would convince her it was the right thing to do.

When he had met Barbara, she had been working as a prostitute, sharing a premises with Molly Bondo. But he had given her a better life and had never regretted it. For a few years she too had seemed content, but recently had wanted more. The rented house in the small side road, leading nowhere but the railings of the allotments, had been wonderful at first, but now the cloak of respectability that had covered her past had given her confidence to seek more. She craved a more exciting life, and talked of Cardiff, Bristol or even London.

He was afraid he might lose her, so the series of robberies in such a short time, which added greatly to the danger of being caught, were to make sure she had all she needed for herself and the girls.

Percy slipped into the back lane behind the

shops and walked, unhurriedly, to where he had left the car. Best not to look anxious, or show impatience; that way people remembered you. He cursed when he heard voices and moved extra slowly for fear of a rattle revealing the contents of his pockets.

He was leaving the lane when he met Edward and Megan, who were coming to inspect the condition of the fence around the garden of the shop. He nodded and touched his cap deferentially. Edward nodded casually, uncurious about his presence and when Percy turned back after walking a few paces away from them, slightly exaggerating the stoop he affected, he saw them looking at the broken fence that had been made to swing back and allow access to cats, dogs and himself. He hoped they wouldn't fix it just yet. Not until he'd recovered the rest of his cache. Climbing a fence took longer, specially with clothes filled with breakable, oddly shaped items, and was more likely to arouse suspicion.

★ ★ ★

Having telephoned her mother for the second time that day, to tell her she wouldn't be home for dinner, Megan went back with Edward and ate at Montague Court. His way

48

of saying thank you for her assistance that day. When she finally reached home, she saw the bruises on her mother's face immediately.

'Mummy! What happened?'

'I fell darling. Clumsy old me, eh? On the landing while I was carrying dirty linen. I tripped on the end of a towel I think and caught my face on the edge of the newel post.' Sally was pleased with the lie. She had been embellishing it in her mind all day.

'Oh, why wasn't I here? I should have come home for lunch as I promised instead of phoning. Why didn't you tell me?'

'I'm all right. Come on. It's me who should be fussing over you. I've put a hot-water bottle in your bed and if you're ready to go up, I'll make you a nice milky cup of cocoa.'

When Megan was in bed, Sally sat for two hours, frequently glancing at the clock, watching the minutes build into hours until the grandfather clock in the hall struck eleven-thirty. She told herself she would give Ryan another hour then she'd have to go to bed.

He made it with three minutes to spare, walking in and passing her without a word. She stood in the hall after locking the door and followed his movements by the sounds he made. Into the bathroom, then up and up, to the top floor where the spare beds were located in case of need.

There was no bedding in the room and she hurried towards the stairs to follow him and make sure he had all he needed, then she stopped. What was the matter with her? Making sure he was comfortable after what he had done? She must be crazy; programmed like some mindless doll, to perform as required. She went to the room she and Ryan had shared all their married life and locked herself in.

★ ★ ★

Rhiannon was married to Charlie Bevan and lived opposite her mother, Dora Lewis, in Sophie Street. She worked at the Temptations sweet shop on the corner and, until recently, had looked out for Charlie's son Gwyn every afternoon when school finished. Now Gwyn had left school and had started work in Windsor's garage with his father.

The shop was experiencing the lull between busy times, and in a quiet moment she glanced out of the shop door towards the house where she now lived and wondered whether she dare close the shop for a few minutes to let Gwyn's dog out into the yard. Seeing Gertie Thomas outside her grocery shop on the opposite corner, she locked the door and asked Gertie to 'keep an eye'.

The dog was sleeping on Gwyn's bed, something not allowed in the family rule book, but something of which no one could cure her. Rhiannon changed the drinking water, put down a few biscuits and, leaving the door open into the back yard, hurried back to the shop. It was only for an hour, she'd be back at one o'clock.

* * *

The old man walking along the back lane heard the door open, and saw the dog's nose poking through the bars of the gate. He stopped and talked to the lively animal and, from his pocket, produced a sweet which Polly ate with enthusiasm.

He recognised Rhiannon and watched as she filled the dog's drinking bowl, then through the open door, saw her head towards the front door. She wasn't going to leave the back door wide open was she? He waited for several minutes then, coaxing the dog to be friendly, he stepped inside the gate. Approaching the door he listened and, hearing nothing, stepped inside, still talking soothingly to the dog.

He didn't take very much. Just half a loaf and a pot of Marmite, and a partly used packet of butter. Hiding them under his coat and stuffing a few biscuits into his pocket, he patted the dog, gave her another sweet and hurried back to the cheerless room where he lived.

★   ★   ★

Before she reached Temptations, Rhiannon realised she had left the shop door key on the kitchen table. She stepped into the hallway just in time to see the shabbily dressed figure closing the gate. She presumed it was someone selling out of a suitcase. There were several people in the town begging in the guise of salesmen.

Made aware of the danger of leaving the door open with only a soppy dog to guard the place she called Polly inside and closed the back door before returning to the shop.

★   ★   ★

Rhiannon's stepson Gwyn was working as an apprentice in the garage where his father worked. Earning only fifteen shillings a week but hopefully learning a trade that would keep him in work all his life, he was very content. Having spent years in the care of his great-grandmother, Maggie Wilpin, he was thrilled to have Rhiannon as a stepmother and Dora Lewis as a doting 'gran'.

His mother had run off when he was very young and his father had spent several years in prison for burglary and similar offences. Now, all that was behind him and Gwyn was happier than he'd dreamed. Yet, something was wrong. Sensitive to Rhiannon's every mood, he sensed that there was something she wanted to discuss with him.

He racked his brain trying to think of something he had done that might displease her, but he failed. He couldn't ask outright and neither could he approach his father. He knew married people sometimes disagreed, but hoped and prayed that he wasn't the cause of any problem.

That evening he discovered the reason Rhiannon had been somewhat distracted. Blushing furiously, she asked him how he felt about having a brother or a sister.

They were sitting around the fire, drinking their late-night cup of cocoa, and when Rhiannon and then his father mentioned the possibility of a baby in the family, Gwyn's face became redder by several shades to those of Rhiannon and Charlie.

'We realise that with you now fifteen, it would seem a bit odd,' Charlie said, 'And with such an age gap you could hardly be close friends, but Rhiannon and I would like to have a child.'

'How do you feel about the prospect, Gwyn?' Rhiannon asked gently. 'We wouldn't want to do anything that you'd hate.'

Gwyn's reply surprised them. 'I think you should have two, not one. Then he wouldn't be lonely.' He grinned then, staring from one to the other and Rhiannon saw such a strong likeness to Charlie her heart filled with joy. She jumped out of her chair and ran to hug him.

'Gwyn,' she said with a sob threatening to hold back the words, 'you and Charlie — you make me so happy. I love you both, very very much.'

For a fifteen-year-old boy, hugging was difficult to cope with, but Gwyn managed. In fact, he quite enjoyed it.

Lewis came in at that moment and was aware of an atmosphere, sensing he had interrupted something, and, giving the lame excuse that he was tired, he went to his room.

The closeness of the three people downstairs upset him. It reminded him of the emptiness of his own life. He stood for a long time staring out of the window across at number seven, where his wife Dora lay, also alone. How could he persuade her to take him back?

There had been a temporary ceasefire when Dora had agreed to him moving back in, but when he had slipped into her bedroom convinced of a loving welcome, he had been thrown out again. Yet he knew she still loved him. She really was a difficult woman, punishing herself as well as him.

Common sense told him he should move away and find someone else but when was common sense a factor in his life? He sighed.

The following morning, while the four of them ate breakfast, Rhiannon, Charlie and Gwyn discussed a plan to cycle down the vale and take a picnic lunch on the following Sunday.

'The weather is warm enough, if we find somewhere out of the wind,' Charlie said.

'Pity we can't take Polly,' Gwyn said. 'She'd love to paddle in the river.'

'I'll take you if you like,' Lewis offered. 'I have the car and there's plenty of room for us all including the dog.' He smiled at Rhiannon, 'There's room for your mother too, if you can persuade her to come.'

Rhiannon and Charlie shared a glance, assessing each other's mood without the need for words. They wanted to refuse. They valued these family outings and were both aware that once Gwyn started meeting friends, he would soon stop joining them. This time of special closeness would be gone. But Gwyn spoke first.

'Great! Can we, Dad? I'd love to take Gran. D'you think she'll come?'

'She has a lot of work to do on Sundays, working every other day in the café,' Charlie warned.

Lewis leaned over and winked at the boy. 'I'll bet you can persuade her,' he said.

It was as she began to make sandwiches for Charlie and Gwyn to take to work that Rhiannon noticed the missing food.

'Did you get up in the night and have a midnight feast?' she asked Gwyn jokingly, remembering how he used to sometimes wander around at night and prepare a snack which he would share with Polly. Gwyn looked surprised.

'No, I haven't got up in the night for ages. Since starting work with our Dad I'm too tired!'

Frowning, Rhiannon thought of the shabbily dressed man at the gate and wondered whether Polly was too friendly, and had allowed him to come into the house. The thought made her shiver, but she said nothing to the others. Best to be sure before worrying them about what must have been an opportunist, someone desperate enough to take a chance. If that was what it was, it was unlikely to be repeated.

* * *

Dora was reluctant to go out for the day, as Sundays were her only opportunity to deal with the housework, fill in the accounts and make sure the orders were in place for the coming week, but, seeing Gwyn's hopeful face and realising, like her daughter had, that the time was fast approaching when he would not want to be a part of family outings, she agreed.

It was difficult for her to be in Lewis's presence for more than a few minutes and this would be for several hours. She loved him and wanted him back and knew that if she said the words he would do so. Only pride was preventing her being happy, so she usually ended up quarrelling with him. She would try to be calm and indifferent for the day, for the sake of Gwyn, Charlie and Rhiannon. To refuse would be childish.

There were a few cakes and pasties left at the Rose Tree Café that Saturday evening and instead of sharing them as she and Sian usually did, Dora was given them all to swell the picnic. With sandwiches wrapped in greaseproof paper and damp tea towels and several bottles of pop, they set off at ten o'clock.

Dora and Lewis bickered all the way and it was with relief that they saw Lewis head off for a walk along the beach as soon as the car stopped.

Selecting their position on the beach took a few minutes and as they began to set out their belongings, colonising the area for the duration of their stay, Gwyn asked, 'Rhiannon, can I go with Mr Lewis?'

'He might like to be on his own,' Charlie warned but Gwyn replied quickly.

'I don't think he likes to be lonely.' Accepting his father's nod as agreement, he ran along the road that skirted the beach and soon caught up with Lewis who hadn't gone far, but was sitting on the tufty Maram grass-covered dunes staring out to sea.

'He talks a lot about loneliness, doesn't he?' Dora said as they watched Gwyn run to find Lewis. 'I don't think he'll ever forget the months when you were in prison, Charlie.'

'I can't believe I treated him so badly,' Charlie said sadly. 'Or how lucky I am now.' He hugged both women affectionately. 'You two have more than compensated for his misfortunes.'

'We asked him last night, how he felt about having a brother or a sister and he said we must have two so they won't be lonely.'

'Marvellous idea!' Dora's blue eyes glowed. 'Tell me when to start knitting!'

★ ★ ★

Gwyn sat beside Lewis and offered him a sweet from a packet Rhiannon had given him. The tide was high and the sea moved slowly and gently. Selecting stones from the line below the dunes, for a game of ducks and drakes, they stood and threw them into the water, skimming them and counting the number of 'jumps' they made. The record was five and Gwyn admired the older man's skill and asked him to show him the technique. Aware he was being flattered in the hope of being pleased, Lewis smiled, ruffled the boy's hair and demonstrated until they were rivals, boasting of their superiority like equals.

★ ★ ★

'Not a bad kid, young Gwyn,' Lewis said to Dora as he carried the blankets and empty boxes back into number seven.

'A wonderful boy. And,' she added, her blue eyes glaring, warning him not to disagree, 'Charlie's a good man.'

'As long as he doesn't revert to his former

59

ways and let Rhiannon down.'

'You're the one who let Rhiannon down, Lewis Lewis! Going off and having an affair with Nia Williams. Fine example you are! Charlie's changed but I doubt that you have!'

'Nia's dead!' he reminded her angrily. 'There's no chance of my reverting to my former ways!'

He dumped the remnants of the picnic on the floor and left.

3

After discussing his situation with the estate agent and his bank manager, as well as an enthusiastic Megan, Edward decided to be bold and buy the shop rather than rent it. At the end of April, with the aid of a bridging loan until Montague Court was sold, he was the owner of number sixty-eight Highbourne Road, known locally as the High Street.

'I won't be able to tackle the refurbishments until I have more money,' he explained to Megan as they stood looking into the dreary little shop one dark evening. 'I have moments of panic at the enormity of what I've taken on.'

'When you look at it, try not to see what's in front of you,' Megan advised. 'See in your mind's eye what will be there once you can make a start. Pendragon Island will have the surprise of its life when you have finished here and the shop is open for business.'

'If ever,' he sighed.

'Edward — ' she warned. 'No more panics. You can do it. Remember I have faith in you.'

'I haven't really looked at the surveyor's report,' he admitted with a wry grin. 'I thought it would sound too daunting.'

'I believe they usually do. Bring it to the house tomorrow and we'll look at it together.'

'Eleven o'clock?' he suggested. Then, seeing a frown gathering on her brow he quickly offered her an excuse to refuse. 'But you have other plans, I'm sure. Don't worry, we can look at it some other time, I mustn't keep bothering you with my troubles.'

'Would you like me to look through the report with you?'

'Well yes, of course, but — '

'Then Edward, stop sounding as though you don't!'

'If you're sure you have the time,' he said, still hesitantly.

'If I didn't want to I wouldn't!'

'Eleven o'clock?' he repeated with a smile.

'No. I have a doctor's appointment to make sure all is well with The Lump. Then there's the clinic visit at three. You see, he has a social life before he's even born. What an upheaval he'll make in my life.' She frowned before adding, 'If you aren't helping the dreaded Margaret and my delinquent Uncle Islwyn with lunch, what about eating at the Rose Tree Café at twelve-thirty?'

* * *

62

When the surveyor had looked at William Jones's old draper's shop, Edward had been given a surprise. There was a basement he hadn't noticed on his earlier inspections. It had been bricked up, he was told. Inside the back room, one of the large floor slates had been replaced with wood and when lifted, led to worn wooden steps. The outside access had been so well hidden by the overgrown trees, bushes and grass, it obviously hadn't been used for a long time. It was only when the deeds were studied that he'd been made aware of its existence.

'Mr Harvey the surveyor hasn't opened it up,' Edward told Megan the following day when they sat in the Rose Tree Café eating lunch. 'He suggested I do so immediately, to give the place some air and prevent the damp, which smells strongly in the back of the premises, from becoming worse. 'Always allow air through the underfloor area and it will help prevent damp problems,' he told me. So, that is where I'll make a start. It won't cost much and it's best to get the worst over first.'

'If it's been closed for years you might regret opening it up,' Megan warned. 'But, if you insist, we ought to go at once and ask Frank and Ernie Griffiths if they want the job.'

never before witnessed: chickens wandering and being casually shooed out, dogs and cats coming to satisfy their curiosity. The worn furniture was covered with clothes spread to dry near the roaring fire. Janet snatched the newly washed garments into an untidy pile and threw them onto the table, embarrassed by the presence of Edward Jenkins from Montague Court.

Edward was embarrassed too, but sensing her stronger unease he smiled, picked up a shirt that had fallen, added it to the pile and said politely, 'Washing day is such chaos, isn't it, Mrs Griffiths? I don't know how you ladies cope.'

He noticed that Megan was, surprisingly, quite at home. She was so outspoken about things of which she disapproved that he expected her to complain, but she was obviously a regular visitor to this unlikely place. Megan was certainly full of surprises. He watched as Joseph-Hywel slid down to go and play with a toy. Megan picked up a cat and began to nurse it. He did the same with another which came to investigate the newcomers in the inquisitive way of felines, and began to relax.

After being plied with tea and cakes which they were too full to enjoy, and hearing all about Janet and Hywel's grandchildren, and answering questions about The Lump, they were finally able to explain the reason for the visit. Janet assured them the boys would be there on Saturday afternoon.

Before they left they were invited to admire the menagerie outside and, stepping over Frank, who was sleeping, propped up against a sack of logs in the porch, they walked around the various sheds and were introduced to the goats, including Ermintrude, the most affectionate one who followed Frank around whenever she had the chance.

Edward was surprised to realise he had enjoyed the visit and hoped to be invited to go there again. When he told Megan how he felt on the drive back to town, all she said was, 'Of course you enjoyed it. Everyone does. Even stuffy old bores like you, Edward.'

He laughed but couldn't resist asking, 'Am I? A stuffy old bore?'

'Not any more you aren't. You're shedding your inhibitions at an impressive rate, and finding it fun, I think.'

'Being with you is making it easy to turn away from the old life and look towards the new, Megan. Thank you.'

'Silly old thing,' she said patting his arm, leaving it there for a moment.

He felt the warmth of her touch for a long time.

If Sally was aware of the time her daughter was spending with Edward Jenkins, she didn't remark on it. She was so anxious about Ryan's abuse of her, she hardly noticed Megan's comings and goings. At bedtime she went through the usual routine, putting a hot-water bottle in her daughter's bed and making cocoa which she took up to her, but instead of staying beside the bed and talking to her for a while, she put the cup and saucer down and returned downstairs, anxious to get into bed and lock herself in before Ryan returned home.

She was wary whenever Ryan was around, still half expecting a repeat of the blow to her face, which was still tender to the touch. As much as possible, she kept out of his way and when they did meet, she avoided saying anything apart from the mildest of comments. Sometimes he replied, mostly he did not.

The post brought a demand for an unpaid repair bill on Saturday morning and she knew she would have to speak to Ryan about it. She was certain it had been paid but was unable to find the receipt. Forcing herself to stay calm, she waited until he was settled in his armchair with the morning paper, and, carrying a cup of coffee that a shaking hand threatened to drop, she said, 'Ryan, this came this morning but I'm sure it's been paid. I don't know what to do.'

He took the statement of account from her without looking at her and she waited while he read it. To her surprise he then looked up and smiled at her.

'They've made a mistake, I'll telephone them for you, shall I?'

'Please Ryan.'

He made the call, sorted out the error, and followed her into the kitchen. 'It's all right, you can throw this away, it was a simple mistake. The monthly statements were made up before the account was settled.'

'Thank you,' she said softly.

'Sally, I'm sorry,' he surprised her by saying. 'I don't know what caused my fury on that day. I was almost insane with rage. A build-up of several things I think.' He moved towards her and she shrank from him.

'Keep away. I can't trust you not to do it again,' she said, panic raising the tone of her voice.

'Don't say that, Sally.'

'Sorry Ryan, you can continue to stay here with Megan and me, but I don't want you near me.'

'What d'you mean I can stay here? It's my home!'

'My father bought it for us, and I'll only have you here under certain conditions.'

She was trembling. This was a part of her character never before revealed. She steeled herself to continue even though the look on his face had changed from apologetic to rising anger and was frightening her. She should have waited until someone else was in the house. Megan was out and none of the guests would be home until dinner time. She took a step towards the door but he touched her arm and she froze.

'What conditions?' He spoke softly but there was an edge to his voice.

'Megan, for one,' she said. 'You have to accept this child she's carrying and stop treating her like a convict.'

'You expect me to beg to be allowed to live in my own house and condone the disgusting behaviour of your daughter?'

Sally noticed he referred to 'her' daughter and not theirs. She noticed also that his voice was more gritty and the grip on her arm was tightening. She tried to pull away and reached for the door handle to make her escape before he stopped her and turned her to face him. She tensed against the blow, but it didn't come.

'Sally, please don't look at me like that,' he said and slowly, like a stranger, he pulled her into his arms. 'I'm sorry, sorry, sorry. The truth is, I can't cope with Megan's condition. I try but I can't. You'll have to help her, I know that, and I want you to. But I can't talk to her knowing what she's done. That's why I snapped the other day. It'll never happen again, I promise.'

Slowly, in a confused state of mind, Sally relaxed against him. She wanted to believe him so much.

* * *

So far, Frank had made very little difference to the garden behind the old draper's shop. He had started to drag some of the fallen branches from where the tangle of grasses held them like a vice, but most of the time he had sat and thought about the best way to deal with the problem.

Megan went to see Janet and told her to remind Frank that it was payment by results. With Edward and Megan in attendance, Frank and Ernie Griffiths arrived on Saturday afternoon to break through and see what secrets lay behind the concealed entrance to the basement.

But the first task was to cut back the rest of the foliage. A start had been made, but by pulling up things long hidden in the

Thanking Dora Lewis and Megan's Aunt Sian for their meal, they drove out of town to the cottage where the Griffiths family lived. The small cottage was surrounded by small sheds and outbuildings and fenced-off areas, most of which were occupied by livestock. Chickens roamed freely, a couple of geese were hissing like over-filled kettles, the plaintive sound of goats wanting company filled the air and above it all, dogs were barking fit to pop one's eardrums.

Janet came out, a small woman with grey hair straying from its bun and flying around her head like an unravelling halo. Drying her hands on her apron she waved for them to come inside. Tipping a cat from a chair she wiped the seat ineffectually with a flap of her skirt, and invited Megan to sit.

A little boy came into the room and stared at them until, recognising Megan he walked across and leaned on her knees, raising his arms to be lifted.

'Hello Joseph-Hywel,' Megan said, helping the 2½-year-old to climb up. 'This is Caroline's son, Janet and Hywel's grandson,' she explained to Edward. Hywel came in then and, seeing the visitors, nodded a greeting and disappeared.

Edward was uneasy in the untidy and shabby room. It was a scene such as he had neglected garden, and throwing them down somewhere else, Frank had created a worse mess than before he'd begun.

'This will need more than shears,' Ernie said as he hacked his way through the smaller branches of buddleia and ash and sycamore that had grown sturdy over the years of neglect. Megan pointed at the saws and axes and tilting her head on one side, waited for them to begin. Edward couldn't stay, he had to be at Montague Court to deal with the lunchtime rush.

He and Margaret still worked together although Islwyn was slowly learning how to be useful. Edward watched Islwyn sometimes and guessed that his show of enthusiasm was false; he could see he found the work tedious and boring and would soon tire of it once it was a full-time occupation. For a moment he felt sorry for Margaret. She was leaning on a man who lacked the strength to support her.

Although they shared the various chores as they had always done, Edward and his sister rarely spoke to each other. So used to each other's ways they had little need, but besides the familiarity of the tasks, there was a tension between them. Margaret was so resentful of what she pompously called the abdication of his responsibilities, she wanted to shout at him, argue that he should stay and

71

do his duty to support the family's endeavours; even though the family was reduced to just the two of them plus a grandfather who showed no interest and cousin Terrence whom they both disliked.

Edward sometimes still felt a surge of guilt and was on the point of relenting, accepting her arguments, prepared to give up on his dream; but since Megan had begun to take an interest, these moments of weakness were becoming less frequent.

Since being invalided out of the RAF with his hopes of becoming a tennis player dashed by a leg injury, he had done what the family wanted. Now it was time to live for himself.

He had never aspired to great sporting heights, had known he hadn't the talent to become a top-class player, but believed he had been capable of succeeding in the local and regional tournaments. He had quickly realised that even without the leg injury he couldn't have indulged himself. His time and energy had been needed to prop up the ailing family fortunes. The money had by that time all but gone, the family were reduced to earning a living by opening their home to strangers.

Once persuaded back into the family business he gradually gave up a hope of any other life. But a chance had come to do something for himself and if he didn't break out now, he knew he would be trapped for the rest of his life.

★ ★ ★

Frank and Ernie worked for several hours in the jungle that was once the garden of the draper's shop. They cut and sawed and chopped until the area was covered so deeply with the hacked-off branches and the debris of years of grass growth and wild flowers they were almost hidden. As they opened up the gate which led into the back lane, it fell off, and Frank toppled out into the rutted lane, followed by a sack filled with chopped wood intended to be sold as firewood. Long dangling legs waving in the air like a demented spider, he landed at the feet of his father who had come to help.

'God 'elp us, Frank,' Hywel laughed. 'Can't you find anything better to fight than a sack of wood?'

Hywel's sons were well known for arguments that ended in a fight and a court appearance, but today their energy had been spent. They hadn't even the breath to reply.

Hywel Griffiths was not a tall man, but he was heavily built and with his grizzly beard, his missing teeth and a leather belt slung

73

aggressively across his large belly, he looked like trouble. He took off his jacket and began helping his sons.

They began removing the enormous pile of wood, pulling out grasses and dead flower stalks and unearthing long-lost items such as chimney pots, buckets, an old zinc bath and an enormous collection of rotten wood, unidentifiable pieces of rusty metal and empty boxes. By six o'clock, they had succeeded in taking away most of the thicker branches and burning the smaller ones. The metal had been piled inside the gate which led into the lane.

Without going home to change or wash, Frank and Ernie headed for the Railwayman for a reviving pint. Although he had only worked for a couple of hours, Hywel went with them.

Hywel's other son was there. Basil worked in a small factory making the new plastic kitchen and toilet items, like buckets and washing-up bowls as well as combs, assorted brushes and soap dishes. Although he had always been a man for the outdoors, Basil had accepted the factory job without hesitation. All their lives the Griffiths men had lived on their wits: a deal here, a bit of poaching there, and all the time balancing on the very edge of honesty.

Now Basil was married to Eleri and they had two sons. That was sufficient reason for him to forgo the freedom of the fields and the pleasures of casual work, and settle down to regular hours in, what was to him, an alien environment. His brothers Ernie and Frank had yet to do the same. His father Hywel never would.

The mention of the mysterious basement room was enlarged upon by Frank. He succeeded in his intention to intrigue his brother Basil into offering to help. The next day being Sunday, Frank, Ernie, Basil and their father Hywel all agreed to report for work early in the morning.

★ ★ ★

A figure had been watching as the men removed the results of their clearing. Badly dressed and obviously wearing more than one layer of outer clothing, he was short and the extra padding gave him a distorted shape. On his feet were boots that seemed too large. His dark eyes shone with interest as the garden was gradually emptied. He stepped forward once or twice and listened to the lively chatter and the laughter, but stepped back when there was a possibility of being seen.

He saw the broken gate propped up when

75

they finished and after the men had gone he went over and pulled it aside and entered the sad-looking garden. He stood for a long time, staring around with curiosity, then he gathered some pieces of wood and revived the fire.

It was getting dark. He took from his roomy pocket a knife, half a loaf and some cheese, and sitting down on an upturned bucket, the sharp edges protected by a piece of matting, he began to eat. He stretched his hands out towards the blaze, and continued to add pieces of wood, enjoying the warmth.

* * *

Once Sunday breakfast at Montague Court was over, Edward went to join the Griffithses. To his surprise the garden was cleared. Hywel's van had carted away two loads of wood and the debris of the bonfire and disturbed earth was all that remained of the flowers and shrubs that had made the place into a mini jungle. The van was loaded with the last of the metal and the rusted items, ready for disposal.

Edward saw that the bricked-up doorway was clearly visible, no longer hidden by the living screen of foliage. It was made more obvious by the fact that the bricks that had sealed the basement were of a different kind from the rest of the building. Frank and Hywel were waiting for him, poised, each holding a four-pound hammer.

'Say the word, Mr Jenkins,' Frank said, 'and we'll start bashing.'

'Go ahead,' Edward smiled. The faces of the men showed expressions like children opening a surprise parcel which, in a way, it was. 'Be prepared for disappointment, though,' he felt forced to add. 'I don't suppose there'll be anything inside.'

They didn't answer. Frank and Hywel were already enthusiastically wielding the heavy hammers, and the others stood expectantly by.

Once the bricks had been loosened, eager hands helped to clear the opening. The bricks and cement were thrown aside and Hywel was the first to poke his head inside. He popped back out swiftly, coughing and complaining.

'Bloody 'ell, boys! The place stinks of dead mice and mildew!'

They knocked out a few more bricks and Hywel looked inside once more. 'Look at this!' he said to Edward. 'The place is full of junk.' With an effort Hywel tore himself away from his examination of the dark room and stood back for Edward to inspect the place.

Edward stepped forward, shining the torch he'd had the forethought to bring, and he swung the beam around piles of cardboard boxes of various sizes and condition. Some appeared intact. Others had been weakened by dampness or nibbled by nest-making mice and had collapsed, spilling the contents onto the tiled floor.

'Hang on,' Hywel said and calling Basil to help, he collected a large board from the van and set it on the earth. 'Bring a few out so you can see what's in them,' he suggested eagerly.

Four heads were leaning over as Edward opened the first of the boxes. There was a chorus of groans as the contents were revealed. Collar studs. Hundreds of them.

Examination of the other boxes showed nothing of greater interest and sadly the Griffithses went off to dispose of the last of the vegetation and rusty metal in the heavily laden van.

Edward spent all the time he could spare that day looking into the odd assortment of abandoned stock in the basement. At four o'clock, using the board Hywel had left, he covered the entrance and set off back to Montague Court to begin preparations for dinner.

He was late and he knew Margaret would

be annoyed, but even so, he made a detour and went to see Megan.

'I can't stop,' he said when she opened the door. 'I thought you'd like to know we opened up the basement.'

'How exciting, Edward. What did you find? Spiders, beetles, mice and kindred things?'

'Those in plenty,' he told her with a smile. 'But there are dozens of boxes filled with an assortment of odd things, like packets of pins and needles, rusted into their paper. And buttons, and collar stiffeners and cufflinks and the like. Pounds and pounds worth, or they would have been. Now they are useless junk.'

'Can I have a look? It must be like an Aladdin's cave,' Megan said.

'I have to work tomorrow morning to make up for the time I took today, but if you're free tomorrow evening?'

'Seven-thirty.' she said in her abrupt way.

★ ★ ★

The lonely diner revived the fire in the garden of the draper's shop and set out his meal on a plank of wood propped up as a makeshift table. Then he removed the wood blocking the entrance to the basement and edged his way inside. The hour was late and it was impossible to see anything, so he began taking one or two boxes at a time, carrying them to his seat and examining the contents by the flickering light from the fire.

After a while he sat dreamily nursing a box filled with once white collars. He cried silently when the weakened box collapsed, spilling the contents into the flames. When the fire died down, he ate the food he had brought and shuffled off to the sad room in a cheap boarding house that he called home.

★ ★ ★

Sally and Ryan began the slow return to a normal routine. Ryan still slept in the attic, Sally had insisted on that. And she still locked her door. She lay there that Sunday night afraid to sleep, watching the door handle, half expecting it to turn as her husband made his way to his bed, but it didn't.

The rage seemed to have dissipated once he had confessed it had been the situation with Megan that had caused it. She watched him anxiously but he showed no sign of wanting to hit her again, although the calm expression in his eyes, the occasional smile, didn't prevent her heart from racing with fear every time he came near her.

Sally's most urgent desire was to prevent

her twin girls becoming aware of the estrangement. For this reason, she rose early and left her bedroom door open. Ryan, with tacit agreement to keep the situation secret, would go into the bedroom for his clothes and leave his laundry in the basket near the bedroom window as he always did. If Megan was aware of an atmosphere in the house she did not mention it.

In fact, she and her twin hardly noticed their mother and father. Joan was involved in running the family's wallpaper and paint shop with her husband Viv, and Megan was wrapped up in thoughts of the sports shop and Edward.

Besides, parents were a part of the scenery, not like friends whose every nuance of mood they registered. They were there, as they always were, whenever they were needed. As with most young people, their parents just existed on the periphery of their days. They had no reason to expect anything to change, and nothing happened to attract their attention to a serious rift.

Sally fussed over Megan as usual, and Megan ignored her concerns. Sally was anxious about the baby, anxious about future plans, of which Megan had none. She worried about her daughter's health, and about what people were saying. And the effect of the pregnancy on her mother, Gladys, who had been so distressed by the announcement and was trying to be brave.

Megan did notice how little was said in the presence of her father and how careful her mother was to avoid discussing anything to do with the baby, but she presumed he was yet to forgive her.

'Daddy will come round, I know he will, fathers always do,' Megan said to her sister one day when they were sipping coffee in the office of Weston's Wallpaper and Paint.

'He'll have to!' Joan said sharply. 'He can't sulk and pretend it isn't happening, for the rest of his life.'

The sisters were in the shop on a Sunday, while Viv and one of his assistants were sorting through some old stock with the intention of having a sale.

'I know the baby will change my life,' Megan told her, 'but I also know that, in spite of the undisguised fact that I — one of the Weston Girls — should have succumbed to such terrible weakness, my family will be there with as much help as I need. And that includes Daddy, and you.'

'I was shocked at your stupidity, I'll admit,' Joan said. 'Especially with the awful Terrence Jenkins of all people. But, although I don't want a child of my own, in a way I envy you.'

'Terrence isn't so bad. I just can't imagine being married to him. He's weak and I could have persuaded him, but we were both glad to end it.'

'He will be registered as the father, won't he?'

Megan grinned wickedly and whispered, 'What if I put down 'father unknown'?'

'You wouldn't! People would presume you're a tart! Unable to decide who was responsible!'

'No, I wouldn't do that, but it's a useful threat when Mummy starts fussing,' she smiled. 'Has Daddy spoken to you about the baby yet?'

'No. I don't think he will. Unless he changes his attitude when The Lump becomes a little person.'

'He will, won't he?'

'Unlikely,' Joan said sadly. 'He hasn't forgiven *me* yet, for marrying Viv!'

★ ★ ★

Viv Lewis visited his father later that evening. In Rhiannon and Charlie's house, opposite where his mother lived, Viv found Lewis sitting in the sparsely furnished front room listening to the radio. Lewis was so pleased to see his son, that Viv felt mean for not calling before.

'Sorry, Dad. I should have popped in before this, to see if you're settled in all right. But with the shop all day and the books to do in the evening there isn't much time.'

'Don't worry, son. I'm all right and I know where to find you if I need you.'

'Fancy coming to the Griffiths's? The Railwayman is closed, being a Sunday, but Hywel is usually stocked up in readiness. Basil and Frank and Ernie Griffiths were booked to break open the basement of the old draper's shop this weekend. They'll be full of what was found.'

'Yes, I'll enjoy a chinwag.' Lewis took his jacket from the back of the chair and combed his hair. 'That's me ready.'

Viv was aware that his handsome and charming father was subdued, despite his earlier reassurance. 'Is everything okay, Dad?'

'Well, not really. Nothing serious,' he added as Viv looked startled. 'We'll talk about it on the way.'

Viv called 'cheerio' to Rhiannon, Charlie and Gwyn, but his father shook his head.

'They're out on their bikes. Never in more than long enough to eat. I'm stuck here on my own for hours on end, and there's your mother only a few yards away across the road on *her* own. It's daft. That's what it is. Daft. I can't stay there,' Lewis said as they hurried through a clear, May evening to join their friends.

'Isn't Rhiannon looking after you?'

'Rhiannon does all she can to make me comfortable, but it's no use kidding myself, Viv, I'm in the way.'

'Have you talked to Mam?' Viv asked. 'She might be reasonable now Nia Williams is no longer here to — ' The pain on his father's face at the mention of Nia stopped him.

'I've tried. But reasonable isn't a word I'd use to describe your mother, much as I love her.'

'You love her? It isn't because Nia died, and — Sorry,' he added quickly. 'Forget I said it.'

'I don't expect you to understand, I don't know that I do! Although Nia was the one who made me happiest, I've never stopped loving your mother. But Dora's such a prickly and hot-tempered woman that she's hard to live with. Nia was quiet, calm and always loving and gentle. Two such different women and I've loved them both.'

'Try telling that to Mam,' Viv suggested softly.

'I'd have to tie her up and gag her first!'

'Now, now, our Dad. We'll have none of that!' Viv teased. He smiled but he was

85

thoughtful as they made their way across the fields. There had to be a way to get his parents back together, and reminding Dora that Rhiannon and Charlie didn't want Lewis as a lodger, might be the best way.

'It won't work,' Lewis said when Viv suggested it. 'I've already tried; saw through me in a split second she did. Accused me straight off of moving in with them just so she'd take pity on them and have me back.'

'As if you'd be that devious,' Viv smiled.

'As if my Dora would be that easy to fool!' Lewis sighed. 'She did give me a chance though, and typically I blew it.' He sighed again and added, 'I wonder how long — if ever — before I get another?'

★ ★ ★

Edward and Megan met that evening after the restaurant's dinner session was over and they went to the dark, dingy room behind the shop. A ladder had been brought and fixed in the opening the surveyor had disclosed in the floor, as the old wooden steps were unsafe. With a Tilley lamp and the aid of a powerful torch Edward carried some of the boxes up into the shop, and they began sorting through the contents.

It was a dismal collection of abandoned

stock. Button hooks once used to fasten the line of buttons on gaiters and leggings. Hat pins no longer fashionable. Snap fasteners and hooks and eyes, sewn onto paper gone brittle with age. And box after box of buttons in every colour and size. Stiff, wing collars curled in their boxes, heavily starched, severely folded and looking lethal. Garters, and arm bands once used to hold sleeves back from the wrists. Dozens of socks, rotted and nibbled by vermin. They opened box after box and felt sad.

In larger boxes they discovered shirts no longer wearable, in styles that had gone out of fashion years before. They also found women's skirts and blouses and wrapover aprons that fell apart when lifted out of the box, waistcoats, trousers and even a few once smart jackets. There were lisle stockings chewed and discoloured. In a corner they found piles and piles of paper carrier bags, as dry and brittle as dead leaves.

'This isn't just the stock of a draper,' Edward frowned. 'I wonder where it came from?'

'It might have been a clothes shop before Mr Jones took over. Or he might have decided to change the business.'

'Whatever, there's a lot of money gone to waste.'

When Edward moved the last of the boxes, a metal container was exposed. He carried it up the ladder to throw with the others and when Megan opened it she gave a cry of surprise. It was filled with money.

'Thank goodness it was in a metal box or there'd have been some very expensive mice nests under your floor!'

'We'll have to find Mr Jones and return it,' Edward said.

Megan looked at him and burst out laughing. 'Frank and Ernie will be furious!'

Edward smiled. 'I think it best we don't tell them. They'd never forget how close they were to a fortune. It would ruin their lives. There must be at least five hundred pounds there.'

When they counted it, there was five hundred and sixty-two pounds and ten shillings.

'Sorry Edward, but we *must* tell Frank and Ernie. I just have to see their faces when they realise what they missed! Besides, they might know where the retired draper is living.'

'Ah, and now comes the problem,' Edward sighed. 'Where on earth do we start looking for a Mr William Jones?'

'Post office?' Megan suggested. 'He's probably drawing a pension.'

'And how many William Joneses do we

have to interview before finding the right one?'

Megan tilted her head in that fascinating way and asked, 'How many buttons are there in these boxes?'

4

Barry Williams sat in the silence of the late Sunday evening, staring out of the window to a garden he could no longer see. The house was so silent he wished the radio was playing but he couldn't make the effort needed to turn it on.

The house in Chestnut Road had seen many changes since his mother Nia had moved out of the flat above her sweet shop in Sophie Street, and brought them here. Then the house had been filled with noise and music and laughter — especially laughter, he remembered sadly. Joseph, his prankster of a brother had seen to that.

Friends called and were made welcome, Nia sang as she worked in the house and the garden, the house had a heart and was filled with contentment. When first his brother Joseph and then his mother had died, the house had died a little too.

During the on-off marriage to Caroline Griffiths the place had begun to revive a little; there was a sensation of a living, breathing home. The little boy, Joseph-Hywel, was not yet three and if he and Caroline had stayed together, things would have continued to improve. But Caroline couldn't live with him, and had returned to the Griffiths' inconvenient, over-crowded cottage, preferring its many disadvantages to this modern, well-furnished house with him in it. He missed them, but in a perverse way didn't want them back. They demanded too much of him.

If Caroline had accepted what he was, had helped him to achieve his ambitions it would have been all right, but she wanted him to give up on the business he was building, give more time to her and little Joseph. If she'd trusted him, given him more time . . .

He had started a photographic business which had been beginning to show promise of success, but he had given it up in an effort to make his doomed marriage work and play the part of a devoted husband. To please her he had taken a job he hated, in a plastics factory, but Caroline had still left him and now he had nothing but an empty house redolent with ghostly echoes of happier days.

Not even that, he reminded himself; the atmosphere was no longer a happy one. There was an unnerving melancholy about the empty rooms. Shadows leaned towards him, whispers filled the air, the fire failed to warm the hollow spaces. Small, ordinary sounds were alien, threatening.

Barry shrank away from the blank window and looked around the shadowy room. In a rare moment of sensitivity he knew the house didn't want him there. It needed children, the chaos and clutter of family life. He didn't want to spend another night in the place. It was dead to him, his ghosts had fled and the house was silently awaiting new beginnings.

'Tomorrow,' he whispered to the walls, 'I'm putting the house on the market.' He was relieved to have made the decision, and went straight away to the desk that had been his father's and wrote to Caroline, telling her of it. He assured her that, as his wife and the mother of his dead brother's child, she would receive half the money.

He started to go up the stairs but stopped halfway up. The shadows were oppressive, the emptiness reminding him he was an unwelcome presence. He went back down and slept on the couch and dreamed of Caroline.

★   ★   ★

Caroline was lying on her bed listening to the laughter from below as Lewis, Viv, and her brothers Frank and Ernie and her parents talked over the events of their day. She had read stories to Joseph until he'd been ready to sleep but instead of going back down, she had stayed with her son, unable to disguise her unhappiness and join in the noisy good-natured bantering.

In her melancholic mood she had been saddened rather than amused by the story of the abandoned stock in the old draper's shop. A failed business — almost as sad as a failed marriage. And, she reminded herself guiltily, because of her, Barry had suffered both.

When the house fell silent she went down and made a cup of tea. She opened the back door and stood for a long time staring out into the darkness as Barry had done, her thoughts winging across the night sky.

* * *

Edward was getting into his car in the car park of Montague Court in the afternoon following the weekend discovery of the money in the basement of his shop. He intended going to the police in the hope of finding the owner of the five hundred plus pounds, and was irritated when a voice hailed him. He didn't have much time before his evening duties began. He turned to see Mr Leigh Grant approaching. Hoping that the man's visit meant he was about to close the deal on the purchase of Montague Court he went forward with a hand outstretched.

'What the 'ell's the matter with that sister of yours?' Leigh Grant demanded.

'Margaret?' Edward frowned.

'She's the only one you've got isn't she? Thank goodness too. You wouldn't want a whole tribe of 'em!'

'What is the matter?' Edward asked, leading the man towards the main door.

'Today, my solicitor had this.'

'This' was a letter and Edward read it with growing alarm. Margaret had stated that the price of the house had increased by a thousand pounds.

'I don't understand. She said nothing of this to me and I certainly wouldn't have agreed. Come with me will you? We can get this sorted straight away.'

Muttering about the uselessness of women in business and the irritations of the same, Leigh followed Edward through the main door, along the passage and into the kitchen where Margaret and Islwyn were preparing sandwiches and arranging small cakes on plates ready for afternoon tea.

'This won't do, Margaret,' Edward said striding towards her. 'You can't do this!'

'I already have, Edward,' she replied with a smile. She didn't look at him and neither did she stop setting out the small cakes.

'But we have an agreement for Mr Grant to

buy the house. At the price stated.' He didn't know how to deal with Margaret at the best of times and this could turn out to be the worst of times, with a heavy bridging loan to consider.

Mr Grant stepped forward and edged Edward out of the way. He caught hold of Margaret's arm and turned her to face him. 'What the 'ell's going on? You either want to sell the house or you don't. You're wasting my valuable time. D'you realise that?'

'I saw another agent, this time in Cardiff,' she explained, 'and they said the place was being sold too cheaply. I informed Oakland Estate Agency and demanded they adjusted the price accordingly.'

'You can't do this,' Edward said weakly. 'We gave our word.'

'Nothing is signed.'

'But I've spent money and I'll make damned sure everyone knows about your dishonest ways. You'll never sell.'

Margaret looked at Edward then, and smiled. 'Now wouldn't that be a pity?'

'I'll offer one hundred and fifty more and if you don't sign contracts today the deal is off.' Leigh Grant strode off and at the door, he stopped and waved Edward to join him.

'I mean it. I can't waste any more time on this.'

'I'll do everything I can, Mr Grant. I want this sorted too.'

It was nearly too late now to go to the police regarding the money. He wasn't in the mood to start on the preparations for the evening meal. He returned to where Margaret was now slicing cucumber and tomatoes to garnish the sandwiches, and spoke to her calmly.

'Margaret. You have to sell. I will never change my mind about leaving here. You might wait months and then get a much lower sum. Whatever you plan to do once this is sold, you need as much money as possible to make a start, don't you?'

'I'll discuss it with Issy,' she said.

Holding back on the need to argue and show his frustration, Edward looked at the vegetables waiting his attention and the fish under its cover that needed boning and cleaning. He couldn't face it. Not after this.

'Great,' he said with a grim smile. 'Then I'll leave you in peace to talk it over with Issy. I'm going out!'

'But Edward! It's your turn to deal with this!' She spread her arms to encompass the work that needed urgent attention.

'Not tonight it isn't, and I dare say I'll be less and less reliable until the contract is signed.' He walked over to the car. If he was lucky, the police station wouldn't be busy and someone would be willing to listen to his story. The old draper's shop had more interest to him than the work at Montague Court.

On the way to the police station he had to pass the estate agency and he stopped and went in. A brief discussion assured them that the sale to Mr Grant was still on and that Margaret would be in the following day to sign the contract.

* * *

Edward didn't get to the police station. The urgent sound of an approaching fire engine made him curious and he followed it to the main road through the town. Dense smoke filled the air and the cloying smell of burning made him close the car window. A second appliance arrived and a police car followed. He parked in a side street and went to see what was happening. It was soon clear that the large department shop facing the main square was on fire. Palls of smoke poured out of the roof and flames were seen leaping in frightening intensity through broken windows of the first and second floors.

The usual crowds had gathered and he saw the police and fire officers push them back. He presumed this was to allow the firemen to deal with the fierce blaze. But to his surprise he saw that cameras were on the scene. The BBC outside broadcasting van had been in the town to cover the opening of a new playground, and had taken the opportunity to add the fire story to the item filmed for the local television news.

Lewis Lewis was standing in the crowd and Edward went to join him. 'Mr Lewis? This is a first, isn't it?'

'Being present as news is made? Yes. And we'd better smile in case we're caught on camera.'

They both watched as the roving lens of the camera travelled past them and on around the crowd, then back to the action outside the blazing building.

Flames were doused with jets of water that sparkled in the spring sunshine of the late afternoon, and gradually died down. The chattering crowd dispersed and the two men nodded to each other and went their separate ways, Lewis to a lonely evening in the house of Rhiannon and Charlie, Edward to smother his guilt at his dereliction of his duties at Montague Court. He decided to postpone reporting the money found, and instead, call on Megan.

★   ★   ★

98

When Lewis reached the house in Sophie Street he looked across at number seven as he always did and saw his daughter coming out of the door.

'Dad,' she said, 'I've got a whole week off next week. Barry is coming to look after the shop and I'm going to decorate the house. Or at least some of it,' she added with a smile.

'I can help you at the weekend and in the evenings, love. I'll be glad of something to do.' Rhiannon looked doubtful and he said, 'I'm not useless you know. Your old dad used to keep number seven in good order, didn't he?'

'Of course you did, it's just, well, Mam has offered. I couldn't tell her not to come, could I?'

'Then I'll do what I can and I promise I won't do anything to make your mother lose her temper with me. Right?' He smiled at her and added in a whisper, 'Damned hard it'll be, mind, knowing how easy it is to make her mad. We all know she isn't a redhead for nothing.'

'Charlie, Gwyn and I are going to see our Viv on Saturday afternoon to look at paint colours and wallpapers. Exciting, isn't it?'

Lewis wondered sadly whether they were planning on decorating a nursery. He couldn't accept his daughter's marriage to a man who had seen the inside of more than one prison, even though she seemed utterly happy. He was certain it couldn't last.

Gwyn watched his stepgrandfather and wished he could make him a friend. He loved Rhiannon and her mother Dora, but Lewis seemed unwilling to accept him, apart from rare occasions like the game of ducks and drakes at the seaside that day. Childlike, he wished something would happen to persuade Lewis he was worth a few minutes of his time but what that something was, he had no idea.

'Want to help me wash the car?' Lewis asked, an hour later. But that was not the Something Gwyn was hoping for. Besides he had promised to see Dora.

'Sorry Mr Lewis, but I've said I'll go and see Gran. She's bringing home some leftovers from the café for our tea.'

Lewis shook out the pages of his newspaper and hid his disappointment in its shadow.

* * *

Margaret didn't go to Oaklands Estate Agency the following morning, even though Edward had told her the time of the appointment and waited for more than an hour.

When he walked into the kitchen, Margaret

held up a hand to stop the words about to burst from him.

'I know, I should have been there, but things happen here and I just couldn't make it. You'll have to rearrange it for next week.'

'And you'll stall and stall until the Grants give up. Is that it?'

'Edward, you can't honestly want to see this lovely old house in the hands of the Grants? Did you know they were scrap merchants? And that Mrs Grant ran a second-hand clothes shop? Issy checked on them and it's true. They've been dealing in old metal and other people's unwanted junk, for heaven's sake! How can they take on a place like this? We have to wait for someone more suitable. Mummy would be broken-hearted seeing it go to people like the Grants.'

'Nonsense, Margaret. They are perfectly decent folk.'

'Decent maybe, but can you image what this wonderful old house would look like in a year's time if we allow them to buy it? They'd tear out eveything that's beautiful and change the decor to 'contemp'ry'.' She mimicked the voice of a simpering woman. ' 'Contemp'ry' carpets instead of these wonderful Axminsters, and 'contemp'ry' curtains with jagged patterns on material you can see through. I can just imagine the plastic 'egg chairs' in the lounge can't you?' She turned for Islywn to share her disparaging laughter, but it wasn't Islwyn who stood in the doorway, it was Annie Grant.

'I don't intend to change anything in this historic house apart from more modern plumbing, Miss Jenkins,' Annie said in her quiet voice. 'And if my taste lacks the necessary polish, I'm not too proud to seek advice. In fact, I have already instructed a professional designer to come and look at the place and help me arrange the few quality pieces I've already bought, and assist me in finding the rest.'

As she walked out, Edward glared at his sister. 'If you don't sign that contract today, I'll burn the place down, Margaret. Contents and all! The house might be beautiful but you are not!'

★ ★ ★

Sally returned from shopping to find the back door wide open. She couldn't keep the place completely secure because of her guests coming and going at odd times, but she thought she'd locked it. Then as she thought about her movements she remembered she had gone out through the front door. She couldn't have left the back door unlocked, surely. Things like checking doors and windows before going out were automatic. Perhaps one of the boarders had called back for something? No, she admitted to herself, if anyone forgot, it was me.

Even with the thought she might have done it herself, she couldn't shake off a feeling of unease at finding the door open. Standing in the kitchen, afraid to go any further, she called for Ryan. Then she noticed that the carved table that had stood near the bottom of the stairs was not there; neither were the two valuable porcelain bowls that had stood on it. Surely they hadn't had a break-in?

Slowly, still calling her husband's name, she went through the hall and into the lounge. There she could see quite clearly that they had been robbed. She backed out and went to where the telephone now sat on the floor, its table missing from the corner.

When they had first been married, there had been plenty of money and she and Ryan had chosen some beautiful antiques for their home: some Georgian silver, and elegant lamps and small tables and chairs that they had found at auction rooms. China too had become an interest and she looked around, tiptoeing into the rooms as though she were a stranger there, and saw that most of the best items were missing.

She returned to the hall and as she knelt to pick up the phone to call the police, the thought flitted through her mind that Ryan might have taken them to sell. He was always complaining about having no money in his pocket. They were his as much as hers. Perhaps she should wait to speak to him before calling the police. She replaced the phone.

'Why haven't you called the police?' Ryan demanded when he came in a few minutes later and learned of the robbery.

'I thought, well, I didn't know whether you'd decided to sell them.'

'What? You're accusing me of robbing my own house? Like your father, eh? Burning down his shop and claiming the insurance? Is that what you think of me?'

Frightened now, her tongue tripping over the words, she tried to explain that, as they were his he had every right to sell them should he wish to do so. The words came out disjointed, making no sense.

★ ★ ★

When Megan went home she called as usual as she stepped through the door but her mother didn't answer. She had been in for more than an hour and had started peeling

104

the potatoes which were standing in a bowl ready, cutting them into chips for the usual Friday meal, before Sally appeared.

'Mummy. I was wondering where you were.'

'I was having a lie down, dear.'

'Are you ill?'

'No, but I fell again and hurt my head.'

'Tomorrow you and I are seeing the doctor.'

'No, dear. It's all right. I wasn't dizzy or anything. I was overloaded, trying to save myself a journey, you know how it is. A lazy man's load your grandmother would call it.'

Megan sniffed the air and frowned. 'I can smell vinegar. Have you spilled any?'

'Perhaps when I refilled the bottles a little while ago.'

Megan glanced at the shelf where they kept the condiments used for the tables. The vinegar bottles were far from full.

'Where's Daddy?' she asked.

'He's — I don't exactly know, I've been asleep,' Sally excused. There was weakness in her voice and Megan wondered with some alarm whether she had been crying.

The front door slammed and Megan saw her father hurrying down the drive. She knew something was wrong between her parents, but couldn't imagine what it could be and daren't ask. She would talk to Joan about it.

A little later, she went into the bathroom and smelled again the sharp, unmistakable smell of vinegar. In the small litter bin in her mother's bedroom she found a pad of brown paper that had been saturated in the stuff. The words of the rhyme came to her.

' . . . he went to bed to mend his head
with vinegar and brown paper.'

It was what boxers and others used to help reduce bruising. If that was what her mother had done, why had she lied?

* * *

Rhiannon started work on the living room on Monday morning after Charlie and Gwyn had gone to work. Stripping wallpaper off was a tedious task but by lunchtime she had managed to clean two walls. Her father came in at three o'clock and insisted on helping.

'Your Mam won't be home from the café until six so I've got about four hours,' he said, after changing into old clothes.

When Charlie and Gwyn came in at six the walls were clean and the ceiling had its first coat of white paint.

'Thanks, Mr Lewis,' Charlie said, pleased

with the result of the first day. 'I feel awful about Rhiannon doing it while I'm at work, but she insisted on having a go.'

'And I feel awful too,' Lewis told him. 'She's only a young girl and she was intending to do that high ceiling herself.' His voice was harsh, the words came out as a criticism.

'It wasn't my idea, but Rhiannon wanted to try,' Charlie protested. 'I wouldn't tell her she couldn't do it. She makes her own decisions. I respect her too much to tell her what to do.'

Lewis was angry — but with himself and not Charlie. He had intended to say he was glad he'd been able to take a few hours off and help. 'I'll give the ceiling its second coat before I go to work in the morning,' he said gruffly.

'Thanks for your help,' Charlie uttered.

'You're welcome' didn't seem a suitable reply, so Lewis said nothing.

When Dora came at seven o'clock she was dressed in overalls and wore a scarf around her fiery red hair. Seeing the walls were all stripped and clean, she suggested they sized them ready for the paper.

'I'll do that, Dora,' Charlie said, 'but first I'm taking Rhiannon and Gwyn for a walk and to get some fish and chips for supper. Will you come?' He glanced at Lewis as he spoke but Lewis presumed the words were for Dora alone and didn't acknowledge them. Dora shook her head.

'No thanks. I'll just get all this wallpaper into a sack for the rubbish and go home. We'll do the sizing tomorrow evening, shall we?' She had guessed from the atmosphere that Lewis was out of favour. The three went out leaving Lewis and Dora alone. 'Have you upset them?' Dora demanded as the door closed.

'Not intentionally, no.' He started to explain what had happened, but instead he said, 'It's no use, Dora love, I don't trust the man with our Rhiannon. He's a jailbird. He's broken into people's houses and stolen from them. He stole from the shop where Rhiannon works. How can I welcome him as a son-in-law?'

'By looking at Rhiannon and seeing how happy she is.'

'What about you, Dora. Are you happy?'

'I'm enjoying the cafe, and working with Sian is pleasant enough.'

'That wasn't what I asked.'

'Yes,' she snapped, 'I'm happy! Right?'

Lewis burst out laughing. 'I asked an innocent question and you flare up as if I'd asked you to murder someone.' He went into the kitchen and put the kettle on to boil. 'If I ask if you'd like a cup of tea, will you shout at me?'

'No. But I'd refuse.' She picked up her coat and he held her back.

'Please, Dora. Stay a while. I'm damned lonely.'

'And whose fault is that?'

'Mine,' he said sadly. But she stayed.

* * *

Margaret stalled for a few more days but signed for the sale of Montague Court on the twenty-third of May. She had always known the house would have to be sold. Once Edward had backed out and demanded half of the money there had been no hope.

'He let me down badly, Issy,' she said as she and Islwyn were getting into bed. 'I can't bear the thought of leaving my home. What shall we do?'

'Sometimes things that seem ruinous turn out to be for the best. This house would always have been a drain on you. There would never have been a moment in all your life when you were free of money worries. A place like this eats money like water pouring down a drain in a storm.'

'I know all that, but I love it so. Besides, we do have to earn a living. What can we do?'

'Open that restaurant you've often talked about. You're a particularly talented cook, my dear, and I'm quite capable of doing all the less skilled jobs.'

'A cafe,' she said despondently. 'Like your wife, Sian.'

'A restaurant very *unlike* my wife Sian's. You'd soon earn a reputation for first-class cuisine. Dora and Sian run an unimpressive caff!'

'I have considered a small, exclusive restaurant,' she mused.

'Then think again, of a *large*, exclusive restaurant. Something that will make Edward's pathetic little shop seem like a joke.'

He had hit on the one thing to cheer her. 'I'll pay him back, Issy. I want to see him suffer for the way he's behaved.'

'Don't waste energy on petty anger, my darling. You're bigger than that. Stronger. More dynamic. A visionary endowed with imaginative skills. You'll be so successful you'll be able to forget you ever had a brother Edward.'

'Maybe, but I don't want Edward to forget me.'

★ ★ ★

110

With the sale of Montague Court set to go through, Edward's activities in the restaurant were reduced. He spent hours each day working with Frank Griffiths and occasionally Hywel, getting the shop emptied and cleaned.

'Can you imagine this ever being a garden in which we can sit and relax?' he asked Frank one morning when they threw even more rubbish out of the house and into the once cleared area.

Frank laughed. 'Every time we clear it, we start filling it again, but it'll come. The last few bricks from the dividing walls will take another day to clear, but then we'll get Dad and Ernie with the van, and we'll empty the garden for the last time.'

'Don't you get tired of dealing with jobs like this?' Edward asked as Frank added more bricks to the pile that almost covered the small back garden. 'I'm fed up with mess and confusion and I've only had a few weeks of it.'

'It depends on what you want from life,' Frank the philosopher replied. 'Now me, I don't like responsibility, see. I give Mam as much as I can afford each week and she does the rest. I never get a bill, she tells me when I need new clothes, she feeds me and I help Dad keep the place going. For me, perfect. Now our Basil's different. He's married to Eleri and they had two little boys and he's in his oils. Never been happier. So there it is, it's what you choose.'

Edward was surprised. He'd never heard more than half a dozen words from Frank before; in fact all Frank usually offered were monosyllabic grunts.

'It sounds as though you've thought about life very seriously,' he said.

'Seriously and long, Mr Jenkins. And I know I'm not the sort to be a reliable husband. Sad,' he added, 'but true.'

'I never thought I'd marry,' Edward replied, 'so I told everyone, including myself, that I didn't want to.'

The remark hit home to Frank, who had begun to think he was unlovable and would never find a girl who could love him. He didn't reply for a long time and as both men were working hard sorting the bricks and stones into piles, Edward thought the conversation was over. Then Frank said, 'You're right.'

'Am I?' Edward frowned. 'Right about what?'

'Right in thinking I'm pretending. I do want to find a girl and marry her but I don't think I ever will, so I tell myself I don't want to. Sad, eh?' he said with a wry grin.

'It seems perfectly normal to me. I suspect we aren't the only ones, Frank. There must be many people who do just that.'

Frank stopped shovelling and stared at Edward, who in spite of the physical work he was involved in, still managed to look smartly dressed and elegant, wearing overshoes to protect his footwear and gloves to protect his hands. 'You know, you aren't half bad for one of the gentry, mate.'

'One of the gentry? The Jenkinses? Not any more I'm not, but thank you.'

When he left Frank finishing the clearing, and got ready to go back to Montague Court, Edward's thoughts were on Megan. Something about his strange conversation with Frank had brought his feelings for Megan into focus. Not one of the world's great thinkers, but Frank had certainly highlighted one of his own worst fears. Like Frank, he didn't want to face the rest of his life alone.

* * *

Similar thoughts were keeping Lewis's mind from his work. At two-thirty he rang up his last two customers and cancelled his appointments, then he headed back to Sophie Street. He knew Dora would still be at the cafe, but Rhiannon should be at home finishing off the decorating. Opening the door he called and was rewarded with seeing Rhiannon coming

out of the kitchen followed by the enthusiastic dog.

'Dad. This is a surprise. Don't tell me
you're mitching again?'

'I know you want to get the room finished
today, so I thought, while you did that, I'd
make a start on Gwyn's room. I'd like to do
something for the boy.'

Pausing only for a sandwich, Lewis set
about cleaning the walls and washing the
ceiling in the boy's room, hoping that, besides
helping Rhiannon, it would please his
stepgrandson. He was impressed with the
paper the boy had chosen. Cheerful but not
overpowering. He must remember to con-
gratulate him on his choice. The walls had
already been scraped clear of wallpaper, and
Lewis sized the walls and painted the ceiling
before stopping to eat.

When Dora came at seven, he asked her to
go with him to the pictures instead of
working on the next stage of the decorating.
Prepared for arguments and reasons for
saying no, he could do nothing but stare
when she agreed.

At once Gwyn asked whether he could go
with them and Lewis glared at him and said,
no. The boy's face crumpled and Lewis felt
ashamed. Unintentionally he'd upset the boy
again. 'Any other time I'd love you to come,

son,' he said. 'But tonight, I want to talk to your Gran.'

'Let him come, Lewis,' Dora said. So it was the three of them who set off an hour later, to a film none would enjoy, each aware of the disappointment of the others.

One day, Lewis thought, one day I'll do something right!

★　★　★

Three times Margaret and Islwyn thought they had found the perfect position for their restaurant. Each time they were refused permission to change the use from residential to business. All the time as they searched and were thwarted, she blamed her brother for their trouble.

'It's all right for him,' she complained to Islwyn as they closed the door on another disastrous property. 'He chose when to leave. He had something all ready and waiting. No thought for how difficult it would be for us.'

'There are a dozen properties that would do for what Edward has planned, dear. We need something a bit more select.'

They were walking back to the car along the road overlooking the docks and the railway sidings when he stopped to examine the details of the final house for that day.

'Not far,' he said, 'we might as well walk.'

It was situated in a quiet street which was lined on either side with tall trees. The properties were large and had once been imposing, but most were neglected and run down. The area was not one to appeal to the clientele they hoped to attract. Sadly they retraced their footsteps and headed back to the car.

They drove around, remarking on the possibilities of certain streets and the hopelessness of others. On reaching the beach they stopped and decided to walk a while. That was when they saw a 'For Sale' notice they hadn't seen before. It was beside a path which led down to a small bay not far from the pleasure beach and with a garden that overlooked the sea.

The house itself was detached and with a wide drive shaped like an upside down Y, with two gateways marked 'in' and 'out'. Thrown into the shrubbery they spotted a dilapidated sign stating the place had once been called Waterside Restaurant.

'At least there won't be difficulties about change of use,' Margaret whispered excitedly.

The man who showed them around the three reception rooms and five bedrooms was vague. His wife was shopping he told them and he kept looking around as if expecting her to suddenly appear, like a genie from a lamp.

The rooms were clean and elegantly decorated and furnished, and at once they knew it had possibilities. A week later they had arranged to buy it. A survey had been carried out and an architect consulted to deal with the enlargement of three rooms into one with a series of arches.

For a while, Margaret forgot her aching need to revenge herself on Edward.

* * *

In the garden of the old shop, Frank was scraping rubbish together with two large pieces of wood, using them like paddles to draw the assorted oddments together before picking them up and putting them into a sack. Something stuck against the wood stopping its movement and irritably he pulled at the rubble and dead branches and long, dead grass and found a wrapped candlestick. It looked rather fancy and for a moment he thought of taking it to sell, but conscience prevailed and he put it aside to show Edward.

They went together to the police station and showed them the candlestick and it was quickly recognised as being a part of the haul when Sally and Ryan's house was robbed.

Megan came to tell him and she was still there when the police came to interview Edward about how it had been discovered.

'All I can tell you is that it was found among the rubbish when Frank Griffiths was scraping up the last of the rubble from the building work,' Edward told them. 'If you speak to Frank he'll be able to give more details. I can't tell you how pleased I am that at least one item has been found. Perhaps there'll be a clue as to where the rest is hidden?'

'We'd like permission to search your property, sir. Here and Montague Court.'

'My property? But of course, although as it was found out here, there doesn't seem much point.'

The stony-faced policeman then asked, 'Can you give me your movements on the afternoon of the robbery, sir?'

Alarmed, Edward thought a moment then shook his head. 'My movements are no longer regular I'm afraid. I spend a lot of time at Montague Court with my sister, and a lot of time here, with Frank Griffiths. It's impossible for me to remember exactly where I was at a given time.'

Quirking an eyebrow, the policeman asked, 'You wouldn't be thinking of using Frank Griffiths as an alibi would you?'

'Why not? He found it and handed it in, didn't he? I've found Frank to be hard-working and honest, so I can't allow you to make me say otherwise.'

'This property, sir,' he waved his arms expressively, 'it's an expensive undertaking?'

'I can cope, constable.'

'I'm sure you can, sir. Thank you for your help. We'll be in touch.'

'He thinks I did it!' Edward gasped.

'How exciting,' Megan laughed.

★　★　★

When the shop basement was finally cleared, Frank and his father found a sink with a tap, previously hidden in a corner, and also what looked like a junction for a gas appliance on an opposite wall. Both had been boarded up but the sink drained satisfactorily, and water gurgled, spluttered and eventually flowed, brown and rusty, from its solitary brass tap. They showed it to Edward with great pride, as though they were responsible for it being there and were offering it to him as a prize.

'Someone must have lived down here at one time,' Edward said when he showed Megan. 'Perhaps I could rent it out and earn a few pounds to help things along. Frank said his brother Basil might be able to find a bed

119

and table and the rest, although I might get what I need from Montague Court. We will want it decorated though.'

'Another job for Frank Griffiths,' Megan smiled. 'D'you think he'll cope with such regular work?'

'If he does, I gather it will be the longest gap between court appearances since he was nine!'

5

The police had called on Sally and Ryan and begun their investigation of the robbery.

'There have been a series of break-ins to houses where good quality items are likely to be found and, surprisingly, this their seems to be a rather well-dressed, well-spoken man himself,' Inspector Leonard told them. 'Perhaps someone who knows these houses, has been a guest at some time. He seems to get in and out fast, suggesting he knows what he's looking for and where to find it.'

He looked at Sally, standing beside the couch on which Megan was sitting, then at Ryan, on the opposite end of the elegant room, leaning on the windowsill and looking down at his highly polished, expensive leather shoes.

'If you think of someone in your circle, sir and madam, or you Miss Fowler-Weston, someone who might be desperate for cash, someone who might need money badly enough to commit these crimes, you would tell me?'

'Of course,' Megan said sharply, 'but

there's no one we know who'd be capable of this.'

'Tell me about your brother-in-law,' the policeman glanced at his notebook and went on, 'Islwyn Heath-Weston is it? He's now living with — er — at Montague Court, I believe?'

Sally was staring at Ryan and didn't respond to the question. Ryan continued to look down at his shoes, so it was again Megan who answered him.

'He is, Inspector, and if you require details of his movements you'd better ask him; we don't see him and have no idea what he gets up to.'

'He's a fool, we all know that, but he wouldn't be involved with this.' Ryan spoke for the first time.

Sally looked at him, her eyes staring intensely. 'Who knows what another person is capable of. We don't really know anyone, do we?'

★ ★ ★

The police searched Edward's shop and his room at Montague Court, but found nothing. Edward was anxious, Margaret angry at the impression their investigation gave to the Grants, and Megan was amused.

122

'Imagine them seeing you in the role of burglar, Edward. With your injured leg and the ancient car you drive, you'd hardly be ready for the quick getaway, would you?'

He smiled ruefully. 'I wonder how they can think me capable of doing anything fast. I'm the slowest thinker on record. I'd be caught standing outside the house wondering whether to turn left or right.'

'Don't put yourself down, Edward, you're smarter than your sister believes for a start, and you're going to be one of Pendragon Island's most successful businessmen. I insist on it.'

Besides searching the newly cleared shop, the police went through the other empty properties on the row and found that one had been used as a shelter.

'Probably a tramp,' Constable Gregory told them. 'There were some boxes and a stub of a candle and a few old clothes. I think someone must have slept there, perhaps during the winter. Nothing more recent than an April newspaper anyway.'

'Will you need me for anything else?' Edward asked.

'It's possible, I can't say, sir,' was the disconcerting reply. 'It depends what comes up during our enquiries. Just as long as we know where to find you if we do, you needn't worry any further.'

'They *do* suspect me!' Edward whispered as the last of the constables propped up the fallen gate and left.

★ ★ ★

Sally had managed to cover up the real reason for the bruise on her face and although movement was painful, no one except Ryan knew of the larger bruises on her body. After the first time he had been careful not to hit her where it was likely to show. The blow to her face on that second attack had been caused by the side of the dressing table when she had fallen over.

She wasn't sure why he hit her sometimes and on other occasions was kind and gentle, praising her, even offering to help with the work she did in keeping the house running and the meals coming for her boarders. After the first occasion when she had asked him to make the cup of tea he wanted, she had been careful not to ask him to do anything. Yet on three separate occasions he had suddenly lost control. She tried to puzzle out what had caused it. But there didn't seem to be a pattern. The saddest part was her inability to talk about it to anyone.

Her mother would be very distressed and

even Sian, her twin, to whom she would normally have run, couldn't be told. She wouldn't have been able to hold back from interfering. Whatever had caused it, she was the one at fault. She must have done something to make a placid man suddenly turn into a monster. She must have changed; in some way she had caused him such irritation that he had become a different person. So, she reasoned, it was up to her to change him back.

She took on an extra assistant, intending to make sure she had more time to spend with Ryan. The girl, Judith Parry, was employed to help clean the house and deal with the laundry during the morning and prepare the vegetables for the evening meal. The idea was for Sally to sit in the lounge with Ryan and talk about their day, share the activities of the house that had been their family home.

For the first three mornings he went out as she entered the room. On the fourth, she had followed him upstairs to ask whether he would like to go into town and help choose some new curtains for the room that would be the nursery when their grandchild was born.

'We won't have to spend much, dear,' she assured him, reaching for her coat. 'The window isn't large, but it will please Megan that we have bothered. Perhaps a rug as well. What d'you think?'

She hardly felt the first blow, as her coat was bunched up around her shoulders, but the second, a punch to her stomach had her bending over and trying not to be sick.

Then she was against the wall, trying not to make a sound, curling her head under her arms and staying there for long after he had gone.

'I shouldn't have mentioned the baby,' she chided herself between sobs. 'It was my fault. He told me how much it distressed him. How could I have been so stupid?'

After that incident she hardly spoke to him at all. She rose early and went to bed late and locked herself in. She presumed he slept in the loft room and also guessed he had been careful not to be seen leaving it, as Megan said nothing about the arrangement.

★ ★ ★

Constable Gregory went to Montague Court and asked to talk to Islwyn.

'Sorry to bother you, sir, but I wondered whether you'd seen anyone hanging about, you know, someone who shouldn't have been where you saw him? It's a long shot, but sometimes the small piece of the jigsaw is the one that leads to success.'

As the policeman was leaving, Margaret followed him and said, almost apologetically, 'I don't suppose it will help, but my brother Edward's movements are rather erratic these days.'

'How d'you mean, Miss Jenkins?'

'Well, until a few weeks ago I always knew where to find him, but now, he's often absent during the day. I've had to do his work on several occasions, you can ask Islwyn. And at night. He's often very late.'

'What are you suggesting, miss?'

'Oh, good heavens, I wasn't suggesting — oh dear!' She put an embarrassed hand to her mouth. 'No, I didn't mean — I just thought that he's a more likely person to have noticed someone 'hanging about' as you put it. That's all.' She was smiling as she returned to the kitchen.

★   ★   ★

The local papers were filled with reports of the spate of robberies. In Dora and Sian's café they heard the gossip and the rumours and the exaggerations, both thankful they had no valuables for anyone to covet.

'I've never had any, and you disposed of yours when you sold your big posh house, didn't you?' Dora said to Sian.

They were also among the first to hear that Gwennie Woodlas, who owned the gown shop in the town, had disturbed the thief as he was gathering together the items he'd chosen. She came into the café after the police had examined her home,

'Too distressed I am to go and open the shop today.' She answered their questions cheerfully though, proud of the fact she had prevented the burglar from getting away with her cherished ornaments and silver.

'Smartly dressed he was,' Gwennie told them. 'I remember how shiny his shoes were, top quality leather too. And such fine worsted trousers and blazer. I can recognise quality when I see it. I didn't see his face, he wore something over it; frightening it was mind.' She frowned at the memory then added, 'He spoke, you know. Called me a stupid woman would you believe! Me with a business and a grand house and him having to steal what isn't his, and he calls me stupid!' She lowered her voice. 'The thing is, I'm sure I'd recognise his voice again. He wasn't the usual kind of man to steal from houses.'

'What's the usual type?' Dora asked, thinking she was about to hear a criticism of Charlie, and preparing to retort.

'He was more the Raffles sort of criminal.

You know, a gentleman thief. His voice was very upper class.'

★ ★ ★

The police visited Charlie and, after several visits and blatant checking of his story, were apparently reassured that he had nothing to do with the thefts. Dora was upset, worried about the effect on her daughter's marriage, of the constant threat of police suspicions. She was there one day when PC Gregory called to tell Charlie they probably wouldn't want to see him again.

'I should think so too!' Dora commented. 'Fat chance of allowing people to forget previous mistakes with your lot barging in every time something disappears. When will you leave the boy alone?'

'Sorry, Mrs Lewis. I like the lad,' the policeman replied, 'but we have to check on ex-criminals.'

'At least you refer to him as an ex!'

'This time we have a description and, well, the man was described as tall, which you are not,' he said turning to Charlie, adding with a grin 'expensively dressed, polished shoes, carefully pressed clothes, well spoken and charming, all of which you are not!' After a final discussion of Charlie's movements, the

129

constable said, 'All in all, this one's a bit out of your class, boy. The items stolen aren't your 'quick sale, ask no questions' type of robbery. No. Fancy stuff like this bloke takes, needs some real good contacts. Although,' he added warningly, 'don't think you're out of the frame yet. Who knows what contacts you made in prison, eh? We're watching you, remember that.'

Lewis was embarrassed when he heard about the latest inquisition and he went to number seven Sophie Street to talk to Dora.

'It's humiliating living in a house where the police call whenever something like this happens. And our daughter being married to a criminal! Who'd have thought we'd end up like this, with the police around every corner 'making enquiries'? It's not right, Dora. We ought to do something.'

'Charlie's not a criminal! He's given up all that and you well know it! Our daughter's happy, Charlie's good to her, Gwyn loves her too. Think about it, Lewis. Do you want to do something to spoil that?'

'I know. I just wish — ' He sat down in the chair that had always been regarded as his when the family lived at home. 'I just wish we weren't mixed up with the police. What if he *is* guilty? What if he — '

'Don't say any more,' Dora warned, waving

130

a threatening finger. 'Just support them. They're a lovely little family and they're ours. Right? Besides,' she added more slowly. 'There's a bit of a look about Rhiannon that makes me think she might be telling us some exciting news very soon.'

'You mean — ?'

'I mean you might be a grandfather next year. Make you feel old does it? Too old for women? Perhaps that'll stop your shenanigans, eh?'

'Oh Dora,' he laughed. He stood up and opened his arms to her and she went to share in a hug.

* * *

Annie and Leigh Grant went to see Edward and demanded that he dealt with the latest of Margaret's tricks.

'Only taken the chandeliers hasn't she!' Leigh shouted as soon as he found Edward in the shop. 'They were clearly marked as part of the sale. I want them back. Pronto. Right?' The man's rage startled Edward.

'But nothing's been moved out of the house, yet.'

'Go and look if you don't believe me. Annie and I went to check a few measurements. You know what the women are like for getting ahead of themselves.'

Locking the shop, Edward went to find Margaret. She was nowhere to be found but the chandeliers were indeed missing. In their place, simple lamp holders had been fixed. As well as the lights, other things had gone too.

On Margaret's desk Edward shuffled through papers and found scribbled on a margin a telephone number with the name Browns beside it. He dialled the number and found it was a curtains and loose covers agency. Determinedly he rang several other numbers he found and on his fourth attempt reached a Cardiff antiques dealer.

A threat of the police, a firm assurance that the goods were in fact stolen, and it was quickly agreed they would all be returned, and an invoice sent to Margaret with its own threat of police involvement.

When he told Margaret she had to repay the money he didn't hear her reply. Anger blotted out everything but his determination to beat her every time she tried to cheat on the Grants.

* * *

In the old draper's shop, progress had been fast. By the end of June, Frank and his father, with occasional help from Ernie, had cleared the rubble and emptied the basement. The builders had completed the rearrangement of the rooms by removing a wall and adding a new doorway to another. The shop fitters were already finished and the place was looking completely different from the sad place Edward had first seen.

'Heard anything about that money yet?' Frank asked.

'We've tried everywhere we can think of but William Jones, retired draper, seems to have vanished.'

'I asked Mam and Dad but they don't remember where he went. Probably dead,' Frank said lugubriously. 'Best you spend it.'

'I won't give up yet,' Edward smiled. 'Megan's going to every shop in the road and asking if they remember the old man. Someone will eventually give us a clue I'm sure.'

Megan came in just then. She shook her head. 'No luck yet,' she told them, and Frank hauled himself up off the floor where he had been touching up the skirting boards, and went to find some liquid lunch.

'I'm so grateful for your help,' Edward told Megan as they looked at the completed display area. 'I don't think I'd have made such excellent use of the space without your ideas.'

'I haven't finished yet,' she said in her sharp manner. 'So don't dismiss me like an unwanted employee!'

'Thank goodness for that,' he smiled. 'I was hoping you'd go through the orders and make sure I haven't forgotten anything.'

'You're brave to have decided to cover all sports including golf, and the increasingly popular ski holiday goods, Edward. They're expensive and there's a risk of money lying idle in the stock you'll have to carry.'

'You think I'm wrong.'

'Not at all. Confidence is the key and will certainly pay off in this case. Edward, I'm proud of you.'

They sat together in the basement at the table Basil had brought in, enjoying the sun shining over the rooftops and warming them. Edward flicked through the pages of orders he'd completed. Sports clothing in every size from school sports wear to extra large adult garments. Tennis rackets and cricket bats, through darts and table tennis and bowls equipment and even skipping ropes and, when they could find room, fishing would have its own section too.

'Whatever there's a demand for we'll stock it, that'll be our motto,' Edward said.

'*Our* motto?' Megan queried with a tilt of her head.

'Ours if you want it to be, Megan. In fact, I can't imagine running the business without you on hand.'

'I'm afraid The Lump might have other ideas.' She patted her distended belly with a small sigh.

'Don't be sad about becoming a mother.' Edward put a hand over hers. 'The little one won't stop you doing anything you really want to do. He'll be much too considerate.'

There was a glow of excitement in his eyes as he reassured her about the baby, an inner fire that seemed to grow as her body swelled with each passing week.

'You're quite as excited about the birth as I am, aren't you?' she said curiously.

'I suppose I am. But only because it's yours. I've never been involved in the development of a baby before and I'm longing to see this little mite.'

'He'll probably look ugly, I'm told they often do. Red and wrinkled and quite awful.'

'How can he be anything else but beautiful if he's yours.' He seemed suddenly to realise the compliment was too impertinent and turned away, rustling the pages of the order book as if searching for something elusive and important.

'Thank you Edward. That was a lovely compliment,' Megan said with a wide smile.

She placed her hands over the page he was pretending to read. 'You're a kind man and I'll be sorry when you don't need my help any more.'

He was trembling and he almost ignored the opportunity to tell her how he felt. He glanced at her and there was something in her expression that implied she was ready to listen. 'Megan, I won't ever be content without your help. I want you with me always.'

'Always, Edward?'

'Not only in the shop. Every moment. Do I stand a chance of keeping you with me always?'

'Ask me again when the baby's born, will you?'

He thought she was turning him down gently, but she was afraid that imagining a child looking sweet, all white frills, and scented with soaps and powders, to admire and nurture, would be different from the actual situation. A baby that cried and demanded attention, and grew in his need of her would disrupt his life in a way he could not comprehend at this moment.

Even though she thought he was in love with her, he could end up feeling trapped and in utter despair. No, it was best to wait, even though she could imagine nothing more wonderful than to spend her life beside this shy and gentle man.

'Just until August and you see what life with a baby is really like,' she said softly. 'I suspect it will be a shock to us both.'

★ ★ ★

Sian and Islwyn's son Jack was a schoolteacher and he had startled his family by falling for his grandmother Gladys's maid, Victoria. A further surprise had been their elopement and marriage at Gretna Green. Victoria had been overwhelmed and terrified by Gladys's interpretation of what their wedding should be and she and Jack had taken matters into their own hands. Yet another revelation was how happy they were. Even Gladys, who thought marrying beneath you was a recipe for disaster, had to agree that Victoria had made Jack content.

Victoria's mother, Mrs Collins, was a widow with six children still at home. She taught piano on an instrument bought for her by Jack and also did some domestic work as her daughter had done. She had agreed to deal with the last minute cleaning of the old draper's shop for Edward.

Most of the clearing and initial cleaning had been done by Frank, but she gave the shop area a final spit and polish, and straightened the displays with enjoyment. The place still held some dust and she found satisfaction in making everything sparkle. She knew that the basement remained filled with clutter and guessed that the dust which coated everything was probably coming from there, with the back door open to freshen the place and dispel the smell of new paint. She finished long before the time Edward had given her so she decided to go and see whether wetting the basement floor would help settle the dust and assist in keeping the place dust free for longer.

There was a sack of sawdust in one corner, left by the carpenter and forgotten by Frank when he had cleared up. Wetting some by putting a few shovelfuls into a bucket of water, she mixed it up and threw the wet sawdust all over the floor then began slowly to sweep it up, taking with it the worst of the dust and the few remaining pieces of rubble.

The steps to the shop from the basement were new and freshly polished. To avoid marking them with wet feet she placed pieces of cardboard on each tread as she went up and down the stairs.

She looked around her, satisfied with her morning's work and went up to wash out her dusters in the kitchen that was part of

Edward's new home. The flat above the sports shop was sparsely furnished but she knew that once the sale of Montague Court was completed, Edward would bring what he needed from there, sharing the contents with Margaret and selling what they neither of them wanted.

She stood for a while imagining how she would furnish the place if it were hers, then, as the town clock struck twelve, suddenly remembered the children coming in from school for lunch. Grasping the dusters and some pegs, she ran down to hang them on the clothes line, slipped on the cardboard on the steps and fell to the bottom.

It was her son-in-law Jack who found her. When she didn't arrive to take the youngest children from Victoria who was looking after them, he went to the shop to look for her.

There was no reply to his knocking and he couldn't get in, so he went around to the back garden, where he found the broken gate propped up. He pushed it aside and went in. She was sitting on the basement steps, pale and obviously distressed.

'I'm all right,' Mrs Collins assured him hurriedly. 'It's only my wrist. I felt a bit shaky that's all.'

'No piano lessons for a while then?' he said, trying not to show his alarm. She was bruised all up one arm and the side of her face had been scraped on the rough slate floor. 'Come on, let's get you home.'

* * *

Margaret heard of the accident and immediately used it to her advantage. 'It's an unlucky place and I don't think the business will succeed,' she told anyone who would listen. She was in the Bluebird Cafe in town one morning when she knew it would be crowded. Her sole reason for being there was to spread gossip. 'It's an unlucky place that shop of Edward's,' she remarked to the woman behind the counter. 'That business will never succeed you know. I tried to warn my brother but he's so stubborn.'

The woman nodded understandingly. 'Men so often are, is my experience.'

Several women for whom superstition was never far below the surface of their minds, listened intently. Gladys Weston and Megan were drinking tea at a table near the window and Margaret hadn't noticed them.

'Mrs Collins slipped on cardboard placed on polished steps. Careless that is, not unlucky!' Megan said sharply. 'She said herself that she should have had more sense!'

'Fancy coming in here brazen as you like,

after stealing your Uncle Islwyn from his wife and family!' Gladys whispered softly. 'How she has the nerve to show her face I don't know.'

Trying to appear unconcerned by the unfortunate encounter, Margaret ignored them and, speaking to the assistant, went on in a loud voice, 'No one knows what happened to the previous owner, you know. Disappeared, leaving all his money. Poor Edward. No one will support him. Anyone with sense will go into Cardiff for their needs, where there's a better choice — and no fear of reprisals from a restive spirit either. Yes, it's haunted. How d'you think that poor Mrs Collins fell down those stairs? An unhappy spirit pushed her. Keep away, that's my advice.'

Megan stood up and glared at her. 'What rot you talk *Miss* Jenkins. But what can I expect of someone who stole someone else's husband? Too unpleasant to find one of your own, aren't you, *Miss* Jenkins?' Followed by an embarrassed and tearful Gladys, Megan left the cafe.

Margaret left soon after, having restored her confidence by repeating her warnings. When she got back to Montague Court she telephoned Edward's firm of shop fitters and advised the manager to get his money as quickly as he could as there was some doubt about all the workmen being paid. The same with the builder, and with Frank Griffiths. It was Frank's mother who guessed what Margaret was trying to do and she told Edward, advising him to scotch the rumours of financial problems immediately.

He wasn't sure what to do, and he had as yet done nothing when Margaret saw one of the suppliers' reps going into the still unopened shop. She called to him and invited him to share a cup of coffee at Montague Court. There, she warned him of the risk involved in letting her brother have goods on the six weeks' credit arrangement.

'He hasn't sufficient funds, you see,' she explained in mock sorrow. 'He was depending on my helping him out, but with this lovely house so slow to sell and our difficulty in finding a place for the restaurant we plan to open, the money simply isn't there.'

Playing the worried and supportive sister was easy; laughing about it later with Issy was hilarious.

★　★　★

With the bank behind him, Edward paid all demands immediately, but the stock was a

142

problem. He had depended on that six weeks' credit in the hope that the sale of Montague Court would be completed and the money would be there.

Putting aside his anxieties he went to see Mrs Collins to make sure she wasn't too badly hurt. At first she made light of it, but seeing her hand bandaged and some bruises on her forearm, Edward insisted on knowing the full story.

'Unfortunately it's my hand and, as I teach piano to a few pupils it's made things difficult,' Mrs Collins admitted. 'But it's only for a week or so. I'll manage,' she said.

'I'll pay for the lessons you miss,' he assured her and put a crisp white five pound note into her hand. 'Please tell me if there's more practical help I can give.'

She stared at the note long after Edward had gone. She'd never owned one before. 'I don't think I can bring myself to spend it,' she laughingly told her daughter Victoria, when she and Jack called later that evening.

★ ★ ★

'What am I going to do about Margaret's stories?' Edward wailed to Megan. 'I've had several firms asking for payment in advance of orders being sent. It's never heard of!'

'Have a big extravagant party,' Megan suggested.

'What d'you mean, a party? I don't even have a home in which to hold one. I can hardly hold it down in the basement!'

'Why not? Advertise a great opening do, invite reps and managing directors of the firms you hope to deal with, and tell anyone who's interested to come.'

'I couldn't do all that.'

'Mrs Collins and Janet Griffiths could. And if they don't want to, there's always my Aunt Sian and Dora Lewis. They run the Rose Tree Cafe and do anything else in the catering line they're asked to do. They did Joan and Viv's wedding didn't they? Go on, it will show everyone you're up and running and will quash rumours of a shortage of money.'

'Here?'

'Here!'

★ ★ ★

Rhiannon had a suspicion she was expecting a baby. She said nothing to Charlie, afraid of disappointment. In a few more weeks she would go to the doctor and only then would she tell him and Gwyn, and her parents, and her brother Viv, and Joan and — She stopped, the list was too long. What fun it would be sharing such wonderful news with all her family and friends. It made her realise how fortunate she was to have so many people who cared for her.

She wondered how her father would take the news. He was not really happy about her marriage to Charlie. She crossed her fingers and thought how wonderful it would be if the baby's arrival brought her parents together again. Dora living across the road in what had been the family home, running the cafe and pretending she was happy. Her father living with them, also trying to pretend he was happy. How much simpler life would be if they were together. How wonderful it would be for Lewis to go back home and for her and Charlie and Gwyn to have the house to themselves, be a proper family before the baby arrived. She sighed. Every time her parents met, they seemed to spark each other off within minutes and part in anger.

She knew the present difficulties were mainly due to her mother — Dora, with her red hair, and the touchiness of temper that reputedly went with that wonderful colouring. Dad would go back, she was certain of that, if only her mother would forgive him and try to forget his past weaknesses. He might even manage to stay constant now his Nia was no longer alive. That he would not was her mother's greatest fear, she knew that. Rhiannon sighed and began peeling potatoes for their main meal. Charlie and Gwyn finished at one-thirty on Saturdays.

Three rooms were now newly decorated and she was pleased with the appearance of her home. Having time off had unsettled her a little. She liked her job, but after being home for a week she had enjoyed not having to go out at a quarter to nine every morning, and not having to spend evenings and weekends rushing to do the routine chores of the house. Her hands were still, the potatoes neglected, as she stared out of the kitchen window and imagined being home all day, with a small baby to care for, and having time to sit and talk to Charlie and Gwyn. Be a proper housewife.

Her thoughts turned again to the problem of Lewis living with them. She loved her father and couldn't bear the thought of him going back to live at The Firs, a rather drab boarding house, but she did wish he didn't live with her and Charlie.

She saw the back gate begin to open and expecting to see her father, she turned away from the window to put a light under the kettle. He liked a cup of tea when he came in. She didn't see an old, whiskered face peering in through the kitchen window, or see the oddly dressed figure scuttle away. She only caught the briefest glimpse of a black coat and a heavy black boot disappearing through the gate. She ran out but saw no one. It was probably a tramp, perhaps hoping to steal something he could sell. She shivered nervously and went back inside.

Lewis came in through the front door and they met in the passageway.

'Someone came into the garden just then,' Rhiannon said anxiously. 'I thought it was you and put the kettle on and when I looked again he was disappearing through the gate.'

'Don't worry, love. He probably mistook our gate for his own.' He went to where the kettle was singing and poured water on the tea leaves. He seemed unaware of her alarm.

'But Dad, with these robberies I was frightened.'

'Nonsense. There isn't much to steal around here, love. Charlie home yet?'

'Not yet.' She was a bit upset at the casual way he had dealt with her fear. Charlie would have talked to her, reassured her. 'I'll lock that gate once they're home. Keep it locked during the day. It's best don't you think?' Lewis didn't reply. 'I'd better get on with these potatoes,' she said. 'Charlie and Gwyn won't be long.'

'I want him to look at my car. It's not

pulling as it should.'

'Is it a big job? We're going out on the bikes tomorrow.'

'Won't take him long. He'll have to do it tomorrow, I need it for Monday morning.'

Rhiannon felt unaccustomed anger towards her father. Once she wouldn't have minded him demanding that Charlie did some repair on his car, but now it was a growing irritation: 'I want him to look at my car', not 'I wonder if he would be kind enough . . . ' as it had once been.

She recognised with a shadow of dismay that the period when she accepted her father's presence with equanimity was gone and resentment was starting to mark even ordinary things like asking Charlie to look at his car. How long before her resentment grew into open hostilities? And what then?

She knew that a part of the change in her attitude was the possibility of a baby. Although, even without that complication, offering him a home had only been a temporary plan. She and Charlie had hoped that her mother would have seen the difficulties approaching, and taken him back.

The earlier brief easing of the situation hadn't lasted long. Within forty-eight hours Lewis had been back, having been thrown out by Dora yet again.

Barry Williams had made a few decisions while he was working in Temptations, the shop that had once been his mother's and before that his grandmother's. Apart from certain periods, the shop was fairly quiet. Rhiannon used the quiet spells to clean, but he did nothing but think. He looked back over the last couple of years and what he saw was a series of mistakes. He wondered how many of them he could put right.

He had put into motion the sale of the house on Chestnut Road. It was too large for just himself and there was no possibility of his wife, Caroline Griffiths, ever coming back to share it. He wouldn't want to live there if she did. That was one move.

The second was to give up the factory job he had taken in the hope of saving his marriage. He hated it and would stay there only as long as it took him to start up again as a photographer. Selling the house would give him the capital to support himself while he built a business again. That and the profit from the sweet shop. That was two moves. Giving up a house in which he no longer felt comfortable and a job he hated — they were easy ones.

He felt quite light-headed at the methodical way in which he was dealing with all that was wrong in his unhappy life. His third move was a literal one. He would move back into the flat here, above Temptations.

His fourth move was not such an easy one. The decision was a shared one and he didn't know whether the other party concerned would think it worth the effort.

Having married Caroline Griffiths when she was in despair, expecting the child of his brother who had been killed in a road accident, he now knew it had been doomed from the start. He hadn't approached the marriage with any confidence, any hope of succeeding. He had felt the shadow of his handsome, light-hearted brother always at his side. He believed Caroline had compared them and found him wanting.

Caroline had made him feel over-large and unattractive, dull and unimaginative, selfish and uncooperative. Thinking about it now, with time to go over it all in his mind, he realised that most of the negative thinking had been of his own making. He had entered the marriage expecting it to fail.

When the shop closed that Saturday at six o'clock he began sorting out the rooms above with the exciting feeling that he was rebuilding his life. Encouraged by his decisions, he decided to go over to the Griffiths's the following day and start some rebuilding there too, in the house to which Caroline had returned and which she shared with her parents and brothers, plus cats, dogs, chickens and goats. He'd made a workbench for young Joseph, complete with a set of small tools. He'd take that over and . . . the success of his fourth move would be in the hands of the fates.

★ ★ ★

Edward had a room at Montague Court but Margaret was making it increasingly difficult for him to use it. Sharing out the furniture, most of which had been in the family for several generations, had been difficult. Knowing what he needed, Margaret made sure she claimed it before he could decide. Then making up his mind for him, she had filled his room with more and more of the items she didn't need until he could hardly get inside.

Megan told him to telephone her and have a moan. 'Better than bottling it up and trying to sleep with anger on your mind, Edward.' He thought it unlikely that he would, but they made an arrangement that he would allow the phone to ring three times and wait for her to ring back if she felt able to talk. Amusing and childish, but that was how Megan made him feel. A happy child.

He went home one night after taking Megan to the pictures and for a meal, and he couldn't even get to his bed for the 'clutter'. He rang Megan and she answered his ring almost immediately.

'Make a noise, move everything and bang it about,' she suggested.

He tried sleeping on the couch, but at five past one in the morning, he gave up trying, and began moving stuff out of his room. That it was late, and he was disturbing his sister and Islwyn didn't bother him at all. In fact he enjoyed it and made as much noise as he could.

Margaret stormed out of her bedroom, hair in curlers, dressing gown half draped around her, eyes blazing with anger.

'What a time to come in! You have no consideration for others, Edward. It's after one o'clock!'

He had been home for more than two hours but he didn't bother to explain. 'What d'you expect me to do, sleep on the landing? What on earth have you done to my room?' he demanded.

'You should have been here to help. There's a lot of sorting out to do. In case you've forgotten, brother dear, we're having to move out!'

A few minutes later Islwyn joined them, dressed in slacks and a jumper, his hair neatly combed. He was still embarrassed at showing they slept together. Everyone knew it but displaying it so blatantly was something he couldn't manage.

'What sort of woman has Megan become,' Margaret went on. 'Staying out half the night and her carrying a bastard.'

'Don't you dare talk about Megan like that!'

'Oh,' Margaret said softly, 'getting fond, are we? Well don't get too optimistic, she'll soon discover what a wimp you really are.'

'That was a bit much, Margaret,' Islwyn muttered.

After a brief, one-sided row, Edward being silenced at the abuse of Megan, Margaret went back to the bedroom followed by Islwyn. After a few moments Edward heard an argument taking place.

Margaret was always in a worse than usual mood when she was tired. He silently wished Islwyn luck for the following day.

A week later he did it again. Noisily dragging chairs and tables around. Then after making sure he had woken them and caused as much annoyance as he could, he went and slept on the couch.

6

Rhiannon and Gwyn prepared to cycle to the pebbly beach and the park beyond, at two o'clock on Sunday. The weather was overcast but with the air warm and cloud lifting, there was the promise of a breakthrough into a sunny day. Charlie had agreed, willingly, to look at Lewis's car, although Rhiannon had been less than pleased.

'Can't it wait, Dad?' she pleaded as she packed bats and balls and the last of the small picnic into her saddle bag and fastened the straps. 'Gwyn's so disappointed not to have his father along. They climb trees and jump about in streams, explore the woods and look for foxes dens, you know what boys like. It isn't the same for him without Charlie.'

'Oh, come on, love. One afternoon won't hurt him. He works with his dad and spends most of his time at home, he'll be glad to get away from him.'

'No, Dad. He won't!' She patted the dog, whose eyes showed disbelief at not being included on their excursion, and gave her a biscuit which Polly refused to eat on principle.

With her mind on the selfish attitude of her father, she rode for a while with hardly a word to Gwyn.

'Didn't you want to come, Rhiannon?' he asked. 'We'll stay home if you like?'

'I want to go, I've been looking forward to it, but I wish your dad was with us, that's all.' She smiled and added, 'Lucky I am to have you. I'd be on my own otherwise, wouldn't I?'

Cheered by the assurance that she really wanted to be with him, Gwyn challenged her to a race.

They waited until they reached the country roads, where the sharp bends made extra fun and there was little traffic to concern them, then they increased speed.

For a while Rhiannon concentrated on winning but then she relaxed a little and enjoyed the simple pleasure of speed with no effort as she coasted down a steep, winding hill to where she knew there would be a glimpse of the sea. Even without Charlie this was good. Gwyn raced on, his feet pedalling so fast they were a blur. He disappeared around a bend in the lane then she saw him waving at her from the top of the next hill and waved back. He was standing beside his bike and leaning it against himself; he waved again, this time with both arms and she smiled. He was boasting at how much better he was than she.

Rhiannon knew the road well and remembered how it snaked around in a tight bend then travelled close to a small stream at the bottom of the hill. Gwyn was now out of sight, lost in the line of tall trees that sheltered the fields above. Increasing her own speed, she smiled as she thought how she would surprise him by how fast she'd catch up. A sharp turn left and she would have to begin the long climb to join him.

To help her up the approaching hill she pedalled as fast as she could and enjoyed the sensation of the wind brushing past and enticing her long hair out into a trail behind her.

Because of the baffle effect of the trees and the bend in the lane, she didn't hear the van. As she turned left, riding wide to make the most of the last of the downhill run, she suddenly faced it. The driver turned into the hedge on his left and she sailed past with inches to spare, lost control and went down the bank and into the stream.

Suddenly slowed by the deep water she was tipped off and thrown into the chill mud at the furthest edge. She wasn't hurt apart from a scratch on both arms from the smaller branches of the roadside trees. Although the shock of the cold water made her gasp it had also softened the fall.

She was surprised to see Gwyn running through the water to help her even before she had recovered from the shock sufficiently to stand up.

'Are you all right? Oh, heck! You're bleeding! Our Dad'll kill me if you're harmed. I was trying to warn you. Didn't you see me waving?'

She began to laugh then. 'Waving?' she giggled. 'Of course I did. I just waved back.' It was all so funny that it was some time before she realised that a man was standing on the other bank, watching them.

'The van driver,' Gwyn whispered, gesturing with his thumb.

Still laughing, Rhiannon stood up and, recognising Arfon Weston, her brother Viv's father-in-law, she quickly assured him she was unhurt.

Arfon's wife, Gladys was in the passenger seat of the van and her most urgent worry was embarrassment at being seen in the unsuitable vehicle. And, by one of the common Lewises. As the head of the Weston family they had a position to keep and this awful van was not designed to impress. She urged Arfon to hurry home and get her out of it before anyone else saw her.

'We can't drive off and leave them,' he protested mildly.

'Look at the girl,' she hissed, nodding a head towards Rhiannon who was trying to rescue her bicycle with Gwyn's help. 'I knew we shouldn't have allowed our granddaughter to marry one of the Lewises! Can't you take me home first, Arfon?'

'No, love, I can't. What's wrong with being seen in the van anyway? It's ours and fully paid for!'

'If you don't know, dear,' she sighed, 'I won't try to tell you.' Arfon looked at the bedraggled Rhiannon and began to chuckle.

In his loud, rather pompous voice he called, 'I think I should give you a lift home, young lady,' he said. 'For one thing, you can't go wherever it was you were going, looking like that.'

Rhiannon looked down at the once white blouse, the neat blue shorts and the sandals that were now thickly spread with mud. It was so funny she laughed again and this time a relieved Gwyn joined in.

Gladys groaned in what she hoped was a ladylike manner and accepted the inevitable. With the Lewises involved, everyone would know she had driven around the countryside in a van!

* * *

It was her father who saw Rhiannon first. He gave a shout of alarm as Arfon and Gwyn lifted their bicycles out of his van.

'They've had an accident!' he shouted and Charlie threw down the spanner he was holding and ran to where a still laughing Rhiannon, unrecognisable at first, was walking towards them. At once, Lewis began accusing Charlie of not looking after her as they ran to see what had happened. He tried to edge Charlie out of the way and get to Rhiannon first, but Charlie ignored the mud and hugged her, speaking softly, anxious for her not to be involved in an inquest until she was bathed and warm and fed.

After Rhiannon's arm had been looked at and she had assured them it was nothing worse than a scratch, Arfon offered an apology and prepared to leave. Gladys looked pained and enbarrassed, having tried and failed to stay out of sight, as they drove away.

Lewis's demands to know what had happened had finally been quashed by Charlie's terse 'Shut up, Lewis! Let's get her inside and make sure she's all right. Shall we?'

Outraged and offended, Lewis had left

them and run to knock on the door of number seven.

His anger as he told Dora what happened didn't receive the reaction he expected. 'He doesn't look after her. That's the truth of it!' he almost shouted, expecting Dora to agree.

Scrabbling for her coat, a comfort rather than a need, Dora said, 'You've got the fault for this Lewis! Doing something to *your* car wasn't he? Something you could have done yourself and then Charlie would have been with them!' She pushed him out of the way and ran across to see her daughter. Lewis began to follow her but stopped and sat in his chair beside Dora's fire instead. He wasn't wanted. What a bloody life.

He made himself a cup of tea then sat staring into the fire, poking it occasionally, adding more coal, pushing a few sticks into the parts where ash had collected, concentrating on the simple and unnecessary tasks as if his mind were empty of thought. But behind the handsome dark eyes with their blank expression, he was feeling mean.

He had insisted on Charlie working on his car deliberately to spoil his day out. He didn't like Charlie and wanted his daughter to come to her senses and leave him. Surely she'd thank him one day? His mood softened, the guilt that had been half recognised grew and

160

almost overwhelmed him. He began to face the unpleasant fact that he was hoping for his daughter's life to be ruined.

Rhiannon loved Charlie and young Gwyn. She'd be unhappy to lose them. What sort of a father was he, that he could wish for her to be miserable? After an hour he went back to Charlie and Rhiannon's house and asked how she was feeling.

Assured she was feeling no effect from her muddy fall, he touched her arm and said humbly,

'I'm sorry, love. It was my fault. If Charlie had been there he'd have been looking after you and this wouldn't have happened.' The reaction to his apology wasn't what he'd expected either.

'*I* was looking after her! I did what I could,' a distressed Gwyn retorted. 'It was an accident. Dad said it was no one's fault.'

'Gwyn's right,' Charlie said with an edge of anger in his voice. 'No one was at fault. Certainly not our son.'

'Tell me what happened, Gwyn,' Lewis said, ignoring Charlie. He listened to the full story and then, trying to make Gwyn feel better, he told the boy he had been very quick-witted to signal a warning. The pity was that Rhiannon hadn't realised what it was. 'Fancy her just waving back, eh?' he said coaxing a smile.

'I was looking after her,' Gwyn said again, rebelliously.

'I know you were. She's lucky to have you. I know that. I was upset earlier, the words came out all wrong. I didn't mean it to sound like I blamed you, Gwyn. Sorry.'

Gwyn said nothing; his young face still looked troubled.

'Thank goodness you were there,' Lewis persevered. 'Things would have been much worse if you'd stayed to help your dad, wouldn't they? You certainly guessed she was in trouble and got to the stream fast.' Gwyn still didn't looked convinced and Lewis asked, 'Swallow any fish, did she?'

'She didn't half look a mess,' Gwyn said as a smile reluctantly appeared and slowly widened.

Lewis glanced at Dora and was relieved to receive a nod of approval.

* * *

Edward's shop was set to open at the end of June and as the day drew near he worked hard, getting the tables and chairs set out ready for the opening party on Saturday the twenty-fifth of June. Mrs Collins had recovered from her fall and was helping, and the catering was being dealt with by Megan's aunt, Sian Weston, and Dora Lewis. To Edward's surprise, Lewis Lewis came with Dora on Wednesday afternoon with a selection of sweets with which to decorate the tables. He didn't know that the gesture was to please Dora and not him and he thanked Lewis and invited him to the party.

'Margaret's efforts to discourage people have failed,' Edward told Megan thankfully. 'All the invitations have been readily accepted by everyone we chose to invite.'

'You'll do well, Edward. I'm sure of it.'

'If I succeed, it's down to you,' he smiled, his growing love for her showing in his eyes and the almost shy twist of his mouth.

'D'you know, Edward, you look a different person when you smile at me. You could be two people instead of one. Your formal, stiff-upper-lip, serious side is wiped away like magic with your wonderful smile. Two personalities, and — ' she added, lightly kissing his cheek ' — I like them both.'

'Then will you — '

She stopped the words with a finger. 'After The Lump makes his appearance, we'll talk. Not before.'

He looked at her. She was confident, brave and so beautiful. More so now, with that wonderful glow of pregnancy. And way out of

163

his reach. He was fooling himself thinking otherwise. She and her twin Joan were very outspoken; they were famous for it. But he comforted himself that she at least felt something for him, enough to let him down lightly. The thought had a sweet melancholy.

To his relief, Annie and Leigh Grant had exchanged contracts on Montague Court. The sale had gone through without a hitch. Margaret hadn't contacted him since they had signed away their home, but he heard from others that his sister, and Sian's truant husband, Islwyn, were planning to buy a rather large house where they could boast a view of the sea. He felt content enough to wish them well, although he hadn't invited them to the party.

'Perhaps you should,' Megan said when he remarked on it. 'Now the arguments about whether or not to sell Montague Court are settled, there's no point in you two behaving like pouting children any longer, is there?'

'Did I? Behave like a child?'

In reply she looked at him with her pretty head tilted and he acknowledged the accusation with a nod. He remembered the way he had thumped furniture about late at night and nodded ruefully. 'I'll write and invite her. Although, wait a minute! I can't have Islwyn there as a guest with his estranged wife doing the catering, can I? Confrontation with both sides armed with sticky buns. It doesn't bear thinking about!'

'Yes, I'd forgotten about my delinquent Uncle Islwyn. Perhaps it's better to leave it and say the invitation must have been lost in the post,' she laughed.

The day before the party, when everything was set and only the food was to come, Edward invited Megan to go to the pictures.

'Thank you Edward, but I don't think I will.'

'Are you feeling ill? Is everything all right with The Lump?' he asked anxiously.

'He's behaving impeccably, kicking to remind me he's there, but nothing more than that.' He put out a hand and waited until the baby moved and his gentle face softened with pleasure.

'Do you think he'd like to go for a stroll instead?'

'A stroll would be wonderful.'

As the day had been rather dull, the pleasure beach wasn't crowded; just a few strolling couples and two or three families carrying an assortment of bags and beach games, making their way back from their picnic and day out.

They walked along the promenade, before stepping down onto the warm golden sands to follow the edge of the tide, hand in hand. They hardly spoke, content in each other's company and their own thoughts. Although, if they had discussed them they would have realised how close their thoughts were, both going through last minute details of the shop's grand opening on the following day.

When they got into the car to drive home, Megan noticed a sizeable parcel on the back seat. 'What's that, something for tomorrow?' she asked.

'Silver light-fittings for the windows and stronger light bulbs for the flat and the basement,' Edward told her. 'I'll fix them tonight. The ones there at present are too weak. We need to make everything look as bright and cheerful as possible for the party, don't we?'

'Can we drop them off at the shop now?'

'It's late and you should be getting to bed. The Lump needs his sleep.'

'You have remembered that we're calling at Grandmother's early tomorrow to collect the cot and all the bedding she and Grandfather have bought for me? We'll need the space in the car.'

'Perhaps we *should* take them now then. It won't take long.'

He parked outside the shop, told Megan to stay in the car and unlocked the door. There was a strange sound and he paused as he pushed the shop door open.

'What is it?' Megan demanded.

'Stay there. I can hear something down in the basement.'

'I'm coming with you.'

From her tone he guessed it was useless to argue but he made her walk behind him as, putting on the shop lights, he went towards the basement stairs. In a steady stream, beginning halfway down, water from a hosepipe was making a waterfall of the new, polished wooden stairs.

Below, they could see that a couple of chairs were overturned, the tables had been piled up in a corner and were bare of their decorations. Balloons cheerfully filled a corner and a glass bowl, still containing a few sweets, floated like some jaunty little nursery rhyme boat. The floor was completely awash and the tablecloths which Mrs Collins had made and put in place were moving sluggishly in the flood.

'What on earth has happened?' Edward gasped.

'At a guess, I'd say Margaret has 'happened',' Megan said angrily. 'The furniture hasn't been moved like that by the water. Someone has deliberately pushed things about to make as much mess as possible, wouldn't you say?'

Edward couldn't take his eyes off the disaster scene that had once been a room prepared for a party.

'Now, Edward,' Megan said, in a cold, calm voice. 'Are you going to stare at it all night? Or will you go and shut off the tap?'

★ ★ ★

After driving Megan home Edward went back to the ruins of his opening party. He threw all the furniture outside and piled the once pristine tablecloths, stained with the crêpe paper table centres, into a galvanised bucket for Mrs Collins to wash.

By the time he had brushed the worst of the flood outside, dried the floor and wiped down the furniture, it was after four o'clock. Too late to go back to Montague Court, where, anyway, his bed would probably be covered with furniture once again.

He had no clothes into which he could change and he was very chilled, so he went up to the room that would soon be his bedroom, turned on an electric fire with fingers crossed that the water hadn't touched any of the cables, and tried to sleep.

If Margaret was responsible for this, why

was she still so angry? Selling up had been inevitable; in spite of her protests she had known that. It should have happened years before and would have if their father hadn't been so determined to let their mother finish her days there. Edward drifted off into sleep thinking that if it weren't for Megan, he would probably have been weak enough to allow Margaret to talk him round. She was so strong and she would have battled until he had given in and agreed to stay and work at making Montague Court into a viable business. It would have failed, he was sure of that, and they would have ended up penniless. Megan had been his salvation. He smiled as dreams took over and Megan's face swam into view. He was so glad he hadn't given in to Margaret. Megan was equally strong, but with her decisions were discussed, shared. And besides, with Megan, life was much more exciting.

★　★　★

The party was cancelled. Edward gave Gwyn Bevan a pound to go around on his bicycle and tell those people he couldn't reach by telephone. He went to see Dora and Sian himself.

'What d'you expect us to do with all the

food we've prepared?' Dora demanded.

'Whatever you wish,' Edward said sadly. 'I'll pay for it, of course, but if you can think of anyone who would like it, well, I'll leave it to you.'

Sian and Dora exchanged glances. In chorus they said, 'The Griffithses!'

Hywel and Janet greeted the news with excitement. 'A ready made party?' Janet said. 'No problem for us, eh, Hywel?'

No invitations were written. There was never any need for the formalities. The television was moved into the shed, logs for the fire were brought in, and logs to be used as extra seating appeared from under the stairs. Caroline unwrapped the plates she and Barry had been given as wedding presents and had never used. Caroline's nearly three-year-old son, Joseph-Hywel, was promised a 'late pass' by his uncles, Ernie and Frank, and Hywel had a bath.

In the inexplicably speedy way of such things, everyone who should be told was told, and by lunchtime, the talk through the small town was of the 'do' that night in the small cottage on the edge of town.

'I think I might go,' Megan said when she went to see Edward later that day. 'Will you be there?'

'At the Griffiths'? You surely aren't going to

170

spend the evening in that awful hovel, are you?'

'I most certainly am! It won't be the first time, and don't get on your high horse, Edward. They're really rather good fun!'

Edward went on with his task of washing down the stair-case and didn't reply. Even for Megan, one of the famous Weston Girls, for whom the outrageous was to be expected, he still thought visiting the Griffithses socially was a bit much.

At five o'clock that afternoon, Edward went back to Montague Court. It no longer looked like his home. Furniture had been moved or was missing altogether. The walls were sadly marked with the paleness and staining where pictures and furniture had been moved after many years in the same place. The carpets showed indentations filled with dust where heavy cupboards had once stood, and there were several dark stains, their origins long forgotten.

He decided not to mention the flooded basement. Better not to know for certain that it had been Margaret's doing. He forced himself to speak normally when Margaret appeared.

'Annie and Leigh Grant will have a difficult task getting ready for reopening, won't they?' he said to Margaret.

'They had a bargain, thanks to you. You don't expect me to clean it for them as well, do you?' she snapped.

He didn't bother to reply, overcome by a feeling of isolation. As the day of departure drew near he had bouts of sadness and Margaret's attitude was an added reminder that with the end of their life at Montague Court, he no longer had a family. Margaret was so bitter he doubted whether they would ever overcome their differences.

As he began checking the lists of items he and Margaret had decided to keep and started planning their removal, Margaret and Islwyn came through from an adjoining room, staggering under the weight of a grandfather clock.

'Where were you last night?' Islwyn asked. 'My niece keeping you from your bed? Or are you keeping her from hers, eh?'

'Neither! And I suggest you keep your filthy thoughts to yourself!'

'What time *did* you come in, Edward?' Margaret asked.

'I didn't! I was trying to clear up the mess in the shop.'

'Mess? What mess?'

Again, Edward didn't bother to answer.

He went back to the shop that evening, imagining the food prepared for his party being eaten by the enthusiastic Griffithses. Electric fires were burning and gradually drying the basement, giving the building an eerie glow. He shivered. The place was still strange to him and he wondered how he would settle once he had moved out of his former home.

Megan didn't come and he was at a loss to know why it upset him so. They had become so close, discussing everything, learning to understand each other. He had come to expect her to be there all the time, not to go off to a party he'd said he didn't want to attend.

They had been surprisingly open with each other during the short time they had become friends. He had been embarrassed at first by the way she spoke of personal affairs, but her free acceptance of the weaknesses of both herself and other people gradually made him deal with life with the same honesty and understanding.

He had told her how he had injured his leg while in Egypt, and his disappointment at not becoming a good enough tennis player and how his family had insisted he abandoned his secondary plan to open a sports shop, and concentrate on the family business instead.

He spoke about his fiancée who had rejected him when he returned from Egypt and his suspicions that his family had discouraged Rachel for reasons of their own. He even admitted that for a while he was fascinated by a young woman called Maisie Vasey, who came to live in Pendragon Island, caused chaos, and then moved away.

Megan talked openly about running away from home and her brief sojourn in London with Terrence, Edward's wayward cousin — the father of the child she was expecting. She spoke of her attitude to Terrence and to the baby she carried.

They were the closest of friends, so why had she gone to the party without him? Was he expecting too much? Was he dreaming when he imagined she cared? Of course he was, he told himself angrily. I should be counting the hours she spends with me, savouring them, storing them to remember when we have said our goodbyes.

In his heart Edward hoped for a happy ending, but in his head he knew it was impossible. She was too remarkable a woman to settle for someone as dull as he was. She was simply using him to fill in the time until her child was born, that's all. Be grateful, he told himself. Be grateful.

The evening was going to drag, he knew it. He wasn't hungry and he was too lethargic to do any more cleaning but he didn't want to go back to Montague Court. There was nothing there for him and he wished he'd finished moving into the flat so he could begin his new life. The fires burning warmed the air and made him drowsy and he sat on the top of the basement steps, leaned against the wall and wondered whether Megan was enjoying the party.

★ ★ ★

For Megan, sitting next to Hywel and Janet's daughter Caroline, the talk was of babies. She was uncomfortable, squeezed up to make room for the growing number of people still arriving in a steady stream. Her sister Joan came in with Viv and seeing the expression on Megan's face guessed, wrongly, that it was due to thoughts about the baby.

'Don't worry, Megan,' she said, having peremptorily moved Caroline out of her place to sit beside her sister. 'It's only a few more weeks and they'll soon pass.'

'It isn't the baby,' Megan assured her. 'I just don't feel in the mood for a party.' She didn't explain that the usual Griffiths' fun was not enough to make her forget Edward all alone in the shop.

'Come on, admit you're depressed and worried about the birth pains; I would be.

You'll be fine once he's born. Thank goodness we aren't the kind of twins who suffer for each other,' Joan added with feeling. 'I think I'd hate him long before he's born.'

Janet showed her a coat she was knitting and Hywel and Barry promised to make him his first push-along truck. She thanked them all, asked Basil to go to the kiosk and ring for a taxi and left before what Hywel called the first round — when everyone relaxed and left behind their inhibitions — was over.

Barry was trying to talk to Caroline, but each time he approached her, either someone stole the seat he was heading for or she saw him, sensed his need to talk and moved away.

He played with little Joseph until Caroline declared it was time for him to go to bed, and was refused when he offered to read him a story.

'Not tonight, Barry, thanks. He's had enough excitement for one day. He'll never sleep!'

The sense of rejection was strong and he left soon after Megan.

* * *

At half past nine Edward was thinking of going to find something to eat. He still wasn't hungry but he thought that if he didn't find some food then, he might be hungry later and then he'd be too late. He heard a car pull up, then drive off. Footsteps he thought he knew hurried towards the shop door and then there was the welcome sound of a key in the shop door.

'Edward, will you take me out and feed me?' Megan said as she walked in and sat down beside him.

'Of course, but what about the party?'

'I went, and everyone was there having the usual idiotic fun, but the thought of all that lovely food being prepared for our little 'do', well, it seemed traitorous to eat it. I kept thinking I should be here, being miserable with you. So, here I am.'

They sat for a long time, in a close embrace, with only a low light burning, staring down into the dark depths of the basement.

At ten o'clock, Edward said. 'I was miserable here without you. I should have gone. Forgive me?'

'Only if you buy me fish and chips. I'm starving and so is The Lump.'

He turned to her, his eyes intent and serious as he touched her lips with his own. The kiss, gentle at first, deepened and left neither of them in any doubt of their feelings.

'Megan, I — '

Once again she stopped him saying the words she longed to hear. 'We have to wait my darling. I want you to understand fully what life with me would mean.'

'I don't care what happens, I want you and — '

'Soon, Edward. Very soon.' The kiss that stilled his words was so sweet that he argued no further.

As they were leaving to buy fish and chips to eat in the car, they both heard a noise. It came from the garden and with a terse, 'Stay here,' to Megan, Edward crept slowly down the basement stairs. As he reached the bottom he became aware that as usual, Megan had ignored him and was following.

There were crackling sounds and the strong smell of wood burning and for an awful moment Edward thought someone had set fire to the place. He fumbled with the door, which was new and rather stiff, and by the time he had opened it, the garden was empty. Someone had started a fire, but not near the house. Sticks were burning brightly and beside the newly lit blaze an upturned bucket had been set up as a table, containing half opened newspaper-wrapped packages of food.

'A tramp,' Edward said with a sigh of relief. 'Well, he's welcome to sit and eat his supper, as long as he keeps his bonfire under control. But I think we ought to get that gate fixed soon.'

'We'll see Frank about it tomorrow,' Megan said. She went over and added sticks to the fire which was in danger of burning out. 'Poor lonely man. It makes me realise how fortunate I am, Edward.'

'Me too.' He placed a half-crown coin on the makeshift table and, with their arms around each other, they went back through the shop to go and buy their supper.

★ ★ ★

Percy Flemming was standing in the over-grown shrubbery of the Waterside Restaurant. His innocent informant, the local milkman called Reggie Rogers, had casually mentioned that the owners would be away for a week, before returning to deal with their move.

Having parked the old van in the narrow lane beside the property, he began transfer-ring cases of wines and spirits from the house. The stuff was easily sold but it was a time-consuming exercise and he didn't take the complete consignment.

A quick look around and he picked up two Dresden figurines and some Victorian china before driving off with moderate speed to where he planned to hide the Victorian stuff until he could drive to Newport and deliver it. He hid the van in the garden of an old vicarage where it was well hidden by a high wall and a belt of tall trees. The drink was first delivered to a pub not far from town and at three in the morning he was sleeping soundly.

The police were criticised once more when news of the robbery came to light. They responded with the reasonable excuse that they were simply unable to watch every house in the town, and begged people to be vigilant and report anything suspicious.

* * *

Once the place had dried out and the decoration had been made good, Edward decided to move in. Transporting what he had chosen to keep from the furniture of his former home took most of the day, with Hwyel Griffiths providing the van and Frank and Ernie providing the muscles.

Annie and Leigh Grant had agreed to buy most of the surplus and Margaret was storing what she and Islwyn had selected for their restaurant and future home. The few pieces not wanted by any of them went to a second-hand shop in the town, which did brisk business. Everyone wanted a souvenir of the Jenkins's former home. Vases and pictures of little value were snapped up. Oddments of china, plates, cups and even saucers found a new home. Incomplete sets of cutlery that needed regular sharpening and polishing were tossed in a couple of baskets and displayed to be sold individually as people scrambled for a memento of Montague Court.

Gladys and Arfon Weston bought a huge overmantel in gold-trimmed mahogany. Ryan bought a picture of the Somerset town where he and Sally had spent their honeymoon and gave it to his wife, promising her that from then on their life would be as happy as those early days of their marriage.

Lewis saw an umbrella stand and bought it for Dora to put in the entrance of the café. He also bought a model of a Spitfire that had once stood on a desk in Edward's bedroom, which he presented to a delighted Gwyn.

Through the town, people displayed items from Montague Court proudly as though the ownership of the trifles were prizes captured in battle from the demise of the once great family.

Saddened by the empty rooms and drab remnants of their former home, Edward and Margaret, in a brief moment of togetherness, decided not to go there again.

Spending the first night in his now furnished bedroom above the shop, Edward slept fitfully, the unfamiliar noises of his new property strange: wood expanding and shrinking with the changes of temperature; the wind finding spaces through which to whisper and sigh; traffic causing movement as it passed along the road; a curtain swaying in an undetected breeze.

Creaks and groans startled him on several occasions. Besides the unaccustomed sounds of the building he heard people walking around on bare floors and decided in his half awake state, after calming down from believing they were in the house with him, that they were coming from next door.

The following morning Edward remembered to his alarm that the houses on both sides were vacant. So, what had he heard? Had it been the tramp using an empty house for a comfortable night's sleep? For his own peace of mind he decided that that was what had happened, pushed the worries aside and began to search for breakfast.

Cooking breakfast showed him a serious lack of basic needs. A frying pan was no use without something to fry. A loaf of bread needed a sharper knife than the ones he had chosen to bring from Montague Court. How could he be so helpless?

He made a list and went out to buy what he needed. There was just time to deal with it before he opened the shop at nine-thirty. Megan would be there soon but he didn't want to admit his absentmindedness to her. Not today, when he was opening his doors to business for the first time.

Time passed slowly and he was restless. Returning to the mysterious noises of the previous night he decided to go through the gardens and investigate.

As he had guessed, the house next door was not secure. Pushing open a broken door from which one hinge was missing he went inside. He'd brought a torch but he didn't need it. The place showed clear evidence of someone using it, with clothes and bedding strewn around and in a corner, a cache of food. He left, satisfied that the noises he'd heard were explained.

There was a knock on the shop door and he went to answer it, nervously adjusting his tie. Someone was anxious to be the first customer — it wasn't yet nine-fifteen. When he opened the door, Inspector Leonard stood there with Constable Gregory. They saw Edward smiling a welcome with a dirt-streaked face, and leaves and small branches in his hair from where he had pushed his way through the hedge. There were moss stains on the sleeve of his shirt.

'Mr Edward Jenkins? We'd like you to come to the station with us, if you please.'

'What, now? I'm just about to open my shop.'

'We'd like you to answer some questions regarding your whereabouts on the days and nights of these robberies.'

'I don't understand.'

Inspector Leonard looked him up and down. 'We might begin by your explaining where you've been to get in such a mess, sir.'

7

Edward was questioned thoroughly about the dates on which robberies took place in the town of Pendragon Island and the villages around. At first he was angry but as time went on, and the questions revealed more and more doubt as to his honesty, he began to worry. He was obviously concerned about money, having arranged to buy a property before the sale of Montague Court had been settled, so it was easy for them to make a case for his stealing to support his financial commitments.

'My sister can verify my movements if you ask her,' he said in exasperation after three hours had passed. 'Can you talk to her and please get this nonsense cleared up? I have a shop to open and I've already missed most of my first morning.'

'Your sister, that would be Miss Margaret Jenkins?'

'Of course. You know that very well so why are you asking me?'

'We have to be quite clear, Mr Jenkins. Now, can you tell us where you were on these dates?' The inspector put a piece of paper in front of Edward, and in frustration Edward threw it onto the floor. 'How on earth d'you expect me to remember anything past yesterday! I'm selling my home, refurbishing a shop and beginning a new business. My head's all over the place.'

Slowly and in silence, the policeman picked up the list and replaced it on the table.

Edward calmed down. It was no use getting angry with them and they were completely indifferent to his worries about the shop. With a sigh, he went through the routine of a normal week, describing the hours he worked, the tasks he had undertaken towards the running of the hotel.

'But the hotel is closed, isn't it? Aren't you and your sister in the processs of selling to a Mr and Mrs Leigh Grant?'

'Most of the work still goes on, sale, move, whatever. It's sold as a going concern so although we have refused accommodation while the changeover takes place, we have the restaurant to run. I still have to do certain shifts. Mealtimes come along with great monotony, Inspector. There was never much time between duties.'

'You've recently spent all your spare time working at number sixty-eight Highbourne Road.'

'That's correct.'

'Sometimes with a Miss Megan Fowler-Weston?'

'What has Miss Weston got to do with this?'

'Probably nothing, but we — '

'I know, 'have to be quite clear'! Now, please can I go? I'm starting a new business and it won't look good if I completely fail to open on the first day, will it?'

'Can you tell us again why you were in such a dishevelled state when we called, sir?'

Edward explained about the noises during the night. 'When I realised that the houses on either side were unoccupied I had to find out where the noises came from.'

'And you were satisfied that the rooms were used by tramps?'

'It seemed a likely explanation, yes.'

A constable appeared at the door and after a whispered conversation the inspector and Constable Gregory went out. Left alone in the silent room for a few minutes, Edward began to fume. He was beginning to comprehend who was responsible.

Constable Gregory returned and told him he could leave. No explanations, no apology, only a politely worded request not to leave town without informing them.

The whole morning, the first morning of the sports shop was over. He'd begun by letting prospective customers down. What a mess. What a bloody mess.

He didn't have his car; the police had taken him from the shop in their vehicle so he ran through the streets and along Highbourne Road with a heart threatening to explode.

He'd missed the first morning completely and it was down to Margaret. It was unbelievable the lengths to which his sister would go to to ruin his efforts. It was now after two o'clock and any customers who had bothered to come would have given up and probably gone elsewhere. What a bloody mess.

The shop door was closed and he fumbled with his key, anger making his hands shake. Opening the door he smelled the tantalising smell of bacon cooking.

'Is that you, Edward?' Megan called. He went upstairs to the flat, breathless and dejected, and in the kitchen saw Megan standing near the cooker. It was a sight to revive the gloomiest of spirits. Heavily pregnant, dressed in a loose gown of green, a band of the same material over her dark, shiny hair, her face glowing in the heat from the cooker. His heart began to behave in a peculiar way that had nothing to do with his recent exertions.

She had just lifted a round of gammon and

some mushrooms from the grill pan, and was attending the eggs and tomatoes sizzling in a frying pan. 'I hope you're hungry, I don't suppose you had much breakfast.'

'None. I'm starving and furiously angry at having to stay closed and miss my first morning.'

'You didn't miss it, Edward. I opened up just five minutes late. We took seventeen pounds nineteen shillings and sixpence by the way.'

'But how did you know?' he asked in surprise.

'Constable Gregory, whose daughter Mair Gregory used to work for Grandmother Gladys, told me you'd been taken in for questioning so I came as soon as I could.' She smiled. 'He also telephoned me here to tell me when you were on your way home. I sent one of your customers out to buy this food, will it suit?'

He stared at her, his face showing relief and wonderment, a mixture of frowns and adoration. 'Megan, you are amazing.'

'Yes, I believe I am,' she teased.

'How can I thank you! I — '

She interrupted him with an imperious hand. 'Food first, then we can talk.'

The food was delicious but as soon as he had eaten enough to take the edge off his hunger, he said, 'It was Margaret who did this I suppose.'

'You suppose right, I learned that from Constable Gregory too. But I don't think you'll have any more trouble. I gave them my diary you see. Remember our middle-of-the-night conversations? They'll have a way of checking them, won't they? Anyway, my diary corroborated much of your story, so I think they'll be satisfied on two or three of the nights in question. Weakens their case quite a lot, I imagine.'

While he finished his meal, she went down the stairs, awkward in her movements now she was almost eight months pregnant, and unlocked the door. When Edward came down ten minutes later he had washed, shaved and appeared as calm and cool as the proprietor of a sports shop should.

When they finally closed the door at five-thirty, they had taken forty-seven pounds and had orders for twenty pounds more. Edward hardly took in what Megan was saying as she totalled the figures.

'Megan, my dear, you look exhausted. I'm going to take you home now, and I want you to go straight to bed.'

'Are you ordering me about, Edward?' She looked up, head on one side but she didn't argue. 'You're right. I want to go home and collapse into Mummy's arms and allow myself to be utterly spoilt.'

Locking the day's takings into the safe the builders had fixed into the wall, Edward didn't wait to do anything else; he helped Megan on with her coat and escorted her to the car. Driving home, he chatted quietly — not angrily — about the events of the day. He didn't want her to be upset, and made a joke of it, saying how frustrating it must be for Margaret to know she had been outmanoeuvred so neatly by a superior person. There was no response and when he glanced at her, Megan was asleep.

He left her in the car while he knocked on Sally and Ryan's door. Ryan answered his knock and Edward asked if he would assist him in getting Megan into the house. 'She's very tired you see,' he explained, but to his amazement, Ryan walked away down the hall.

Going back to the car he gently woke Megan and was helping her out as Sally ran down the path. She thanked Edward for taking good care of her, and supported her daughter along the path and into the house. At the doorway, Megan turned and blew him a kiss. In the window of the bedroom above, Ryan watched in a silence that, even from that distance, Edward sensed was hostile.

He rang later that evening and asked Sally

to inform Megan she wasn't to come into the shop the next day. 'Tell her I'm grateful but I don't want her to overtire herself.' Swallowing embarrassment he added, 'Tell her she's too precious for that.'

'She's sleeping now and I'm sure she's all right,' Sally assured him. 'As for tomorrow, have you tried telling either of my darling daughters not to do something they want to do?' She laughed. 'I'll give her your message, Edward, and thank you for bringing her home.'

That night he didn't sleep straight away but he knew that on this occasion he couldn't disturb Megan from her much needed sleep to share his erratic thoughts. He sat for a long time writing out orders and checking the stock they had sold, trying to guess where their greatest attractions might lie. He didn't hear any odd sounds and at two o'clock he extinguished the light and slept soundly until six-thirty.

He woke with a sense of well-being. Downstairs he had a business which, thanks to Megan Fowler-Weston, was up and running. There was nothing more Margaret could do to stop it being a success.

★ ★ ★

In his house on Chestnut Road, Barry Williams decided to abandon most of the furniture that had been his mother's. He had first intended to arrange for a second-hand dealer to come and make him an offer for the lot, but remembered that Basil Griffiths was an expert at finding a home for unwanted items. He met him at the factory where they both still worked and asked him to take a look at the weekend.

He thought of asking Caroline if there was anything she might like but decided against it. If they were ever to begin again, it had to be without anything being dragged along from the past. And that included even bland objects like chairs and tables. It would have to be a fresh beginning with nothing at all to tie them to previous mistakes.

★　★　★

Rhiannon was watching the old man whom she had seen leaving her back yard, going through the gate into the lane behind her house. He was hovering around Gertie Thomas's shop on the corner opposite Temptations and as she watched, she saw him slip a couple of bananas into the front of his outsized overcoat and hurry away.

She was about to run across and tell Gertie

what she had seen, but Barry's van pulling up outside Temptations prevented her. It was too late to catch the man and there was no point in upsetting Gertie unnecessarily. She would tell her later and warn her to keep a better eye on the goods displayed outside her shop window.

Barry stepped out of the van and came towards her carrying a couple of suitcases. He explained that he was selling the house on Chestnut Road and moving back into the flat. Rhiannon contemplated his move with some sadness as he walked to and from the van, around the the back of Temptations and up the steps into the flat, carrying boxes, bags and what she recognised as new photographic equipment. It was almost history repeating itself, she mused. It was like it had been when Barry had worked as a photographer and she had been engaged to him and planning to make the flat above the shop their future home.

She had no regrets about not marrying Barry. She would never have been as happy with him as she was with Charlie and his son Gwyn. The sadness she felt was for Barry himself. He seemed to be constantly changing direction on meeting obstacles that he persistently failed to overcome.

Perhaps the flat was one of those unhappy

places where no one could find happiness, she mused. So many people had come and gone since Nia and her family had moved out. Nia Williams and her sons Barry and Joseph had all lived there contentedly for many years. She tried not to think about her father sneaking in and out and sharing in that contentment.

Barry had stayed on when his mother left to live in Chestnut Road, then it had been intended for Rhiannon herself to move in as Barry's wife. When their plans were abandoned, and Barry had married Caroline Griffiths, he had taken his shy bride there, but that hadn't been a success. He had been out a great deal, on photographic work. Many of his commissions had been in the evenings at parties and dances, and Caroline, coming from a lively family like the Griffithses, had suffered miserably from loneliness and had pined for her parents and brothers.

A young woman and her daughter had lived in the flat for a while. Maisie Vasey and her daughter, little Em, had also been unhappy tenants. They had caused trouble in several families and had returned to where they had come from, unmourned.

Now Barry was moving back, trying once again to build a photographic business, this time without his wife. Rhiannon wondered how long this sojourn would last.

'It's like a game of chess, the way people move in and out of that place,' Rhiannon told Charlie and her father that evening.

'Pity you can't get a job away from that sweet shop, love,' Lewis said. 'Barry is a man who can't make up his mind. I wouldn't be surprised if he gave you notice and ran the shop himself.'

Charlie disagreed. 'I don't know the man well, but I think he'd be bored silly. He wouldn't want to lose Rhiannon. All he has to do is spend the profits, she does the rest. No fear, Rhiannon has a job there for as long as she wants it.'

Rhiannon felt herself blushing. If what she suspected were true, she wouldn't be working anywhere in a few months' time! She'd be preparing for the birth of her and Charlie's baby. She hadn't told anyone yet, although she thought her mother had guessed. In an effort to change the subject, afraid her secret would be revealed, she said, 'I saw that shabby little old man yesterday, Charlie.'

'He wasn't in our back yard again was he?'

'No, he was looking over the fence a few doors away early this morning. Then this afternoon, I saw him steal some bananas from Gertie Jones's shop.'

'I think we should mention him to the

police,' Charlie said. 'He hardly fits the description of the burglar from what you say, but he could be involved, spying out the land, noting when houses are empty, that sort of thing.'

'You can't go to the police, Charlie!' Lewis said, 'you might still be a suspect and thought to be trying to put them off the scent!'

Charlie glanced at Rhiannon but didn't reply.

'It's all very well to look offended, Charlie,' Lewis went on, 'but the facts are, once you've broken the law you're among the first suspects when anything like this happens. So don't go near the police, it's asking for trouble.'

'Rhiannon is worried by seeing the man hanging around. I'll go to the police because I don't want her frightened.'

Charlie's voice was calm but Rhiannon recognised an edge of anger. It was time this conversation was stopped.

'Come on, Gwyn, time we made the cocoa.'

'I'm thankful I've never been tempted,' Lewis went on as she left the room. 'I'd never be bothered by the sight of a policeman knocking at my door.'

'Lucky old you,' Charlie muttered.

A few days later, Gwyn saw the man whom he guessed was the one worrying Rhiannon. Playing a game, he followed him. The wily old man guessed and disappeared through an alleyway between two terraced houses and then through a garden and, unwilling to trespass, Gwyn lost him. Amused at the prospect of playing detective, Gwyn decided he'd look out for him and find out where he lived.

★ ★ ★

In an attempt to please Dora, Lewis offered to tidy up her back garden. When he had lived there it had successfully produced sufficient vegetables for the family, and seeing it neglected, partly dug over and then abandoned, he wanted to put it right.

When she agreed, and even thanked him, he used any spare time he had, clearing dead plants, cutting back overgrown hedges and repairing the mess left by Dora's furious assault on it. Instead of a regular surface, her anger had left it in heaps, and full of weeds.

'What did you dig it with, a Mills bomb?' he asked when he had tamed about half of it.

She laughed, her face eased of tension and

he saw briefly the young woman he had married. 'I was in a bit of a temper when I did it,' she admitted.

'I guessed as much. Dora Lewis in a temper wouldn't need a Mills bomb!' he teased.

They discussed what was to be planted and decided that, with the family gone they could revert to growing flowers.

'Sensible ones like chrysanthemums that you can pick to make displays for your tables up at the café?' he suggested. 'And dahlias, how about some of those? It isn't too late.' Soon Dora was working with him, and to see her parents working amicably side by side was more than Rhiannon and Viv had ever hoped.

They spent several evenings poring over gardening books, choosing and drawing up plans. Rhiannon and Charlie linked fingers and made a wish when they called to see what progress had been made. If only Dora held back her temper they might be freed from having her father as their lodger before too long.

★ ★ ★

Lewis was leaving Dora's one Saturday afternoon when he saw a policeman knocking at Rhiannon and Charlie's door. He glared at

Charlie as he opened the door. 'I told you to stay away from them,' he hissed.

'Mr Lewis Lewis?' the constable said.

'Yes. You'll be wanting to talk to Charlie Bevan I suppose?' He stood back with a self-righteous sigh to allow the policeman to enter and was startled when he was told that it was in fact he, who was wanted.

'Just to answer a few questions, Mr Lewis, sir. Nothing to worry about.'

'Me?' Lewis's look of outrage was so funny Charlie choked on laughter. What a pity Rhiannon was at work and Gwyn was out and were missing it.

'We have a few dates on which we'd like you to tell us your movements.'

'My movements? Whatever for?'

'If you wouldn't mind, sir.'

Lewis went to find his order and appointment books and the constable nodded politely at Charlie. 'I just saw your son, Mr Bevan. Walking that dog of his down past the allotments. Good company for a boy, having a dog.'

While Lewis thumbed through his appointments and the policeman compared the dates with those on his list he shook his head once or twice and frowned as he wrote furiously. He said nothing though, and when he left, thanked Lewis politely and said he might have to call again.

'Just to tie up a few ends,' he told him.

As soon as the policeman was gone, Lewis ran from the house and drove up to Rose Tree Café to tell Dora. She laughed at his outraged expression before reassuring him that several unlikely people were being questioned.

'You fit the description, that's all, and being a rep, you can be here and there in your car without anyone questioning your reason.'

'It's that Charlie's fault! They wouldn't have thought to question me if I hadn't been living in the house of a criminal!'

'Ex-criminal,' Dora corrected warningly. 'Now, have a cup of tea and calm down. And don't let Gwyn hear you talking like that!'

* * *

Gwyn was following the sad little figure of the old man. It was difficult with the dog to manage as Polly always wanted to rush everywhere and Gwyn had to hold her by the collar as he crept around corners and then ran to catch up with the man's movements as he shuffled past the allotments and down a terrace of shabby dwellings in which several families lived in each house. He saw the man go into the house at the end and noted the number before turning to go home. Twenty-one Sebastopol Street. He glanced back as he reached the corner in time to see the old man hurrying off in the opposite direction. Had he been fooled again?

It wasn't difficult for Gwyn to catch him up but keeping out of sight while he followed him was almost impossible. He tied Polly to a lamppost, fed her with some biscuits from his pocket and went in pursuit.

Via a circuitous route he was led to the lane behind the shops in Highbourne Road. From the corner he watched as the man slipped with the ease of familiarity through a fence, across a few gardens and into a house that appeared to be uninhabited. Surely he couldn't live there? Although, if he was stealing food, he might easily be a tramp.

'What are you doing round here, young Gwyn?' The voice, whispering in his ear so close, so unexpected, made the boy jump guiltily. He turned to see Percy Flemming behind him, a half smile on his thin face.

Percy was dressed in corduroy trousers with string tied around the legs just below the knees, and large leather boots; his jumper was covered with earth stains and was torn in several places, and on his hands were large gloves that were stained and smelling unpleasantly of sepsis.

'Dead rats among other things,' he said, in response to Gwyn's wrinkled nose and critical expression.

Percy worked as an assistant gardener at a hospital and dressed sensibly but neatly when he was working there, but when he was doing a very dirty job he wore an ancient outfit, which he would wear until it was too unpleasant, then throw it away.

His wife Barbara went to jumble sales to buy odd waistcoats and jackets and boots specially for work like he was doing today. For his other, more profitable activities he had bought some top quality clothes and fine leather shoes. People judged others in part by what they wore and he wanted to give anyone who met him on his 'other activities', a completely wrong impression.

'What are you doing, Mr Flemming?' Gwyn complained. 'You smell a bit high!'

'I'm unblocking a drain where a tree has broken through and blocked it. There were several drowned rats in there, rotted and disgusting. What a job, eh?' He put a hand in a bucket half filled with a black glutinous mess, as he waited for Gwyn to explain his reason for being in someone else's garden.

'I shouldn't be here really,' Gwyn confessed. 'Our Dad'll tell me off good and proper for trespassing, but I was following an old man who's been hanging around the lanes. Rhiannon was a bit worried. Seen him have you?' He described his quarry, and Percy said,

'You must mean old Willie Jones. He used to live there.' He pointed a glove dripping the foul-smelling black substance, towards the back of Edward's shop. 'That was his draper's shop until a few years ago. Harmless he is mind. You don't want to worry about old Willie. He just wanders about because he hasn't got anything better to do. Poor old fella.'

His questions answered, Gwyn retrieved an anxious Polly and went home.

*   *   *

During the first week of business, Edward was surprised at how busy he was. When Megan wasn't there, he used the lunch hour to reorder and follow up enquiries and rarely had time for more than a cup of tea and a sandwich. When Megan was there they usually managed to have something on toast, or a salad, which she prepared in his kitchen situated at the back of the flat.

Most of Edward's evenings were spent alone. Occasionally Megan and he met up and ate out but this was becoming less regular. Megan's baby was due in a few weeks and she admitted to being very tired after a few hours in the shop.

'Such a pity, as I enjoy it,' she sighed. 'I never thought I would, but it's fun helping people choose. Much more interesting than when I worked in Gwennie Woodlas's 'Gowns for Discerning Women',' she laughed. 'Gwennie is highly successful though, and I suppose I learned something by working with her.'

'You're a natural,' Edward told her proudly.

They went out that evening and before they ate, Edward drove past the property where his sister and Megan's Uncle Islwyn were planning to open a high-class restaurant. There were lights on in several of the rooms and, as there were no curtains in place, Megan dared Edward to go and have a look.

'Knock at the door, d'you mean?'

'No, Edward! Where's your sense of fun? I mean creep up and look through the windows, see what they are doing.'

'What if they see us? We'll feel such fools.'

'Speak for yourself! My uncle and your sister? Why shouldn't we go and look. But we'll try not to be seen.' She heaved herself laboriously out of the car before Edward could get around to help her and together they started up the drive.

They heard voices raised in anger before

they reached the window.

'But I told you we had to wait,' Margaret was shouting. They couldn't hear the lower voice of Islwyn but guessed he had done something of which Margaret disapproved.

Moving closer they saw to their alarm that the room was a shambles. Walls had been removed and beams put in place, modern beams that purported to be ancient. All around the room chunks had been knocked out of the walls exposing myriad wires and the plaster was crumbling almost as they watched. There was a hole in the ceiling large enough to accommodate a small car, and coils of electric cables lay in a jumble on the floor where joists were exposed by boards having been lifted and carelessly cut.

'Poor Margaret,' Edward muttered as he stood with an arm around Megan, and watched.

'She's either been completely misled by her surveyor or has chosen the wrong builder,' Megan whispered back. 'Or both. Poor Margaret indeed.'

When they got back to the car they sat for a moment thinking about what they had seen.

'Anyone else would have said 'serve her right', but you don't think like that, do you?' Megan said softly. 'You're wishing you could help.'

'I'm sorry for her. She was forced, by me, into giving up the house she loved, and now this new venture has obviously gone very, very wrong.'

'I suspect she chose the wrong partner for such an enterprise in my uncle too. He isn't exactly renowned for his enthusiasm for work!'

'Shall we knock? Perhaps there's some way I can help?'

'D'you know, Edward, you're a very nice man.'

'That sounds boring.'

Megan turned his head to face her and kissed him gently. 'Boring you are not,' she murmured.

'Then will you — '

She smothered his words with her lips. 'We'll talk about the future once The Lump shows us what the future will be like. It won't be peaceful and easy. Fun maybe, but life certainly won't be as we envisage it now, without any experience on which to judge it. We both need to adjust to the changes he'll bring.'

A continuing stream of shouting changed their mind about knocking and they went to find somewhere to eat. After they'd eaten, Edward took Megan home. He didn't go in but as usual waited until she was safely inside the door. She usually went in through the front but as they had driven from a different direction she walked up the path and in through the back door. Which was why her parents didn't hear her.

Walking without a sound into the hall she heard a grunt and a low moan of pain. Opening the door she saw a sight she would never forget — her mother cowering against the wall and her father punching her in the ribs and stomach.

'Mummy! Daddy!' she screamed and ran to protect her mother from the blows. Ryan was frozen in the act of aiming another blow, his arm bent and his hand in a tight fist. The expression on his face changed like a kaleidoscope from hate to shock and back to hate again as he moved suddenly and left the room, pushing Megan away from him as he went.

Megan staggered, saving herself from falling by grabbing the newel post. Then she and Sally were hugging each other, both sobbing, speechless with distress. They jumped as the door slammed shut behind Ryan.

And then the pains began.

8

Ryan knew nothing of the sudden onset of Megan's labour pains. Distressed more than he had ever been in his life, he lurched around the streets uncaring where he went or whether he fell under the wheels of the cars that passed him. He was so ashamed. How had he reached this dreadful state when he could hit his wife and not care about his daughter when she was in trouble and needed him?

Crossing the road blindly, he avoided a bus by sheer good luck and found himself outside the hospital. As if his route had been planned for him by some unseen force, he went inside.

He was unable to talk for several moments, mixed emotions, all of them self-accusing, prevented him controlling his breath. Then as he fought back sobs that threatened to engulf him once again, he choked out his words to the nurse standing waiting for him to explain his problem.

'Help me. Please help me, I'm ill.' Without waiting for her to ask questions he raised his voice and went on. 'I'm ill! I've been hitting my wife! Help me, please.' Sobs overcame him and he submitted himself to her care, giving up on the effort of explaining what had brought him there.

Unaware of what happened next, he came to his senses in the office of the matron, with a policeman standing close by. In a panic, he began to rise.

'I'm ready to go home now. I need to go home and make sure Sally's all right.' A restraining hand held him, voices assured him that Sally was safe.

'Your wife is here, in the maternity ward with your daughter.' Matron said. 'We'll attend to her bruises when she is satisfied your daughter Megan and her child are safe.'

This sent him back into despair and confusion. 'Megan's having the baby? Isn't it early? Will Megan be all right? And the baby — will he be all right?'

'It is a little early. A shock will sometimes start things off before time.' There was censure in the matron's voice. She had heard from a distraught Sally what had happened before labour began. 'But so far as we can tell, your daughter is strong and healthy and is now, please God, out of danger.'

'Danger?'

It was a word used deliberately by the firm but kindly matron. The man might be in distress but she saw no reason to let him off lightly. She considered a man who hit his wife, ill or not, undeserving of sympathy.

'It was my fault,' he muttered and his whole body began to shake uncontrollably.

'Calm down, Mr Fowler-Weston. Everything is going normally now. Your grandchild will be born in the next few minutes or so.'

'I hope he'll be all right,' Ryan muttered, repeating it over and over.

When they spoke to him after that, he seemed not to take in what was being said. All he could understand was that his daughter was in danger, her child might be harmed and he was responsible.

He was sitting in the waiting room having been promised an appointment with a psychiatrist, when he saw Sally approaching him along the corridor. He was tempted to run. How could he face her after this?

'There you are,' she said calmly. 'The nurse told me you were here. Come to enquire after your daughter? Pretending that you care?'

'I've come because I need help,' he said, tears threatening again. 'I need help.'

'I hope you find it, because you won't get any from me. Not after this.' She went to the wall phone and he sank back into confusion, only half registering that she was talking to someone called Edward. Who was Edward he wondered vaguely?

Ryan was taken to a small office where a man whose name he couldn't remember asked a lot of questions. He wanted to be helpful and give intelligent replies but with thoughts and words and pictures swimming around in his head completely out of his control, he thought he hadn't made much sense. Trying to pull himself together he said with great authority, 'My name is Ryan Fowler-Weston. How d'you do?'

* * *

News of Megan's labour spread through the family and to others. Sally, the proud grandmother, spoke to her sister Sian, who told Dora. She also called her parents and Arfon handed the phone to Gladys, who burst into tears.

The baby was born with very little fuss and Megan held her daughter and said to Sally, 'Mummy, I don't think I have ever been happier. She's so beautiful, and I want to do my very best for her.'

'She'll have everything she needs, don't worry about that,' Sally said, tears falling onto the cot as she leaned over to put her granddaughter down to rest.

'Now, will you find Edward and tell him I have a daughter?'

Sally made a few calls but Edward wasn't to be found.

★ ★ ★

To Lewis Lewis's embarrassment, the police had come twice more to question him about his whereabouts at the times of the robberies. That evening, he had been asked to go to the police station where they persisted with the idea that he was part of a team, committing only some of the robberies, making sure he had alibis for others in an attempt to confuse the police and throw them off the scent.

'With a job like yours you don't have much of an alibi anyway, do you?'

'An alibi? I don't need an alibi!' Lewis snapped. 'What on earth makes you think I'm involved in the robberies? Is it the company I keep? Is that it? Living with a criminal who happens to be my son-in-law?'

After each visit he had stormed over to Dora ready to talk about his humiliation and each time stormed back again having been shouted at for daring to suggest that Charlie was in any way to blame.

'My life is *hell*!' he said to Edward Jenkins when they met at the police station, neither aware of Megan's labour. Lewis was leaving after the latest round of questioning and

Edward followed him a few seconds later. They walked together along the road, companions in misery.

'What is the matter with them? I've never even had a fine for forgetting to put my driving lights on!' Lewis said.

'Apparently, Mr Lewis, we both match the description given by several eyewitnesses.'

'Both of us?' Lewis looked at Edward; as tall as himself, slim and expensively dressed, but with different colouring and no moustache. Edward, he decided was firmly in the wishy-washy class. Pale and dull looking. He was nowhere near as handsome as he was, even though the man was more than ten years younger. 'Rubbish!' he said emphatically.

'It does seem strange, but they seem to think we're both involved.'

'But we hardly know each other.'

'I think it must have been my sister who mooted the idea that we were working in harness; both involved, taking it in turns to commit the robberies so our alibis were sometimes sound.'

'I think it's because my daughter Rhiannon married a thief!'

'My sister Margaret's very vindictive, and she almost succeeded in ruining my business before it had even begun.'

'My daughter's very stubborn. She can't

really love the man. How could she? A common criminal?'

'I don't know much about love, Mr Lewis, so I can't comment.'

'Oh? I thought you and Megan Weston were more than friends. Not your baby she's carrying, is it?'

'Oh no, not mine.'

'I see, so there's no chance of you becoming more than friends.'

'I wouldn't say that. It depends whether or not I can convince her that I love them both.'

Edward hurried away then regretting putting his private thoughts into words, and to someone he hardly knew. He imagined Lewis telling his daughter-in-law, Joan, and Joan and Megan having a laugh over it. Why had he spoken so carelessly?

When he returned to the shop the phone was ringing. He was surprised to hear Sally's voice and even more surprised to be told that Megan's baby had been born and was a girl.

'Rosemary she will be called,' Sally said, her voice breathless with excitement. 'Megan wanted you to be among the first to know.'

'A girl?' he repeated stupidly. 'We'd always referred to it as a *he*. How wonderful. Is Megan all right? Is the baby all right?'

'Perhaps you'd like to go and see them tomorrow, although Megan asked me to assure you that she doesn't mind if you don't, knowing how uncomfortable some men are in such circumstances.'

'D'you mean she doesn't want me to?' he asked predictably.

'If you can face walking into that ward filled with mothers and their babies, she'd love to see you, Edward. Truly she would.'

Edward replaced the phone, glowing with the thought of meeting the child he had seen only in his imagination. He was smiling, his whole body glowing with the thought of Megan and her child, and Megan, hopefully, now agreeing to marry him. He walked through the flat, considering the place through fresh eyes. He'd have to furnish it properly, but Megan would choose, and the small bedroom would be a perfect nursery.

* * *

When Lewis went back to Sophie Street the news of Megan's baby was being discussed. His son, Viv, was there with his wife Joan, and Joan was describing her beautiful new niece.

'It's ridiculous really, but we all expected a boy. The Lump! As if we'd give a little girl a name like that!'

'That was used to describe Megan,' Dora laughed, 'not the baby. But you're right, we all referred to the baby as 'he'.'

'What will happen to the poor little chap,' Lewis said, 'growing up without a father?'

'Growing up *with* a father isn't always a doddle,' Dora said sharply. 'And aren't you listening? It's a girl.' Charlie touched Rhiannon on the arm and gestured with his head towards Dora. Sharp-eyed as always, Dora looked at her daughter and raised an eyebrow.

'Charlie and I will be having a baby next year,' Rhainnon said quietly. 'A brother or a sister for Gwyn.'

Amid the congratulations, Lewis said with a theatrical sigh, 'Another bedroom to decorate I suppose.'

When Dora took a deep breath to berate him he laughed and winked at Gwyn. 'Only joking, Grannie Lewis! Great news, eh, Gwyn?'

Lewis told Viv about his most recent interview at the police station. 'I met Edward Jenkins, and would you believe they are now considering that he and I are working together, taking turns at the robberies to confuse the police?'

Charlie said quietly, 'It isn't nice being under suspicion, is it Lewis?'

'No it isn't! But at least you deserve it!' At once he regretted his words and he turned to

Dora and mouthed, 'Sorry, sorry, sorry.'

In a hasty change of subject, Rhiannon began a discussion of Edward's friendship with Megan.

Turning to Joan she asked, 'Will Edward still be a friend to Megan d'you think? From what I hear of him he's terribly easily embarrassed. People thinking the child is his would be hard for him to cope with.'

'Megan has been a great help to him; they get on surprisingly well and I suspect he'll stay around. I hope so,' Joan said. 'My sister needs a caring person in her life.'

'Are they still looking for William Jones who used to own the shop?' Viv asked.

'Yes,' Joan said. 'Megan and Edward need to find him to return some money they found that must be his.'

'Willie Jones who was a draper?' Gwyn asked. 'He's the man who's been wandering around here, the one who frightened Rhiannon. I know where he lives.'

'You do?'

Gwyn explained about the man who had frightened Rhiannon by entering the back yard. 'I'll go and tell Mr Jenkins, shall I? Then he can give him back the money he found. Poor dab's in right need of it by the look of him.'

They all left then — Viv and Joan, a

reluctant Lewis, with Charlie and Rhiannon to go to The Railwayman, while Gwyn and Dora went to tell Edward about the discovery of the missing draper. Everyone was in celebratory mood, but Lewis's heart was heavy as he went into the public house. His daughter was expecting a baby. There was no chance of her leaving Charlie Bevan now.

★ ★ ★

Several people called on Sally that day, having heard news of the birth of her granddaughter; they called to bring gifts and good wishes for mother and child. Megan's Aunt Sian was one of the first, having left Dora alone in the café for an hour, and with her were her son Jack and his wife Victoria.

Since their wedding, Jack and Victoria saw very little of his family. Victoria was uneasy in the company of the Westons, especially Gladys, for whom she had once worked as a servant. Gladys had trained the young woman to be her maidservant and was now intent on training her into being a suitable wife for Jack!

Jack was more than satisfied to stay away from his grandparents and allow Victoria to develop any social skills she needed, in her own time. He was utterly content with his shy and loving wife, and was determined that nothing would spoil their life together. As a teacher, he had longer holidays than most and whenever possible, he and Victoria would go away, walking in the breathtakingly beautiful Brecon hills, or the mountains of North Wales. Just the two of them — they needed no one else. He wanted their way of life to go on for ever.

He watched Victoria as Sally described the new child. Was she yearning for a child of her own? He wouldn't mind the changes a child would bring. He saw that event as an added joy, so long as he kept the rest of the family from taking over. He smiled, remembering how Gladys and his mother had been outwitted over their wedding. Controlling the family was something at which he was master. He looked across at Victoria and mouthed, 'I love you.'

Sally avoided questions about Ryan: what he thought about being a grandparent, where he was at present and when he would go to visit Megan. Then the hospital phoned and pretence was no longer possible. Alarm showed on her face and the shock was so great that she told Sian and Jack and Victoria the whole story.

'What did the hospital say that frightened you so much?' Jack asked when the situation had been discussed.

'Only that he's on medication and has disappeared from the hospital, presumably to make his way back here. But he isn't coming in, Sian, I won't allow him in.'

★ ★ ★

When Dora and Gwyn had given him their message, Edward went straight away to find William Jones. The address in Sebastopol Street was a dingy house in a dingy street and he knocked on the half open door with trepidation. A young woman came out and when he asked about the man he was seeking, she told him he had lived there but had moved on.

Disappointed that he wouldn't have news to share with Megan the following day, Edward went home. He decided that he would forget the idea of finding the man and if he hadn't turned up after a year had passed, the money would go to a charity. With a sense of relief that the search had been abandoned, he went into the shop from the front entrance and ran up the stairs in a cheerful frame of mind.

The birth of Megan's daughter gave him a happy feeling. A new beginning for Megan, a fresh start to a life in which he hoped to share. He had succeeded in his attempt to own a business of his own. And there was Megan. He wanted Megan to marry him. Then he would ask for nothing more.

He sat in his small kitchen and planned what he would wear and what he would take on his visit the following day. He realised he would have to close the shop for a couple of hours and having willingly accepted that, he then began to wonder whether there was anyone he could ask to look after it instead.

As his thoughts drifted through the events of the day, he remembered Constable Gregory's daughter, Mair. She used to work for Gladys and Arfon Weston and on occasions for Margaret at Montague Court. Perhaps she would help?

He drove to the Gregorys' house tucked almost out of sight among trees at the edge of the wood, not far from the Griffiths's cottage. She agreed to come at nine the next morning so he could show her the routine.

Altogether it's been quite a day, he thought, as he went once more into the flat above the sports shop. He was in bed by eleven and as he was dropping off to sleep he heard sounds that jerked him into instant wakefulness. Someone was moving about in the shop.

He lay there for a moment or two stiffened with shock, but when the sounds continued, he forced himself to rise opening the door carefully and listening. He recognised the sound of someone moving behind the counter in the shop below and opening drawer after drawer. The irony struck him then, that as a suspect for the burglaries he was now a victim.

He slipped on his dressing gown and made his way slowly down the stairs, keeping to the edge and hoping they wouldn't creak, although a cowardly part of his mind was praying they would make a noise and frighten the man off.

Edward slowly opened the door leading into the shop from the passageway and looked around. There was hardly any light, only a glow filtering through from the street lamps, but he moved his head in an attempt to discern a movement. After what seemed an age but which couldn't have been more than a minute, he switched on the light and stepped into the shop, reaching for a cricket bat from the display and brandishing it, bent in a threatening crouch.

There was no one there. As he grew more and more confident he moved around, looking behind displays and counters, adding more light to the scene, then going — this time noisily — into the storeroom and kitchen beyond the shop. He felt a draught but when he reached the back door, having checked every window, it was all bolted and locked.

He couldn't have imagined it! Angry now, he went methodically through the house, upstairs and down, pulling open every door of every cupboard and upending piles of stock and every other place of concealment. He had to face the fact that he was locked securely in, and quite alone.

He made himself a cup of tea which he took upstairs but for the rest of the night he remained awake, trying in vain to convince himself the sounds had once again been from the house next door.

★ ★ ★

In the property bought by Margaret and Islwyn, there was no sleep either. With floorboards replaced and some hope of getting the place decorated in time for their planned opening in September, they had stayed up all night painting walls. At five o'clock, when they were washing out paintbrushes and preparing to fall into bed for a few hours of sleep, they heard a sound that at first, they didn't recognise. Then they knew it was water.

The water tank in the roof space was old;

they had been warned it would need replacing, but they had hoped it would last a few more months. When Islwyn took a torch and went to investigate he found that it had rusted through. Shutting off the water supply, they went to bed exhausted and dejected.

Margaret didn't sleep. She lay there mentally going over her accounts. At this rate they would run out of money long before they were ready to open. She had to raise more money.

Waking Islwyn from sleep she said, 'Issy, I'm frightened. We're getting more and more into the red and without a hope of earning anything from this place for months. What are we going to do?'

'Talk about it in the morning,' he mumbled.

'I can't sleep. I have to find a ray of hope.'

'Tomorrow,' he said again. She shook him and insisted they talked about it there and then. 'Can't you see that everything is falling down around us? Almost literally?'

His response was to turn away and cover his ears with the blankets.

Margaret got up, switched on the light and pulled the bed covers onto the floor. 'Now, Islwyn. We talk about it now!'

He sat up and rubbed his face, trying to revive himself. 'All right, you've ruined my hope of a few hours of sleep. What d'you want me to say? Don't worry? Everything will be all right? Something will turn up?'

'You could say you'll get a job.'

'I'm needed here.'

'But we can't survive without money. Will you get a job? For a few months, a year at the most. At least then we'll have something to live on. I can oversee the work here.'

'D'you want me to work in a fish and chip shop again, for a pittance? I can't get a decent job. You know that. Not after the publicity the Weston family had after the collapse of the business. I was accused of theft if you remember.'

'I remember,' she said coldly. 'Theft and being too lazy to do what your father-in-law paid you to do.'

'What d'you mean by that?'

'Help us, Issy. I've never asked you for money. I don't want to now, but things are getting out of hand. I think we'll both have to find work. It will be hard to manage a job and oversee this, but I'll do it. Issy, we're in this together aren't we? We have to do anything that's necessary to make this succeed.'

'All this is your brother's fault. He's landed on his feet, ask him for help.'

'I'm asking you.'

Picking up the abandoned bedding, Islwyn

marched into the bathroom and made himself comfortable in the bath. Margaret waited five minutes then turned on the taps. As she squealed with frustration, she heard a low chuckle from Islwyn as she remembered that the water supply had been turned off.

★ ★ ★

The following morning, Edward looked around the shop again, trying to convince himself he'd dreamed the whole thing, that nothing had happened during the night. For a while he was reassured but when he looked in the window, he saw that a display of sports socks had been moved. Instead of a dozen pairs, still in their box, tilted against the back of the window, the box had been removed and the socks had been attractively fanned out in a neat circle with a pair folded and shaped forming the rose-like centre.

Mair came at nine and his mind was taken away from the curious events as he explained to her the intricacies of the till and the stock control system. She was quick to learn and as the door closed for the lunch hour and he handed her the keys he was convinced that she would cope well during the few hours he was away.

With the disturbances of the night and the

mystery of the meticulously arranged display of socks, plus the busy morning serving customers, and in between teaching Mair the ways he worked, he hadn't given much thought to the hospital visit. It was lodged at the back of his mind as something rather terrifying that had to be faced. He couldn't eat, but went instead to buy flowers, fruit and a large box of chocolates.

He had thought about seeing Megan and being introduced to her daughter, but when it came to walking into the ward alongside all the young fathers, he knew he wasn't prepared: all the young women in bed and in their night attire; all the husbands who would presume he was one of them; and worst of all, seeing Megan in bed, nursing her child, probably not even wearing a dressing gown. He wanted to flee.

A glance at the men and the few women waiting for the sister to tell them it was time to go in, made him realise he was not the only one to be ill at ease. He tried to smile at one young man who looked little more than sixteen but to his great embarrassment he developed a nervous tic in his cheek and he hurriedly took out a handkerchief and pretended to blow his nose.

As the doors to the ward opened, he didn't have time to change his mind and leave; he was pushed in with the rest to be left standing in the doorway holding a box of chocolates, a huge basket of fruit and a bunch of flowers, looking helplessly around him. Megan's arm waving from a corner galvanised him into action and he hurried towards her. Once he saw her, she became his goal, and he was oblivious to the rest.

She was wearing a bed-jacket, her hair was neatly arranged and she looked utterly beautiful. Without needing words, he bent over and kissed her, then looked at the sleeping child, and on being given a nod of permission, he picked up the baby and held her. From then on everything was all right.

* * *

Megan's grandparents, Gladys and Arfon Weston, came in about an hour after Edward. He stood at once, apologised for staying so long and prepared to leave. Megan placed a restraining hand on his arm and pleaded with the sister to be allowed an extra visitor for a little while.

She proudly displayed the baby and shared a smile with Edward as she listened to their admiring comments.

'Nothing of that awful Terrence Jenkins

about him dear,' Gladys announced. 'What a relief.' She suddenly realised that Edward was there, but unrepentant, she glared at Edward in defiance; if he thought she would apologise he'd wait a very long time. But Edward smiled disarmingly back. He had no objection to anyone airing their dislike of his cousin Terrence.

The older couple didn't stay long. Edward was surprised to find they were more uneasy than he had been. Gladys was close to tears and Megan knew that however she tried to hide it, her grandmother was embarrassed by the situation.

Megan's family trickled in a couple at a time and she realised that Gladys was organising a rota. Jack and Victoria came, Joan and Viv, Aunt Sian and Dora when the cafe closed. Her mother called each day and Edward, when he was allowed.

One visitor was completely unexpected. She looked up as visitors began to walk through the ward to see her father looking down at the baby. Without addressing a word to him, she at once called for the nurse. Ryan didn't say a single word as he was led away to be returned to hospital.

★ ★ ★

Sally went every day to see her daughter and grandchild but she didn't visit her husband. Ryan, she had been told, had been readmitted to the mental hospital five miles away.

'I have no intention of going to see him,' she told the doctor. 'I have a guesthouse to run and I am preparing for when my daughter and granddaughter come home. These are my priorities.'

Islwyn went to see his brother-in-law but he didn't show sympathy. 'You hit Sally? You deserve to be ill,' was his first comment. 'Pity she didn't swipe you back, coward that you are, that would have cured you,' was his second.

'She says she won't have me back,' Ryan said sadly.

'Won't she? I could walk back into Trellis Road tomorrow if I wanted to. Sian would have me back, no question about that,' Islwyn boasted. With the situation at the restaurant so serious, he had briefly considered going back, but he told Ryan that everything was going well. And having boasted about how wonderful his own life was shaping, and adding to Ryan's remorse and shame, he left.

★ ★ ★

231

At the Rose Tree Cafe, Sian and Dora were beginning to clear up, ready for closing. The door opened and Lewis came in.

'You'll have to hurry, we're shutting the door in fifteen minutes,' Dora remarked.

Sian smiled at him and poured him a cup of tea. 'There's a scone or two if you're hungry,' she said. She nudged Dora as he went to find a seat. 'Don't you ever smile and say an ordinary, 'hello' to the man?'

'Of course I do. Sometimes,' Dora told her unrepentantly, but then she looked across and saw how Lewis's shoulders were slumped and felt mean for her rudeness. 'You're right, Sian. I don't have to be quite so unbearable. It's become an unpleasant habit.' She went across with a tray on which she had placed scones, jam and a dish of clotted cream. 'Have this on me, Lewis. You look as though you have had a bad day. The police haven't bothered you again, have they?'

'Yes. They were waiting when I went to the house at lunchtime.'

'There must be some way to clear this up. Can I do anything?'

'A sympathetic voice helps,' he said, flashing his wonderful smile, widening his dark eyes. ''Specially from you, love.'

'You deserve at least that,' she surprised him by saying.

232

His hand covered hers. 'Thanks. I desperately need your support. I feel as though I'm afloat in a small boat on a wide empty sea, without a friend in the world.'

'No women begging for a moment of your time?' Her voice hardened as she spoke. 'Your charms fading then?'

'No women. Dora, I'll do anything if you'll let me come home. Think of Rhiannon and Charlie if not of me. There's a baby coming and they won't want me hanging around, being in the way.'

'It wouldn't be the thought of disturbed nights with a baby crying every few hours?'

'That too,' he admitted with a smile. 'But the real reason is that I want to be home, with you.'

'I'll think about it when I believe you're genuinely sorry for the misery you've caused me.'

'For God's sake, Dora! You're like a prison warder, handing out promises of a shorter sentence if I can show proper remorse!'

'It isn't like that,' she protested, regretting her stupid and unkind words.

'Number seven Sophie Street is where I belong, with you, in your bed.'

'Eat your scones,' she said sharply, and returned to the kitchen.

Leaving the uneaten scones, Lewis left the

cafe, wanting retaliation and knowing there was only one way to get it. Another flirtation. A rumour that he was seeing another woman was the surest way to hurt Dora. But he'd be hurting himself more and all hope of returning home would be gone for ever.

'From the way you're scrubbing that draining board you're upset,' Sian said to Dora a few minutes later.

'He said I was like a prison warder, doling out punishments.'

'And you think he might be right?' Sian asked.

'I know he is, I treat his need for sex as though it's a crime, pretending mine are non-existent. I won't listen to his worries about Charlie, even though I know it's based on concern for Rhiannon. But I can't see a way of changing things without giving in completely and admitting that I want him back as much as he wants to come.'

'What's wrong with that for heaven's sake? Admit it. Where's the shame in being truthful about loving someone? You're a grown woman, Dora, not a temperamental teenager in love for the first time.'

'But I am. Don't you see? I've always loved Lewis, he *is* my first time.'

'I thought I loved Islwyn, but in a mundane way, accepting that this was my situation, my

234

life, rather than some deep, overwhelming passion. I was married and it's usual for people in my position to stay that way.'

'Nothing more than that?'

Shaking her head sadly, Sian said, 'Nothing more than that. And now I'm free of him. Islwyn walking out after admitting to a long-standing affair with Margaret Jenkins snapped something in my head. Yet you had the same treatment from Lewis and want him back. How different we are, Dora. Although,' she smiled, 'if my Islwyn was as devastatingly handsome as your Lewis is, I might have a different story to tell!'

When Sian reached home that evening she was surprised to see her husband standing outside her front door.

'Islwyn?' she said enquiringly.

'I thought you might not know that Ryan is in the mental hospital.'

'I know, Sally phoned me. He hit her, did you know that?'

'It's unforgivable, isn't it? Quiet, gentle Sally. What a shameful way for a man to behave.'

'Shameful. Two fine men we chose for husbands, Sally and I. You cheated on the family and then on me; Ryan happily letting Sally do all the work while he watched, then hitting her.'

235

'I didn't come to quarrel, I thought we should talk about what we can do.'

'What are you talking about? There is no we, Islwyn. Go back to your mistress. We're well shot of the pair of you.' She went inside and slammed the door. Sian stood there for a while trying to analyse her feelings and was relieved to realise that what she had said to Dora was correct: she felt nothing but relief that he was gone.

★ ★ ★

In a futile effort to make amends, Dora knocked on Rhiannon and Charlie's door and handed the few scones they'd had left to a delighted Gwyn. 'Perhaps you and your granddad might like to come to Sunday tea?' she suggested. 'Then your dad and Rhiannon could do something on their own.' She lowered her voice to a conspiratorial whisper, 'Mums and dads like to do that sometimes.'

Although she waited and waited, there was no word from Lewis to say he would come.

★ ★ ★

Edward continued to visit Megan in hospital. He went every afternoon and the rest of her family went each evening. The first embarrassment did not return and he now marched into the ward and up to her bed with eyes shining with pleasure at seeing her. He held the baby and they discussed her progress like proud parents.

Two days before she was due home, Edward had gone to find a vase for the flowers he had brought and a nurse remarked loudly, 'How many husbands have you got?'

'None,' Megan replied. She hadn't pretended at any time through her pregnancy and she wasn't going to start now.

'Well there's another proud father asking to see you,' the nurse told her. 'He's tall, slim and elegant. Very handsome and by the look of him, he's not short of a bob or two. Ring any bells?'

Megan pulled a face; she knew who it was all right. But why had he come? Surely not to claim his child?

Terrence Jenkins came into the ward smiling widely, armed with flowers and chocolates and a very large teddy bear.

Edward stood in the doorway and felt his happiness drain away. His cousin had come to claim his child. Not wanting to embarrass Megan he decided to slip away without saying goodbye. This was why she had refused to discuss their future wasn't it? She had been waiting, hoping, that Terrence would come back to her. He didn't wait to see Megan's reaction.

'Hello Terrence. What do you want?' she asked ungraciously.

'Congratulations.' He thrust the flowers at her and she handed them to a nurse.

'Give these to someone without any, will you please?'

He gave her the chocolates and she threw them onto the side table without a glance. The teddy bear he placed on the edge of the cot. She took it off and warned him that it could easily frighten the child.

'I came to see the child as soon as Grandfather told me he was born,' he said.

'He, is a she! Well, now you've seen her, would you kindly go, Terrence. I'm very tired and not up to visitors.'

He protested, tried to charm her, but eventually left. When he had gone she looked around for Edward and was told he had gone a few minutes before.

238

9

Megan was saddened by the absence of Edward but told her mother it was what she had expected.

'I was right to ask him to wait before discussing our future,' she said to Sally when, after ten days, she was allowed home with her baby. 'I tried to warn him that once the child was a reality instead of a dream, he would change his mind about wanting me and Rosemary in his life.'

'I'm surprised,' Sally told her. 'I thought he would stay. From how you described his face when he held her that first day, I gathered he was enchanted. His absence isn't anything to do with his cousin Terrence turning up, is it?'

'I don't see how it can be. He knows I have no feeling for Terrence. He was the big mistake of my life. Although,' she added, smiling down at her sleeping child, 'I can hardly consider it a mistake now, can I? I have a lovely daughter and I couldn't be more pleased about that. Look at her, Mummy. She's so beautiful. I don't regret Rosemary for a moment.'

'You don't mind the gossip?' Sally asked.

'That's hardly new for me is it? Remember how often Joan and I were criticised for our behaviour, and called 'Those Weston Girls'?'

'This is different.'

'But bearable, Mummy.'

Terrence called at the house a few minutes later, as Megan was helping her mother by making pastry for the evening meal of steak and kidney pie, to which her mother added grated courgettes and an eggcupful of beer.

'Can I see Rosemary?' he asked as he walked into the kitchen.

'Be quick then, Mummy and I have work to do, and please don't disturb her.' She knew she was being unkind, but she didn't want him to find a hint of interest in her attitude towards him. Terrence was part of the past, and her mother's suggestion that he might be the cause of Edward's non-appearance added to her determination not to encourage him.

Megan suspected that Terrence, like her father, was hoping for an easy life and one during which he didn't need to work very hard. There was no money in the Weston family's coffers now, but he might think there was.

She spoke to her mother about her plans to go to work as soon as she was able, so she could earn the money to keep her child. If Sally thought she was talking nonsense she didn't say so, but following Megan's lead, listened and added a few suggestions about the careers she might try.

When Sally offered him the unwanted remains of the beer left from the pie, Terrence drank it and left, with Megan hardly uttering a word to him.

'I hope he isn't staying in Pendragon Island for long,' she sighed as the door closed behind him.

'Unless he's hoping for frostbite I don't think he will,' her mother replied wryly.

★ ★ ★

Edward hadn't seen very much of his cousin Terrence. He knew he was staying with their grandfather near the pleasure beach and guessed that it was not filial duty that had led him there. He would have called on the old man because he could stay there for free. Terrence was always short of money.

He hoped Megan wasn't going to be hurt by him. There had to be a reason for him coming back. Perhaps Terrence thought the Weston family had recovered their lost fortune and he could settle into an easy life being supported by them?

Edward smiled then, imagining Megan's response to such a suggestion. She had more sense than to succumb to tales of woe from a lazy man; even her mother had finally learned that lesson.

He was re-dressing the window after the shop closed. The evenings were light and the pavement outside was filled with passers-by cheerful in the light-hearted mood and bright colours of summer. Some jokingly stopped and waved a hand to help him adjust a display by an inch or two.

He had two visitors while he worked: Mair Gregory asking whether he wanted help that week, to which he replied 'yes', and Frank Griffiths asking if he wanted him to come and dig over the garden ready for autumn planting, another affirmative reply. Because of their interruptions he hadn't finished the window when hunger reminded him it was almost nine o'clock.

Abandoning the display he put down the beach-tennis sets he intended to place on a small area of sand. For the cricket bats and stumps, the tennis rackets and the clothing to go with them, he planned to set out a piece of imitation grass. But he was tired. It was time to find himself some food. He would finish the window in the morning.

When Edward woke, early the next day, the window display was complete. What was more, the work was considerably better than he would have done it.

For a moment he thought he must have finished it himself, but then he remembered clearly that he had abandoned it to make his supper. He didn't find the prospect of someone wandering around finishing off his job in any way eerie. It was puzzling, but there was no ghostly hand at work here. Someone was getting in. He went to a locksmith and had the locks on the back door and the shop entrance changed. He wished he could discuss it with Megan.

He saw Sally walking past the shop and ran out to ask about Megan and Rosemary. When he had been assured they were well, he almost asked about Terrence, but couldn't. The disappointment of him turning up and ruining his hopes of a life with Megan was a raw wound. He asked about Ryan instead.

'I don't know,' Sally replied, frowning as she spoke.

Edward said, 'But you are concerned?'

'It isn't easy to forget someone you've lived with, shared your life with for so many years, Edward.'

'Would you like me to enquire and report back?'

'Would you?' She looked at him, her head tilted slightly in a way that reminded him of

243

Megan. 'You're such an understanding man, Edward.'

'Nonsense,' he smiled.

'Why don't you call and see the baby?' she asked.

'I can't. Not now.'

He was thinking he'd be unwelcome now Terrence was back. Sally thought he was unable to cope, now Megan's child was a reality.

When Edward telephoned the hospital to ask about Ryan he was told he had been discharged.

* * *

Released from hospital, and having assured the doctors that he was going home, Ryan had set off for Pendragon Island clutching a bottle of pills and wondering where he would spend that night. He went to his in-laws, Gladys and Arfon Weston, and after a discussion between a hissing, disapproving Gladys and the low ponderous voice of Arfon, it was agreed that he could stay until he found somewhere else.

On the following day, he called on Edward and asked for a job.

'Sorry Mr Fowler-Weston, but I don't have anything. I call Mair Gregory when I need extra help but even that isn't regular.'

Edward thought about Ryan throughout the day and decided that, as he was Megan's father and ill, and obviously in need of help, he could at least try and find him a job. Ringing around to some of the people he dealt with, Ryan was promised a sympathetic hearing by a man needing an invoice clerk. Edward went at once to tell Ryan, who promised to see the man later that day.

'The wages won't be high, but you might manage to pay for a room with board,' Edward said.

'Beggars can't be choosers. I've never really thought that would apply to me, but I have to face facts,' Ryan said sadly.

Edward was alarmed at the change in the man — once so haughty, and now chastened and defeated. He rang the house in Glebe Lane and told Sally what had happened.

'I understand you don't want anything more to do with him,' he explained, 'but I suspect you'll want to know how he's coping.'

'Thank you Edward. I am concerned and I'd appreciate you keeping in touch. Do you want to talk to Megan?' she asked.

'Well, yes, if she isn't busy. I want to know how Rosemary is getting on.'

'Why don't you call?' Sally asked, lowering

her voice. 'If you coped with walking into that postnatal ward you can cope with us, surely?'

'I'd love to, but I don't want to intrude. I gather — ' he was about to say, 'that my cousin is there', but changed his mind. 'I gather Rosemary is doing well,' he said instead.

When Megan came to the phone she sounded breathless and he had the feeling he had either interrupted something or that she was embarrassed by his call, so he made it brief. He asked about the baby, she asked about the shop, then they both replaced their receivers in disappointment.

★   ★   ★

Barry Williams's house in Chestnut Road was sold within twenty-four hours of going on the market. Barry had momentary fears that he'd made another wrong decision, but when he counted up how much money the sale would produce, he calmed down. He owned the sweet shop in Sophie Street and the flat above; it was sensible to use it and give himself a second chance to make a name for himself as a photographer.

He went to tell Rhiannon and explain that he would be living above the shop.

'I won't disturb you,' he promised. 'I'll use

246

the back entrance and you won't know I'm there.'

'Have you told Caroline what you're doing?' she asked.

'She knows I'm selling the house. I haven't told her I'm trying again to start a photographic business.'

'Why? She'd be interested to know.'

'Would she?' He sounded doubtful.

'She feels guilty that you gave it up because of her,' Rhiannon told him.

'Then perhaps I shouldn't mention it; won't it make her feel worse?'

'Probably, but better you tell her than someone else.'

★　★　★

Ernie and Frank Griffiths had always been the closest of friends. But with Ernie engaged to marry Helen Gunner, Frank was feeling out of it all. Their other brother, Basil, was married and had two small boys; now it wouldn't be long before Ernie had no conversation apart from wallpapering and babies. If only he could persuade Mair Gregory to go out with him he wouldn't mind so much, but without a girlfriend and no hope of finding one, Frank was miserable.

That evening was particularly bad as

Helen's parents, Gloria and Wilfred Gunner, had been invited to the house to discuss wedding plans. He was amused for a while listening to the diverse ideas of the Gunners' extravaganza and the Griffiths' down-to-earth knees-up style celebration.

'Come for a pint?' he asked Ernie hopefully when the women disappeared upstairs to talk about wedding dresses.

'Come off it, Frank. Can't you see I'm needed here?'

'What's up, son?' Hywel asked. 'Got a face like a double bass you have.'

'If you must know, I asked Mair to come out with me and she told me to get lost.'

'Thank God for that! Her father's a copper in case you've forgotten! He's never forgiven me for selling him that joint of pork from our illegal pig! Ungrateful old misery-guts.'

Frank went to talk to the goats.

The wedding discussion turned into a party when Viv and Joan came with Charlie and Rhiannon and Gwyn, who was carrying some of the Rose Tree Café's left-over sandwiches and cakes.

When Barry walked in, hoping to talk privately to Caroline his spirits fell. He groaned as he saw that all the windows were open and the door was standing welcomingly wide, and the place was full. Fat chance of having a quiet word with Caroline in the Griffiths's house!

But it was easier than he hoped when he realised that Ernie Griffiths's fiancée and her parents were there to discuss final arrangements for the young couple's wedding. It was easy for Caroline and him to go into the garden, tell Frank to clear off, and lean over the fence while Joseph-Hywel admired the goats.

'Don't be upset, Caroline,' Barry began, 'but I have given notice at the factory.'

'I'm glad, Barry. You never wanted to take it. What will you do?'

Again he begged her not to be upset, before he told her, 'I intend to restart my business.'

'Upset? I'm delighted. I felt so dreadful that you gave it all up for us, then we separated so soon after. Such a lot of trouble I've caused you, Barry. I'm sorry. And, I wish you luck.'

'I don't suppose you'd help, would you? I mean do the books, arrange appointments sometimes, that sort of thing.'

'Of course I will. I'd be glad to make amends for the — '

'Not make amends, just helping a friend,' he interrupted. He went home, ignored the chaos of his partly packed up home and slept contentedly for eight hours.

Lewis watched Dora as she set off to visit Megan and the baby and he was filled with resentment. He had offered her a lift but had been told firmly that she would rather walk. In fact she had gone on her bicycle with Rhiannon. Was there ever going to be an end to her bitterness? Out of pique he rang up a lady customer and invited her out for a meal. He'd show Dora he wasn't waiting around for her for the rest of his life. He was still young enough to start all over again. Why should he put up with her temper any longer?

It was a warm evening and August was the month when all the world seemed to be holidaymaking. In a mood of pleasurable excitement he drove into Cardiff to meet Diana Keep. She was waiting for him on the corner of St Mary's Street and wearing a heavy coat in a drab brown, sensible shoes and a hat that could only be described as unfortunate. His optimistic mood faded and when he had parked the car, he went to meet her with a heavy heart.

She was pleasant company, admiring him with her eyes and obviously flattered to be out with him, and when she removed the coat had on an attractive two-piece in a shade of blue he found appealing. But in spite of the promise in her eyes and in her body movements, Lewis's mind was at Sally Fowler-Weston's house, imagining how Dora would look at him if she found out about his date. Paying her back for her unpleasantness by going out with another woman as she so often accused, would rebound on him as usual.

After the meal he made his excuses, thanked her for her delightful company and drove her home. Declining the invitation to stay for a coffee, he went back to Pendragon Island.

It had begun to rain and as he drove towards Sophie Street it increased to a vigorous downpour, suiting his mood. On impulse he drove past Sophie Street and went on to Glebe Lane. There, he knocked on Sally's door.

'I've called to give Dora and Rhiannon a lift home,' he said. 'They can call for their bikes tomorrow can't they?'

'Come in,' Sally smiled and he stood in the kitchen shedding his coat and trilby, before walking into the lounge and greeting them all. Sally put the kettle on for more tea. She had lost count of how many visitors they'd had or how many cups of tea she had made, since the birth of Rosemary.

'I've been to Cardiff, taking a woman

customer out for dinner,' Lewis told Dora at once. 'I'm hoping for a big order when she opens a new sweet shop,' he added.

'Young, is she?' Dora asked pertly.

'Mum!' Rhiannon whispered.

Ignoring both comments, Lewis went over to the cot where the baby lay, and pressed a sixpenny piece into the small, perfect hand, before realising she might swallow it. As he retrieved the coin the baby took hold of his finger and he smiled delightedly.

'Strong grip, and a lovely child. Congratulations, Megan.'

Dora stood beside him, looking down at the baby. 'Remember when ours were this young, Lewis? Lovely they were.'

'They still are,' Lewis replied, smiling at his daughter. 'Our Viv married to Joan and running Old Man Arfon's business for him. And Rhiannon, married to a man who loves her and soon to be a mother herself. They have grown into wonderful people. And our Lewis who died so tragically, well, he'll always be young and beautiful, won't he?' He put an arm around her and led her back to her chair.

Sally brought a tray of tea and when they left an hour later, Dora and Lewis were talking like friends. Rhiannon's hands were aching from crossing her fingers so tightly.

Besides the Rose Tree Café, Sian and Dora sometimes catered for parties and other celebrations. One Friday afternoon they were asked to arrange food for a picnic for local children. 'Most of them are from poor homes or have suffered neglect,' the woman explained. 'I'm so sorry it's short notice, but we suddenly had to change the day from next week to this Saturday. Can you possibly supply individual plates of food for forty children?'

A few phonecalls to order supplies and they agreed. This was something worthwhile and neither woman complained about the extra hours involved.

They had to collect the food they needed on the following Friday evening from a supplier about seventeen miles from Pendragon Island and unfortunately, Sian's car failed to start. Dora ran to find Lewis. He wouldn't refuse to help, not for deprived children. He wasn't there. The car stood at the kerb but there was no sign of Lewis.

'Charlie, can you drive Lewis's car and take us?' Dora pleaded.

'As long as you explain to Lewis, of course I will.'

They were gone a lot longer than they

expected as they had difficulty finding the address. Lost in country lanes with few people about they used up precious time retracing their way again and again. There were few signposts to help them.

'They took down the road signs to confuse the Germans during the war,' Dora grumbled, 'and ten years on they're keeping them hidden to confuse us!' They were both feeling frustrated before finally reaching their destination.

Dora wrote a note for Lewis explaining what had happened, left it on the hall table and she and Sian went back to the café where they had space to work and an efficient kitchen, to prepare the picnic in time for the following day. It was eleven-thirty before they got to bed, and Dora's last thought was that she would make a special meal and invite Lewis to share it, to thank him for the use of the car.

Unfortunately he called at the café during the following Monday afternoon and complained that Charlie had borrowed his car over the weekend without asking and hadn't replaced the petrol he'd used.

'I asked him to take me to a place on the way to Newport to collect some supplies we needed. Didn't you see my note? I didn't think you'd mind.' She felt her anger rising and turned to her partner, 'You tell him, Sian.'

She busied herself in the kitchen while Sian explained to Lewis about the picnic for the deprived children. What had happened to the note, no one knew. Lewis suggested that Polly might have eaten it.

When Dora invited him to come for a meal that evening, some quixotic pique made him refuse; Rhiannon and Charlie and Gwyn went instead and he sat in the car and ate chips, wondering why he'd declined the offer.

★ ★ ★

August was a month for children and the town was filled with families making their way to and from the beautiful sandy bays or the rocky and pebbly beaches; such variety and all just a short distance from the centre of the town.

Buses and trains brought more and more people in and boarding houses and hotels displayed their 'No Vacancies' signs, and still people came. They slept on the beach and washed in the public baths, ate alfresco and enjoyed the freedom.

Edward was busy with smaller, less expensive items for the beach, a part of the business he enjoyed. Twice during the month the window display was changed during the night and he found the goods displayed found favour with the customers.

Annie and Leigh Grant filled their rooms at Montague Court and their restaurant kept their staff busy from seven in the morning until eleven-thirty at night.

For Margaret and Islwyn, things were also beginning to improve. The new restaurant opened and with a small staff and a minimal menu they began to take money. The bank was pressing them; their creditors had been patient but were beginning to warn about an end to supplies unless overdue accounts were settled.

'We only need a good couple of months and we'll start paying everyone back,' Margaret said to Islwyn as they closed their doors one night.

'I can't do any more,' Islwyn said tiredly. 'I'm up at six and working until almost midnight.'

'You could get a job,' she said.

'How can I? You need me here,' he replied.

Margaret said nothing. It was useless to point out that a seven-year-old boy using half his brain would achieve more in a day than he did. She had always known Islwyn was lazy, but had been convinced that when motivated by sharing a growing business that might one

256

day make them rich, he would work as hard and as long as she did. How wrong she had been. If only it had been her brother Edward beside her they would have achieved so much more.

Anger against her brother for being the cause of her problems rose and increased. She hated him for what he had done, losing them their home and causing her such worry, while he plodded along in his pathetic little retail shop.

But Edward's new shop was growing in recognition every week. Instead of going into Cardiff as Margaret had predicted, the local people tried Edward first and his stock soon filled the two rooms behind the shop.

'I foresee the day when I'll have to use the flat for storage and live in the basement,' he told Mair Gregory, as a supply of football and rugby equipment and clothes arrived ready for the new season.

At the beginning of September, when children went back to school, his window was well filled as more footballs and jerseys and socks were added to his displays overnight by his ghostly prowler.

He predicted an extremely busy few weeks. He still employed Mair Gregory two or three afternoons each week and began to think about adding to her hours. When he suggested it to her she was delighted to agree. Until he had asked for her help on the day Rosemary was born, she had only done domestic cleaning. The shop was something she had thought might be boring, but she had been wrong.

Mair's mother was dead and she and her father had continued to live in the cottage they rented, with Mair acting as housekeeper, working a few hours here and there to earn some extra spending money. It was a casual life which she enjoyed. Now, having experienced the interesting sports shop, she wanted to do something more. When Edward asked her to work every afternoon and all day Saturday, for a trial period, she was very pleased to accept.

There was an interesting by-product to his employing Mair for more hours. Frank began calling and offering to do any odd job without payment. From the way he looked at Mair, it was not difficult for Edward to guess why he came.

The garden was cleared, dug and raked ready for the September sowing of grass seed, and the new shrubs and flowers were planted and regularly weeded. In front of Mair, Frank hotly refused payment, but out of her sight, he accepted Edward's 'bonus'.

Edward hadn't seen much of Megan. She

had walked past the shop a few times and waved when he saw her and on two occasions she had been with Terrence. If only she were here, helping him when the baby allowed, staying with Rosemary in the flat when she couldn't leave her. But that was impossible now. Then he met his grandfather who told him Terrence had gone back to London. Gloomily, Edward wondered how soon he would return.

He saw very little of his grandfather. The old man preferred to keep to himself and was glad that Edward and Margaret had never considered it their duty to make regular calls. He was tolerant of Terrence's occasional visits, when the usual reason was to scrounge money, but did nothing to encourage him to stay. He had a woman to keep house for him and a maid who, between a dozen other jobs answered the door wearing a black dress and white apron, cuffs and lacy hat. He lived, and looked, like something out of a novel by Dickens, wearing his heavy tweed suit, even in this hottest of summer weather, his only concession to the season being a rather ancient panama hat. He smoked a pipe and there was usually a stream of tobacco or ash down the front of his waistcoat.

To Edward's surprise, his grandfather called one day and asked to see the premises.

Edward showed him around with pride, the old man commenting on the various things Edward pointed out, nodding and puffing on his pipe. Finally he said, 'You've done well, Edward. Now, will you call a taxi for me to get home?'

Edward asked about Terrence then. When was he coming back? What his plans were. Had he found a job? He was told that Terrence had gone back to London several days ago.

'He only comes to ask for money,' old Mr Jenkins said harshly. 'I told him there definitely wouldn't be any more so this time he's gone for good.'

'Gone? But what about Megan and the baby? He hasn't left them, has he?'

'What d'you mean, left them? He and Megan aren't playing at mothers and fathers so far as I know. He's been staying with me and seeing friends but he hasn't seen Megan except when they bump into each other. Really, Edward, can you imagine Terrence being interested in a child? He walked out on his bride on their wedding day didn't he? There's a baby there he hasn't even seen. Unprincipled waster. He hasn't changed.'

'But he came back to see the child.'

'Nothing but coincidence. He called on me because he was broke, not because of the baby. He pestered and I was determined not to give in this time, but in the end I gave him some money and now he's gone. Good riddance. Worth the money to see the back of him.'

'Megan will be upset.'

'Why should she be? Sensible young woman that she is, she told him a long time ago that he wasn't included in her plans for the future. In fact, I thought that you and Megan — but there, I'm probably wrong about that.'

Edward was amused initially about how much the old man learned about what went on in the family while hardly ever leaving the house. He was wrong about Megan though. Or, was he?

As soon as the shop closed he went to Glebe Lane in the hope that his grandfather had been right, but was told that Megan and Rosemary were away, staying with her other grandparents, Mr and Mrs Fowler, in Penarth.

* * *

That evening, Edward removed some of the window display, but left it untidy and half finished. There were two boxes left with price tickets, ready to set out, and the space for the golf tees and balls was covered with screwed up brown paper. He hoped this lack of order would entice the intruder to return.

This time, when he was woken by the barely discernable sounds from below, of rustling paper, Edward slipped on dressing gown and slippers and went down the stairs. He had been fast and he hadn't made a sound.

He was immediately aware of the unpleasant smell. Dampness and stale food overlaid with sweat and something he thought he recognised as unwashed feet. Some people he'd encountered during his RAF career smelled like this when they first arrived and for days after. Any amount of scrubbing failed to ease away the smell of what he'd always thought of as poverty and despair.

When he saw the figure bending over the display, adjusting the golf tees into a neat circle, and knowing he was responsible for the foul air, he wanted to shout for the man to get out. Instead, he watched.

The golf balls were set out with the price tickets clearly shown; one or two sections of the window arrangement were adjusted to improve their symmetry.

'Mr William Jones?' Edward said as the man finished his task and stretched, groaning softly. 'It is Mr Jones, isn't it?'

The figure shuffled around and said gruffly. 'Can't abide a slovenly window.' He didn't seem startled; Edward had the feeling his presence, as he had watched him work, had been known to the old man.

'That's what made me think it was you,' he said.

'I won't come again, if it bothers you. The nights are long, see, and it passes the time to come and look at what you've done with my old shop.'

'D'you like what I've done?'

'Y-e-e-s.' He sounded doubtful. 'I don't like the fancy shelves, mind. I had glass-fronted drawers. Much better than cardboard boxes stacked like this.' He waved an arm around the shop and the smell of stale, unwashed flesh took Edward's breath away.

'How d'you get in?' Edward wanted to know. 'Through the basement?'

'The door isn't strong enough to keep a mouse out. And you don't bother to bolt the flap in the kitchen.' He looked at Edward in a short-sighted way and asked, 'Chance of a cup of tea, is there?'

Edward followed him into the kitchen and from the way the old man filled the kettle, found cups, tea caddy and the rest, he guessed it wasn't the first time he'd helped himself.

263

When they were drinking the tea and William Jones was tucking into the biscuits he'd taken from the cupboard, Edward told him about the money. At first William didn't believe him. Then his eyes lit up and he began to talk about having a proper room, with someone to cook his meals. Edward promised to help him find a place.

'But first,' he said. 'I'll get you some decent clothes and I want you to take a bath and clean yourself up.' The old man looked doubtful but agreed.

He left at four in the morning and Edward returned to his bed. He didn't sleep, but pondered on the way luck played such a part in people's lives. What had that poor old man done for fate to treat him so shabbily? He wished he could discuss it all with Megan, and wondered whether she would approve of what he was doing or laugh gently and call him a fool.

* * *

Barry emptied the house on Chestnut Road by the simple expedient of telephoning a second-hand shop and selling the whole contents. The few pieces he did want he took to the flat in a series of vanloads, and the flat was untidy and overfull.

264

Once before, Rhiannon had developed the habit of going up the stairs to the flat and tidying up, and now, curiosity took her up there again. What she saw was chaos. Knowing Barry, she knew it would be weeks before he got around to sorting it out. Slowly, she began to do it for him. Between customers and for part of her lunch hour she moved boxes and stacked them, labelling them as she went and soon there was a space in which he could walk, between bedroom, armchair and kitchen.

She decided not to do any more. She was feeling unwell, and besides, the rest was up to Barry. If he was content to live in a tip it wasn't her worry. Her concern had never been for Barry. She simply hoped that if Caroline should call, she wouldn't be discouraged from staying.

'Mrs Cupid,' Charlie teased, when she told him what she was doing. He offered to help but she declined, intending not to go up there again.

'No, I won't do any more,' she told him. 'I've enough to do with the shop and the house and I have a bit of a pain. Only now and again,' she assured him as he looked alarmed. 'I'm sure there's nothing wrong.'

She was in the shop a few days later

when there was a loud crash and the rumbling of something falling. This was followed by a different sound as if a pile of dishes and plates had been smashed. She listened, half expecting to hear Barry shouting for help. He had been there a few moments before.

Turning the key in the shop door she ran up to the flat, dreading what she would find. The door wouldn't open, there was something behind it. Pushing and heaving she managed to get her head around to see what was stopping it. Barry was lying against it, head angled alarmingly, his eyes closed.

In a panic now, she heaved against the door and managed to slide through. Kneeling down she called to him.

'Barry. Barry. Speak to me!' Her mind was working frantically. She would have to phone for an ambulance from the box on the corner. She'd have to tell Caroline.

His eyes opened and a grin widened on his face.

'Fool that I am. I tried to put a box of china on the top shelf and I slipped.' He stood up easily and offered her a hand.

'You're all right? You let me struggle with that door with your weight against it and you're all right?'

'Sorry, Rhiannon. I didn't mean to frighten you, but I felt such a fool.'

The ambulance came that evening, but not for Barry. It was for Rhiannon, who lost her baby.

10

Rhiannon tried not to show her distress at the miscarriage, but when her parents came together to see her in hospital, she burst into tears. Charlie was beside her, his arms consoling her and promising her things would soon come right.

Lewis comforted Dora when they left the hospital. 'Let's visit our Viv and Joan, they'll want to know.'

He put an arm around his small wife's shoulders and for once she didn't complain.

★ ★ ★

There was a week of sweltering heat. The skies were the deep blue of high summer, yet this was September and no one expected it; few could cope. The beaches were abandoned until evening brought hope of respite; even then, the sun was painful to the eyes. No one did much work, animals and humans alike tried to find places where it was cool, but there weren't any. Even in the shadows the sun's heat was felt. There was no movement of air and humidity soared.

Rhiannon lay awake listening to a child crying somewhere, the sound plaintive and lonely. Why didn't someone go and comfort her? She wouldn't leave a baby to cry like that. She fought back tears and tried to think of something other than children. She knew Charlie would be upset if he heard her crying again. She didn't want to make him more unhappy than he was already.

★ ★ ★

Percy Flemming wasn't asleep either. He had no robbery planned, and with so many people awake and sweating away the night hours it wasn't a good idea, yet the thought of all those houses with windows wide open and sometimes doors as well, was too good a one to ignore.

Barbara had been getting restless lately. She was tired of living in a miserly manner, in a small rented house, knowing they had enough to live well. Once they had moved into the new house and furnished it as she wanted, she'd be content.

He wanted to be finished with this place. If his plans went well they would be able to move right away early in the new year; 1956 would be the beginning of the best time of their lives. No more going out at night. No

269

more looking over his shoulder for fear of the police. He usually chose a time when the occupants were out, but tonight would be an exception. Windows wide in welcome, it would serve them right for their carelessness. He dressed and left the house without a sound. A few pounds extra would bring the move that much closer.

★ ★ ★

Barry had shown concern for the loss of Rhiannon's baby and offered any help he could give.

'Tell her to forget about coming back to the shop until she's quite recovered,' he told Charlie, then went to tell Caroline what had happened.

'I feel so guilty,' he admitted, when he and Caroline were out in their usual place, near the goat pen — the only place where they could find privacy in the Griffiths's busy house.

'What you did was stupid, Barry,' Caroline said. 'But I think the baby would have been lost anyway. A baby hangs on determinedly, whatever happens to the mother. There might have been something wrong and the shock you gave her only brought on the inevitable.'

'I still feel ashamed of my behaviour,' he

sighed. 'I fell while I was lifting the boxes and knocked over a pile of books and cameras and the like. One of the boxes was weak and it collapsed, spilling dishes and plates from the high shelf onto the floor. The noise was terrible. It seemed to go on for ages. I stayed where I'd fallen for a moment or two, then Rhiannon came up and — I felt a bit silly I suppose and covered it by joking.'

It was still very hot. The air hadn't cooled as evening drew in. When Barry suggested taking the three-year-old Joseph-Hywel for a walk before his bedtime, Caroline agreed. He wouldn't sleep in this heat.

'I'll be working in the sweet shop until Rhiannon is well enough to return,' he told her as they walked hand-in-hand with Joseph. 'If you're passing, call in and say hello.' It seemed an idiotic thing to say to your wife, estranged or not, but Caroline smiled and said she might.

He went home and spent half the night getting the flat in order in case she did. It was too hot to sleep anyway.

★ ★ ★

Lewis couldn't sleep. He got up at midnight and sat for a while looking across the road to his former home, where Dora was probably

271

as restless as he was. Thinking of the sea and a cooling breeze, he dressed and as quietly as possible went down and got into the car.

In the next bedroom, Charlie heard him and wondered where he was going at such a late hour. He hoped it wasn't a woman. Like Rhiannon, he had dreams of Lewis returning to Dora and leaving their house.

Driving to the beach, Lewis sat in the car for a while with the doors open in the hope of a movement of air. Even waving a map as a substitute fan didn't help, for as soon as he stopped the heat intensified, leaving his face feeling stickier and hotter than before.

He got out and looked towards the sea. It looked tempting and he wished he'd thought to bring his dippers. Then he walked around the headland to a smaller bay, dark and eerie in the almost complete darkness. Standing below the cliffs he blended into the shadows and enjoyed the slight movement of air, which although warm, was soothing to his hot skin.

★   ★   ★

Edward was another who couldn't sleep. He had opened the door to the basement and several of the windows of the flat, but the air was static and stale. He thought of the beach, and envisaged walking along the edge of the tide, barefoot and wearing only an open-necked shirt and light trousers. It soon became irresistible.

He dressed, closed the doors and went out.

Edward soon realised he wasn't the only person wide awake that night. As he drove through the streets, he noticed several lights burning, and in one or two doorways a figure could be seen sitting on a chair, staring out into the relentless dark and heat of the late September night. When he reached the pleasure beach he parked the car and discarded his shoes and socks.

The paving on the promenade was little comfort, the residue of the hot sun was still warm to his feet. Everywhere was quiet and he found himself walking slowly so that his bare feet didn't disturb the silence. The distant sea was hushed, the tall trees surrounding the cricket field were unmoving, the branches and leaves not relieving the silence by a whisper.

The shop doorways issued forth familiar scents of previous meals, and where pavements had been washed, soap and warm sand added to the evocation of the past day, combining to give that unique perfume that in his mind was the pleasure beach in summer.

If other people had chosen to seek a cool breeze, they were invisible in the utter blackness of the still night. A voice called 'Good evening, Mr Jenkins,' but although he answered, he had no idea of the identity of his unseen acquaintance.

Edward walked across the sand, warm, dry and deep at first then hard and ridged by the outgoing tide, and blissfully cool. Reaching the water he waded out and stood enjoying the sensation of it, silky and cold against his legs.

★ ★ ★

Lewis saw Edward silhouetted against his car's sidelights as he went to lean on the bonnet to wipe his feet.

He walked closer before he recognised him, then laughed.

'Been for a paddle, Edward?'

'I couldn't sleep and the thought of it was too tempting.'

'Same for me. I walked around the headland. I'm tired now though and I bet I won't be ready for the alarm in the morning.'

They chatted for a few minutes, but they had little in common — Edward's formality a stumbling block to Lewis's idle chitchat — and soon went their different ways.

The following day was Wednesday and Edward closed at one o'clock. He went to find William Jones and met him near the almost derelict house where he had a room. He looked tidier and was wearing the clothes Edward had given him, although his hands were still ingrained with black dirt, and his skin retained an unhealthy pallor. There was a lacklustre look in his eyes. Neither the sun nor the joys of summer had touched him it seemed.

Edward had found him a room with a widow, Catrin Gwilym, in Brown Street and they went there straight away. Edward had warned the woman that William was in need of comfort and care and after momentary hesitation, she invited them in. Leaving them to discuss terms, Edward went back to the shop and telephoned Sally.

He hoped to talk to Megan but when she answered he was unable to think what to say. 'I thought you and Rosemary were in Penarth,' he said.

'You want to talk to Mummy?'

'Well, yes, but — ' He wanted to say he was glad to hear her voice, that he missed her, wanted to see her, but the phone had been abandoned, she had gone. It was obvious she

275

was no longer interested in him. When Sally came to the phone he told her about Ryan calling on him for help.

'I know you don't want him back and I can understand that, but you did say you want to know how he is,' he told her.

'And he's all right? Recovered from the breakdown or whatever it was?'

'He's lost and doesn't know what to do. I found him a job of sorts, and I wondered how you felt about my offering him the basement to live in? It's completely separate from the shop and I wouldn't see him. But at least you'd know he's got somewhere to sleep. I don't think your parents want him there any longer, do they?'

'Why are you doing this, Edward?'

'No reason, except that the place is there and he needs a base of some kind and you need to live without worrying about him.'

'Thank you. You're very understanding, Edward. I do feel responsible, as I told you before. You can't just pack a few things in a suitcase and expect years of your life to go away, or pretend they didn't happen. I still feel responsible for him. I'll be relieved to know he's safe.'

'Can I talk to Megan again, please?'

He prepared a few words. He wanted to see her and he wanted her to look at the basement and tell him what he needed to buy. Not much of a conversation opener, but it was as good a reason as any to see her again.

The phone was picked up but as he took a deep breath to speak, Sally's voice said, 'Sorry, Edward. Megan seems to have gone out. Was it something important?'

'No,' he said sadly. 'Nothing important.'

★ ★ ★

The news that day had been about the latest robbery. This time, someone had been hurt. The hot weather had meant windows had been wide open and in a house close to the restaurant owned by Margaret and Islwyn, and not far from where Edward and Lewis had met, someone had disturbed an intruder and suffered a blow that had sent him reeling down the stairs. The man was in hospital with broken ribs, a dislocated shoulder and head injuries.

The police came to talk to Edward soon after he had spoken to Sally and it was worrying to think they considered him capable of violence.

'We have a report of you driving off around midnight, sir and the offence took place at that time.'

Relieved, Edward explained about going to

the beach, and meeting Lewis there. At least he had an alibi this time. He told them where he had been and exactly where he had parked and of the brief encounter with Lewis, another one seeking the cooling breezes of the sea.

* * *

Unfortunately, Lewis was so outraged by the suspicion falling on him yet again, he lied.

'For heaven's sake why are you wasting time questioning me?' he exclaimed. 'At midnight I was where all innocent people should be, in bed! *My* bed!'

'That isn't what we understand, sir,' the patient policeman said. 'According to your son-in-law you drove off somewhere at around midnight and didn't return for more than an hour. Would you like to explain why you are lying to us, sir?'

Lewis didn't know that Charlie had already been questioned. He had corroborated a sleepless observer who had seen Lewis driving off just before midnight.

'I was just trying to stop you wasting more time on me,' Lewis excused. 'I did go out, over the beach and I met Edward Jenkins there. He had a paddle, I went for a walk. Anything else you want to know?'

'That's all — for the moment,' Constable Gregory said.

* * *

After questioning Edward, the police still clung to the possibility that the two men were in collusion, sometimes working together, sometimes separately, to confuse alibis and eyewitnesses.

Angrily, Lewis repeated his story, told them exactly what had happened, then went to complain to Dora that Charlie had 'landed him in it.'

* * *

At Edward's shop the police were interested in the basement exit. 'Easy for you to go in and out at night without being seen,' the sergeant pondered.

Edward sighed. 'So why did I go out through the shop, get into the car and drive off? A car in the main road isn't exactly a secret way of leaving, is it?'

'There was a robbery at Montague Court while you were still living there, wasn't there?'

'Yes, and it was fully investigated. But like all the rest, no one was apprehended. When are you going to catch the man? He's doing

279

what he likes and making a laughing stock of you.'

'How d'you know it's a *he*?'

'I don't. It just simplifies any discussion if we give the thief one sex or the other.'

Once they had finished with their questions, Edward left Mair in charge of the shop and went to see Frank Griffiths.

The weather was still very warm, but Janet and Hywel were burning rubbish on a garden fire, watched from a safe distance by an interested Joseph-Hywel. The dogs were too lazy to bark, but the friendly goats called a welcome as Janet led him around the house to where Frank was sleeping in the porch.

'I'd like the decorating finished in the basement,' Edward told him. 'Then I want to see Basil about making a few pieces for the kitchen. A few shelves and a cupboard or two.'

'Renting it out, are you?' Frank asked sleepily.

'I need it ready for the weekend. Mr Fowler-Weston will be using it for a while.'

'What? Him that hit his missus? What're you helping him for?'

'He's ill,' Edward explained. He was uneasy with these people. They spoke their minds in a most disconcerting way.

'I'd give him 'ill'.' Hywel strolled up and

joined in the conversation.

Edward couldn't tell them he was doing it to please Sally and through her, hopefully pleasing Megan.

'Wants a good wallop himself, that'll cure him,' Hywel said. 'Me and my boys'll be happy to oblige any time.' Then the two men listed the various punishments they'd hand out, while Edward stood in an embarrassed silence, and Janet smiled.

'They'd love to think they were real villains,' she whispered. 'But they don't have the heart for it.'

'I'll come this evening, work through the night,' Frank eventually promised. 'Me and our Ernie if he's willing.'

'I'll ask our Basil about the shelves,' Janet added.

Edward nodded, patted Joseph-Hywel's head, gave him a shilling and made his escape.

★ ★ ★

William Jones soon settled into the house of Mrs Catrin Gwilym. She insisted on a twice-weekly bath and filled the tub herself to make sure he was using plenty of hot water, to which she added a good handful of washing soda and plenty of soap, only

281

handing in clean clothes when she was sure he had soaked out the ingrained dirt. She gave him three good meals each day and in a week the difference was remarkable.

Gradually he told her his story.

'The business was failing even before my wife died,' he said as they sat companionably sipping their late night cocoa. 'I took goods in exchange for debts too and that was a big mistake, landing me with stuff I couldn't sell. I just didn't care, you see. Once Mabel had gone, I couldn't see why I was bothering.'

'I didn't let things go when I lost my dear husband, Mr Jones, I'd have thought I was letting him down,' Catrin said.

'Mabel called me Willie,' William told her. 'Except when she was mad at me then I had the full title. Will-i-am!' he smiled.

'Then I'll do the same,' she announced.

When Edward called a couple of weeks after Catrin had taken the old man in, he found them working together in the small garden and chatting away like friends. He smiled as he left them. Sorting out other people's problems was easy, but where was he to start on his own?

Since the phonecall to discuss the basement as a possible home for Ryan he hadn't heard from Sally and there had been no sign of a grateful Megan. Then one morning Sally called at the shop with some of Ryan's clothes and personal items.

Invited down to look at the small bedsit arrangement where Frank was fitting the shelves his brother had made, she thanked him again and told him how grateful she was for the trouble he was taking.

As she left, he asked about Megan and Rosemary and had a proud grandmother's report on the advanced behaviour of the small infant. She said nothing to offer hope that Megan would call. His grandfather had been wrong. Megan was waiting, hoping for Terrence to come back.

While Frank was working in the basement, he often saw Mair and each time she appeared he dropped something, or stuttered or simply blushed. But gradually he began to get in a few pertinent questions about her boyfriend.

'Seeing that Gareth Morgan tonight, then?' he asked when she brought him a cup of tea.

'What's it to you, Frank Griffiths?'

'I wondered, like, if you'll forget him and come to the pictures with me.'

She stared at him for a moment, taking in the long, lean length of him, the rather appealing blue eyes and the poor attempt at a Mexican moustache. For a long moment, hope swelled in Frank's chest. She was going to say yes! He was going to have a date! Then she spoke.

'Get lost!'

Philosophically, Frank went back to his work. He didn't want to get married anyway. He was too comfortable with his mam and dad. But the lie was wearing thin and he remembered admitting to Edward that it was a sad pretence, to cover up the thought that no one would have him.

* * *

At the restaurant things were beginning to look hopeful. Margaret couldn't tackle too varied a menu or a large number of diners yet, but by preparing carefully, she managed to fill the place twice each evening, and with occasional help — poorly paid and illegally employed — they were at last beginning to believe it would succeed.

Margaret worked from six each morning, providing lunches and dinners, ending her day at midnight. Islwyn rose at the same time and worked, albeit reluctantly, throughout the lunches and dinners. He also dealt with the ordering, going to the market each morning to buy fresh vegetables, fish and fruit. He hated it.

As the restaurant increased its popularity,

the more dictatorial Margaret became towards him. He was slow, he was thick and he was often in the way. She was used to working alongside Edward, who knew the routine so well they hardly needed to speak. Besides having minimal experience of how to wait on table, or how a busy kitchen was run, Islwyn was resentful of being told what to do. As business grew, so her hope of their continuing partnership faded. She had to get some experienced help or she would find herself on her own.

★ ★ ★

Lewis and Edward were still under suspicion, even though the police seemed to have no direct evidence against them. They were questioned several times, presumably in the hope of catching them out in either a lie, or with a detail that would lead them to a result. Half of the eyewitnesses were certain they had seen Lewis, the rest equally sure that the person seen running from the scene was Edward.

Instead of being angry with Charlie, Lewis discussed the situation one evening as he was going over the dates on which he was suspected of burglary, trying to remember something that would clear him.

'If I could prove I was far away during one or two of the break-ins, then there wouldn't be much point in them trying to charge me with the rest,' he sighed, 'but my appointment book isn't that specific and nothing I've written sparks off any memories to help me.'

'Why don't you talk to Edward Jenkins? It has to be a time when neither of you could be guilty, remember. The theory is that the two of you work together, or in partnership.'

'If I'm seen talking to Edward the police will only think we're arranging another crime!'

'Then meet at the pub. That wouldn't be suspicious, would it?'

'Grandad,' Gwyn began; he was still unsure of Lewis and although asked to do so, didn't find it easy to call him Grandad. The light of battle appeared in Lewis's eyes every time he said the word. Grandma Dora said it was because he was afraid of getting old.

'What is it, son?' Lewis asked. 'Want some sweet samples do you?'

'Please!' Gwyn replied enthusiastically. 'But I was going to tell you that one of those dates,' he pointed with a greasestained finger, 'that one, was when you and Mr Jenkins were near the news cameras. You remember,' he went on as Lewis frowned in concentration, 'the night you saw the department store burning. I cut the pictures out of the paper and tried to spot you among the crowd but it was too small and spotty to see. There might be a picture of you in the newspaper office mightn't there? If there is, it should clear you.'

Lewis took the pictures from Gwyn's scrapbook, told Gwyn he was a wonder and went to find Edward Jenkins.

'It's worth trying,' Edward said. 'And if I could only find out who said good evening to me on the night we went to the beach, there'd be enough to stop them blaming us and to go out looking for the real thief.'

The police promised to look into it and came back later to say that they were indeed on the photographs. Constable Gregory had also found a man who had frequently dined at Montague Court, who swore he had seen Edward that very hot night. He'd been pulling on his socks and he had spoken to him.

Lewis bought a new saddlebag for Gwyn as a reward, and Edward gave him a pair of roller skates.

★　★　★

Edward was light-hearted, knowing that the suspicion, however ridiculous, had been

287

lifted, and when he opened the door of the basement to show Ryan his new home he felt like celebrating. But not with Ryan, whom he disliked and mistrusted. The only reason he was helping the man was to impress Megan.

His obvious good spirits were reflected on Ryan who hated the thought of living in someone else's basement but knew it was better than staying under sufferance with in-laws Gladys and Arfon, who hardly spoke a word to him, their animosity apparent in every look.

He responded cheerfully to Edward's smiling welcome and was still smiling when Edward ran up the stairs to the kitchen of the shop. Then the smile froze as the bolts were thrown across from above. It was a serious reminder of how close he had come to prison. Fraud and robbery when he worked for Arfon, and now injuring Sally in frustration and temper. He opened the door into the garden and didn't think he would ever be able to live there with it closed.

* * *

Edward was cleaning the window area ready for a fresh display of football and rugby equipment early in November when he saw Megan walking along the pavement with

Rosemary propped up against pillows in her pram. He went out and shyly asked how they were.

'As you see us, Edward,' she replied briskly. 'Rosemary is growing and thriving and already beginning to raise her head and see what sort of world she has been born into.'

'She's beautiful,' Edward said, longing to add, 'and so are you'.

'Isn't she just!' Megan replied proudly. 'Mair is making coffee, why don't you come in and see what I've done to the shop since your last visit?'

He helped her take the pram into the shop where loud banging could be heard coming from the basement.

'Sorry about the noise, I'll ask him to stop, shall I?'

'No need, a baby has to learn to cope with everything; we can't cocoon her from noise. I'd go crazy trying, wouldn't I?'

Edward found her a chair, then agitatedly asked Mair to hurry with the coffee. She returned with a tray while Edward was leaning over the pram admiring the wide-eyed, curious stare of the baby.

'I'll take Frank's down to him,' she said.

'Frank? What's he doing now?' Megan asked.

'Putting up another wall cupboard. There

was need of more storage space so Frank's doing it while your father is at work. Better for him but not for us, eh!'

'My father? What's my father doing in your basement?' she demanded, putting her coffee aside and standing up.

'Living there,' he said in surprise.

'What? Are you mad? Helping my father after the way he treated my mother?'

'But I thought you knew, didn't your mother tell you?'

'Tell me what? That you have given my father a home after he beat my mother? That you are supporting him against her? What on earth were you thinking about, Edward? How dare you! Let me out of here!'

Pushing the pram impatiently, knocking against several counters and display boards, she left the shop and ran up the road without giving him a chance to explain.

'I thought you knew,' he said lamely, to her departing back.

★   ★   ★

Margaret and Islwyn had been very busy all day. Besides the meals they served, there had been some decorating to finish and the clearing up afterwards. Both were feeling tired and not a little irritable.

As the second sitting were reaching the main course stage, Islwyn stepped into the kitchen with empty serving dishes and bumped into Margaret as she lifted freshly fried fish from the deep fat fryer. She shouted in pain as hot fat splashed on her arm, and glared at him, calling him a string of abusive names before cooling it under the tap and reaching for the vaseline, gauze and bangages from the first-aid box. As she did so she continued her abuse of him.

Islwyn put down the dirty dishes, swivelled on his heel and left the kitchen. To her horror she heard the front door slam, followed by the sound of her car being revved and driven down the drive. He'd left her in the middle of the busiest time of the day. 'How could he!' she muttered furiously. 'How could he!'

To add to the difficulties she had a group of awkward customers who thought they were entitled to treatment reserved for royalty. They complained about a spot of grease on the border of a plate; they complained that the napkins were incorrectly folded and the forks less than clean; that the blades of the knifes pointed outwards instead of inwards. She knew they were trying it on, hoping for a reduction in their bill, but she wasn't playing. She needed the money more than they did and blackmail brought out the worst in her.

A few raised eyebrows and a sympathetic nod from a few people who were becoming regulars cheered her and she put up with every complaint with a brighter and brighter smile. They left, threatening never to go there again, and she smiled even wider and thanked them for their promise. There was no tip.

At twelve fifteen Margaret collapsed into a chair, unable to face dealing with the dishes, or even finish clearing the tables. She had managed without Islwyn. But she knew it couldn't, mustn't happen again.

She was so tired that she slept as soon as she got into bed, so she didn't hear him return. The following morning, stiff and tired, she woke and was alone in the big, white bed. For the first time she wondered if he had gone for good. Frantically, she began to list the people who she might call on to help her. She mustn't lose all this, not now.

She went downstairs to make herself a cup of tea, dreading the mess she would find and wondering how she'd find the strength to deal with it. Instead she found Islwyn, wiping down the surfaces, with all the dishes and utensils washed and stacked in their places, the vegetables prepared for lunch and a kettle boiling ready for tea.

'Oh, Islwyn, how could you,' she said as she fell into his arms.

'Margaret, I'm sorry, but I'd just about had enough. Did you have to cancel anyone?'

'I managed, but I don't think I could do it again. Please, Issy, don't do that to me ever again.'

He held her close but didn't reply; the plea hung in the air, both of them aware of the unanswered threat.

While Islwyn was at the market, Margaret telephoned her brother. 'Edward,' she announced, as if it were sufficient for him to both recognise her voice and understand what she wanted of him.

'Hello Margaret, what do you want?' He wasn't pleased to hear her voice. She had tried so hard to ruin the business he now owned that he felt the prickling of suspicion in just hearing that single word.

'I wondered whether you'd be willing to help out in the restaurant occasionally? Just when I'm stuck. You know the business so well and Islwyn, well, he's willing enough, but slow to learn. I'm so busy you see,' she went on, not giving him time to reply. 'I had two full house bookings last night and Islwyn was out and couldn't get back in time to help.'

'Sorry, Margaret. I have no intention of

getting involved with catering again.' He replaced the receiver and smiled as he imagined her outrage.

In despair she rang her grandfather and asked for cousin Terrence's phone number. Terrence's response when she reached him was even less kind than her brother's.

'You are joking, Margaret, dear! Spend my time pandering to people who aren't sure which fork to use? Removing their messy dishes? Washing things? I always thought you were crazy to want to do it. No chance. None at all. Sell the place and find a more amenable occupation.'

Changing tack she said sweetly, 'I just thought, with Megan missing you and wanting you back in her life, and her with rich grandparents who indulge her every whim, that you might like to come back to Pendragon Island. A place to live and an addition to your funds . . . and Megan. Think about it.' This time it was she who replaced the phone.

Margaret rang Edward again. 'I thought you'd like to know, brother dear, that Terrence and Megan are getting together again. He's desperate to come back to her, and she's realised that the baby needs his father. Duty, you see. Such a small word but so important. Goodnight. Sleep well.'

It wasn't a good night and Edward didn't sleep well. He lay awake wondering whether Margaret was telling the truth and by morning had convinced himself that she was.

11

Megan called at the shop the following morning and without waiting to speak to Edward, brought the pram in and found herself a chair.

'I owe you an apology,' she said, as though she were reprimanding him.

Edward smiled. 'Yes, Megan. I believe you do.'

'I went home in an outrage and told Mummy what you'd done and she explained that it was with her agreement and thanks. She also told me that she's concerned for Daddy and won't abandon him completely even after what he did to her.'

'Loving isn't just for when everything is going well. It's a lifetime commitment. The promise made in the marriage ceremony isn't just romantic words. Your mother is responsible for your father's welfare and always will be.'

'D'you think she'll have him back?'

'It's more than likely.'

Mair was in the basement and when she came up and saw Megan, she mimed the making of tea and Edward nodded.

'Would you like to see what I've done with the basement?' he asked.

The baby was awake and looking around the shop, her clear, intelligent eyes absorbing the new surroundings with apparent interest.

'We'll take her with us, shall we?' Edward lifted the child out of her pram and carried her as they went down the stairs into the garden, then through the door into the basement.

There was a television in one corner and a radio beside it. Magazines and newspapers were scattered across a couch and a coffee cup stood amid the casual abandonment. The place looked comfortable and lived in.

'Good heavens, Edward, he won't *want* to come home!'

The warm weather had lingered and it was pleasant in the now tamed garden. They sat in the sun and Megan admired the neat garden with its newly painted fence.

'You've worked very hard here, Edward.'

'No, it's nothing to do with me, it's Frank. He's remarkably keen. I believe it's something to do with Mair Gregory,' he added in a whisper as Mair appeared with a tray of tea. They relaxed, discussed the baby's progress, while Mair returned to the shop to attend to customers.

'Did you know your father has been seeing

a doctor?' he asked after a while, unsure of how much Sally had told her daughter.

'No euphemisms, Edward, he's seeing a psychiatrist, and Mummy thinks he's brave to face the fact that he's ill. Many wouldn't, she said.'

'I agree. After you saw them that day, when he was taking his frustration out on your poor mother, he went straight to the doctors at the hospital, told them what had been happening and sought help.'

'I really don't know which was worse, my father hitting my mother, or Uncle Islwyn leaving Aunt Sian and going to live with that awful — ' Megan broke off, realising she was referring to Edward's sister.

'If you're talking about pride, then I think your mother's the more fortunate.'

'Pride is the very devil to cope with; it makes you do things you know are wrong for you.' She turned her head and stared at him, her eyes melting into tenderness. 'Like you avoiding me when Terrence came on the scene, presuming I no longer needed your friendship,' she whispered.

'Margaret told me that you and he were still in love.'

'What a pain that woman is. I know she's your sister, Edward, but she's an absolute pain.'

Megan picked up the tray and went back up the steps into the kitchen. Edward followed with Rosemary, who had fallen asleep in his arms in the warmth of the September sun and the calm peace of the garden.

For the rest of the day Edward worked in a fog of confusing thoughts. He attended to customers' wants but without really becoming involved, worried by the feeling that he had missed an opportunity with Megan, but not sure what he should have done.

★ ★ ★

Caroline had continued to work in the wool shop in town after her son had been born. Her mother willingly looked after Joseph-Hywel. Janet also made sure that her daughter didn't have to fill her half-day with chores, by doing as many as she could for her.

On a sunny afternoon when she was free for the Wednesday half-day closing, Caroline decided the weather was too good to waste it being indoors, so she took Joseph-Hywel on the bus and called at Temptations. As she had guessed, Rhiannon was there, using the time the shop was closed in cleaning glass displays, going through her birthday cards with a view to ordering more and generally sorting things out.

'Are you fully recovered?' was Caroline's first question. 'I'm sure Barry would continue running things for a while longer.'

'I'm fine and glad to be back. There isn't enough to keep me busy at home, with Charlie and Gwyn out all day.'

Caroline gestured to the stairs, at the top of which was a bolted door leading to the flat. 'Is Barry in? I've brought a toy wooden lorry with a broken wheel he promised to repair.'

In reply, Rhiannon ran up the stairs and banged on the door. 'Barry? I'm putting the kettle on; come and join Caroline, Joseph-Hywel and me.' She pulled the bolt free and called again.

Barry thundered down the stairs and burst into the shop with a wide smile on his face. 'Caroline! Lovely surprise.' He bent to pick up the three-year-old and hug him.

Caroline looked almost shy as she greeted him.

'Tea for three is it? And what about a glass of pop for young Joseph?' Barry took the child and went across to Gertie Jones's shop to buy lemonade. She was closed for half-day, but opened when she recognised her visitors.

'How are things with you and Barry?' Rhiannon asked when she and Caroline were alone.

300

'We're friends, getting along in a more relaxed way. Did you know he's starting his business again?'

'I'd heard. How d'you feel about that?'

'Guilty,' Caroline whispered as Barry and her son returned.

When Rhiannon had made the tea, she suggested that Barry took Caroline and the little boy up to the flat where Barry could look at the broken toy and leave her to get on with her work.

Once inside the flat Barry put a hand on Caroline's shoulder and bent to kiss her. She pulled away and Barry walked to the other end of the room and stared out of the window into the street below, tension in the lie of his shoulders and in the clenching of his hands.

'I wasn't going to attack you,' he muttered angrily.

Caroline knew she had to explain the secret she had hidden away. A secret which kept coming back to haunt her and torment her. It had to be brought out into the open if she were ever to have a contented life.

'This room is where your brother and I used to meet,' she told him, blushing a furious red.

Barry turned and saw her glancing at the corner near the fireplace. In a sudden revelation he knew.

'This is where you and he — where Joseph-Hywel was — ' He forced himself to say the words; they had pussyfooted around long enough. 'Where you and my brother made love and you conceived Joseph.'

She nodded.

Barry walked to the corner, to where her eyes were drawn, and sat down on the floor, leaning against the wall. He spread his arms and Joseph ran to him and he sat him beside his knees; he held out his arms again. 'I think it's time we overlaid old, sweet memories with new ones, don't you, love?'

Slowly, she moved towards him and settled down in the crook of his arm. He kissed her, gently at first, then with longing. She lowered her head onto his shoulder and allowed tears to fall.

Later, Barry drove her home and suggested they met every Wednesday afternoon, making the arrangement a firm one, 'Broken only by dire disaster.'

A few days later, Caroline began to calm down from the mood of hope and happiness, to wonder whether the promise of an assignment to take photographs would persuade Barry to change his mind about their Wednesday afternoons. Feeling a cheat, she telephoned him, and in a disguised voice

302

asked whether he could come on the following Wednesday to photograph about twenty youngsters at a children's party. She prepared herself for disappointment. Barry was a businessman after all and he'd be a fool to turn down such a profitable afternoon, especially working with children. Could he resist it, for her?

As she waited for his response she expected him to accept to booking. Sadly, she wondered what excuse he'd give her, whether it would be truth or invention. To her surprise he refused, told the 'customer' that any other day he'd be delighted, but that Wednesday afternoons were impossible.

Tension fell from Caroline like an abandoned cloak and she trembled with relief; she hadn't realised just how much she'd wanted him to refuse.

During her spare time, she worked on a dress to wear the following Wednesday. Her mother noticed the difference in her lovely daughter and wished for a happy solution. As Janet watched Caroline sewing the dress one evening she heard a call and Mair Gregory poked her head around the door. At once there was a scramble as Frank, who had been reading the paper, sprawled in a chair, dashed past and went out to comb his hair. He returned a few moments later with a sheepish look on his face and offered Mair a drink.

'You aren't proposing to make a cup of tea, are you?' Janet asked in astonishment.

'No, no. I thought we'd go down to The Railwayman.'

Mair declined and showed them the spade with a broken handle that she hoped Hywel would repair for her father.

'I'll do it,' Frank said at once. 'Bring it back tomorrow, shall I?'

When Mair left, with Frank in attendance, Caroline and her mother exchanged looks and said together, 'Smitten!'

'With luck I'll soon be rid of the three of them,' Janet smiled. 'Our Basil married to Eleri, Ernie engaged to Helen Gunner and now Frank throwing his hat at Mair.' She wished she hadn't spoken then, as her daughter's eyes clouded.

'You can't get rid of me though Mam,' Caroline said.

'And there's glad I am. Me and your Dad would miss you so much, love. You and little Joseph-Hywel.'

The wedding of Frank's brother Ernie was planned for the summer after next, but when Ernie and Helen came in later that evening, they looked upset. They sat at opposite ends of the room, and exchanged several frosty glances without saying a word.

'You haven't had a row, have you?' Janet asked finally.

'Hardly,' Ernie grinned, and was rewarded with a withering frown from Helen.

'No we haven't quarrelled, our Mam. We're going to have to get married sooner than her parents wanted, that's all,' Ernie said, blushing furiously.

'The usual reason?' Hywel asked as he entered in time to hear Ernie's words.

'Well what d'you think of that?' Caroline said with a smile. 'A cousin for Joseph-Hywel.'

'And when will the wedding be?'

'Next week?' Ernie said jokingly.

Helen reached out and grasped Ernie's hand. 'We're happy about it. In fact we're glad not to have the fuss that Mam and Dad were planning, but Mam's so upset, and refusing to even discuss it. So,' she went on hesitantly, 'we wondered whether you two would be willing to have it here. It needn't be a big party but — '

' — but it had better be, eh?' Hywel laughed. 'We'd love it, wouldn't we Mam?'

Janet glanced at Caroline. She wondered whether the thought of another wedding in the family while her own was such a failure, would upset her. Caroline stood up, dropping the dress and a tape measure onto the floor, and hugged Helen.

Happily, Janet agreed.

★ ★ ★

At the restaurant, renovation was still continuing. During the hours when there were no customers, builders were making the final touches to the house. The restaurant and kitchen had been in reasonable condition, needing only a few items to update them plus some restoration to cover the scars of the building work. But behind the scenes, decorating bedrooms and hallways and staircases still had to be dealt with. Margaret was tired, and every day wished Edward were there to help. He was so hard-working and a calming presence, and she needed both.

Islwyn appeared to be doing something whenever she saw him, but the result of his day never reduced the amount of work to be done. Besides being slow, he was clearly uninterested. Even unwilling, she admitted to herself sadly.

Before they had sold Montague Court he seemed as excited as she when they made plans for their restaurant. But now that they lived in a partly decorated house, with constant money worries, with exhaustion and no time to relax, the novelty had faded. She faced a growing realisation that Islwyn wanted to give up on their future. She hoped he didn't want to give up on her too.

Having had him sharing her life for a number of years, although until recently secretly, she didn't think she could face being alone again. Would she have to choose? Either giving up on all this and keeping Issy, or staying here and struggling on alone?

It was three o'clock and they had two hours before starting on dinner. Abandoning the work that awaited her, she locked the door, placed a 'Closed until five' notice on it and invited Islwyn to come to bed.

They woke up at five-thirty and at once Margaret was in a panic. Jumping out of bed they ran like clockwork toys gone berserk, unable to decide what to do first. Islwyn ran a bath while Margaret opened the curtains, took out a clean overall, and hopped around looking for a second shoe.

'Issy, go and open the door, quickly! We could be missing customers!' No answer. 'Issy!' she shouted in panic. 'Issy!'

'What on earth is it?'

'The door. The door! There's someone knocking on the door!'

'Give me a chance to dress,' he shouted back, running from the bathroom and streaming water over the carpet. 'I doubt we're missing anyone wanting to book, people usually telephone don't they?'

'Stop dripping on the carpet. It soon gets grubby if it gets wet!'

'Oh give over woman!'

'Well you're making a mess!'

'I came urgently because you called me urgently!'

'I didn't mean you to charge about naked!'

Islwyn dressed at top speed and ran down to remove the notice from the door. A car stood in the driveway. He combed his still-wet hair, adorned a smile and walked across to speak to the driver.

'I'm sorry, were you waiting to book a table for tonight?'

'No, I want to see Margaret Jenkins.'

The man wouldn't give a name or explain his business, he just followed Islwyn into the hallway and waited. When Margaret came down, freshly bathed, dressed and smiling politely, he handed her an envelope. After opening it and reading the contents, she stared at it in disbelief.

'Tell me this isn't true,' she whispered, her face white, her eyes wide and staring. 'Just tell me it isn't true.' When he took it from her shaking hands, Islwyn saw that it was a County Court summons for non-payment of debts.

Edward was surprised when a taxi drew up and his grandfather stepped out. How odd, he thought, for the old man to call again so soon. He went out, paid the taxi and helped his grandfather into the shop. He thought he looked pale and less healthy than when he had last called.

'Are you well, Grandfather?' he asked, as the efficient Mair attended to a customer. 'It's very nice to see you again. Would you like to go out and have tea in the Bluebird Café? It isn't far.'

Mr Jenkins accepted and although they stayed for almost an hour in the café, he said very little. Edward waited, expecting to be told the reason for the visit, but any conversation was confined to discussing the people around them and the food they ate.

They returned to the shop and his grandfather asked a few questions about the business, as if ensuring that Edward's decision had been a good one. Edward still wasn't sure why he had come. Then the old man began talking about the friends he had lost and how, at the age of ninety-six, he had realised he was the only one left out of a group of lifelong friends.

'All gone, Edward. There isn't a living soul

that I've known since childhood. It's a sad world when you haven't any friends left.'

Edward tried to console him, remind him that he still had family, but he wasn't to be comforted with false words. His family had no time for him and hadn't for a long time.

'I've just been to see Wilbert Howells's son,' he said. 'Poor old chap, he's past seventy you know, and ailing. And Harriet Coleman, and Gordon Rees and little Johnny Jones. And that William Jones you told me about who used to run this place. I called on him, too. All gone, the parents I mean. There's no one left. I'm in the front line now and standing alone.'

Edward reminded him of the younger members of the family and the grandchildren of his friends.

'The world goes on, Grandfather, and you have your memories. Besides, you'll be here to watch it for a while yet.' He took out a photograph of Megan's baby daughter that Sally had given him and handed it to the old man. 'Terrence is the father, so Rosemary is your great-great-granddaughter. Isn't that something to be happy about?'

'When are you and Margaret going to start having babies?' he asked gruffly. 'About time, isn't it? Or you'll be my age with no one, friends or relations or memories.' It wasn't until he was leaving that he asked, 'Tell me Margaret's address, will you? I've forgotten.'

When the taxi came to collect him, Edward heard him give the driver Margaret's address. He had a cold, fearful thought that the old man was doing the rounds saying his goodbyes, knowing he was about to die.

* * *

Margaret didn't receive her grandfather very graciously. She was frantically busy, doing the preparation for seven different recipes, setting tables and wondering if she would ever have time to get to a hairdresser, when he arrived unannounced.

'Darling Grandfather, how nice, but you'll have to talk to me as I flit about I'm afraid. I have less than an hour to prepare for the first sitting. Eight covers, three different main course choices, and Issy isn't back from the bank yet.'

'Bank closed hours ago,' the old man muttered.

'Well, he had other things to do besides boring old money to pay in.' She wished Issy would hurry. He could entertain her grandfather while she got on with the meals. Where was he?

The tables were set, with flowers arranged

311

in the centre of each. The vegetable waters were simmering, the casserole finishing cooking and the fish and meats ready to grill, and still the old man sat there. With ten minutes to go before the first customers arrived, irritation simmered faster than the vegetables. Didn't the old man realise how valuable her time was?

In desperation, she asked, 'Would you like to stay for dinner, Grandfather? You can sit in the bar while I finish my preparations. I won't have a spare second to talk for an hour or two.'

She hoped the hint was sufficient for him to be on his way, but he said, 'Thanks. Edward took me out for tea and now you're inviting me to dinner. Quite an eventful day I'm having.'

Margaret ushered him into a small area which was separated by yucca palms and ferns that they called the bar, where people waited until their meal was ready to serve, and silently begged Issy to hurry back. She had served the first course to all eight people and was juggling with the main course when Issy finally came in.

Aware of her agitation he began to tell her where he had been but changed his mind. Better he tried to ease her into it gently. So he said brightly, 'I met Ryan. Seems he's much better and Sally has been talking as though he's forgiven. I never thought he'd get away with beating up his wife, did you?'

'Where the hell have you been?' Margaret shouted. 'No one here to deal with dishes and my grandfather's in there expecting to be entertained. I've been trying to cook for all these people and amuse him while he's drivelled on about all his friends who're dead, and what they died of, and how well Edward's doing and Megan's illegitimate child!' Not allowing him a word, she went on, 'Can't you get it into your thick head that we're running a business here and you're needed?'

Islwyn's response was to turn around, collect the coat he had just taken off, and walk out.

Somehow Margaret managed to survive another evening on her own. A couple of irate diners who had to wait an excessively long time were given a free meal to compensate, but the rest seemed happy to talk for longer than usual, and smile when she apologised with a free glass of house wine.

It was nine o'clock when she saw her grandfather into a taxi and gave his home address, eleven-forty-five before she closed the door on the last of the diners.

Tired though she was, she didn't collapse

into sleep as she had on a previous occasion. This time anger kept her wide awake and impatient for Issy to return home.

He came in at three, stood there as she berated him, then said quietly, 'I've seen the bank and a solicitor, Margaret. We have to cut our losses and sell.'

*　*　*

At number seven Sophie Street, Lewis continued to work on the garden. Gradually a routine developed and Dora looked for him during the times when neither he nor she had office work to do, and she would prepare a meal. They worked alongside each other, sharing the work, discussing each flower bed and each path. The lawn was seeded and regularly watered when necessary. They went to the nurseries and chose rose trees and shrubs and planted them. When the weather didn't allow work outside and on the occasional evening they pored over catalogues and discussed the merits of various flowers.

Across the road, Rhiannon and Charlie metaphorically held their breath.

*　*　*

Edward telephoned Sally and asked whether she would mind if he invited Megan out for dinner. 'I realise it will mean you looking after little Rosemary and I don't know how you feel about that,' he explained.

Sally assured him it would be a pleasure to take care of the baby and then brought Megan to the phone.

'I want to take you out for dinner, to Montague Court. Will you come?'

'When?' she asked in her abrupt manner.

'Tonight? I've already asked your mother if she would look after Rosemary for us.'

'Thank you Edward, but I can speak for myself.'

'I know that,' he laughed, 'but foolish, vain old thing that I am, I didn't want you to accept and then be disappointed when you couldn't come.'

He arranged to call for her at seven-thirty but was there early so he could see Rosemary being prepared for bed. There was something wonderful about the feeling of that fragile little child in his arms; she was so vulnerable, creating such feelings of love and tenderness. He was surprised at the strength of emotion such a tiny person could produce.

The dining room at Montague Court looked much the same as when he and Margaret had owned it, but the table linen was different; Annie had chosen pink tablecloths and napkins, edged with maroon embroidery. And there was a set of antlers over the fireplace; Edward had found them in one of the loft rooms and given them to a delighted Annie. Windows too were bright with generous frills of lace curtains over which maroon velvet curtains were set to be drawn.

A huge log fire burned in the fireplace around which brass and copper gleamed. It looked more cheerful than he remembered, and Annie's greeting added to the feeling of warmth. The place exuded friendliness and a generous welcome.

'Annie and Leigh Grant have changed everything, yet very little has actually been altered,' Edward remarked to Megan.

'Their personality has made the difference. Margaret always resented having to allow people into her home, didn't she?'

'Yes, but she's doing the same thing now, opening a restaurant in what is also her home.'

'Not her home for long, if what I hear is true. They're in trouble and there doesn't seem much chance of getting out of it.'

'Financial?'

'Yes, and caused no doubt in part by the fact that my Uncle Islwyn doesn't like work!'

While Megan went to ring her mother to assure herself that Rosemary was all right, Edward spoke to Annie and Leigh.

'Are you happy now that you've lived here for a while?' he asked.

'Deliriously so,' Leigh replied. 'It's what Annie's always wanted, giving people good food and seeing them go off contented and warmed by friendliness. It's something she's good at, wouldn't you say?'

'Definitely. We noticed the difference the moment we came in.' Edward looked at Annie, rosy-cheeked and smiling, her gentle eyes checking and rechecking the tables to ensure that no one needed anything more. 'What about staff, do you manage all right?'

'With the hotel bookings increasing we need a housekeeper,' Annie told them when Megan returned. 'We have parties booked for the Christmas weekend already. We're offering five-day breaks from Friday the twenty-third until Wednesday the twenty-eighth, then another weekend to include New Year. There's a dance here on New Year's Eve, why don't you come?'

They discussed their evening as Edward drove Megan home.

'I can't help thinking that Margaret and I could never have created such a pleasant atmosphere as Annie has done,' Edward said.

'You have to be happy in what you're doing before you can make others feel the same.'

'And you, Edward, are you happy in what you're doing?'

'I am. I know it doesn't seem much compared with Margaret's grand schemes, but it's what I've wanted and I consider myself fortunate to have achieved it.' She was silent for a while and he asked, 'What about you? Have you thought of where your life should lead?'

'Not really. I have to concentrate on Rosemary for a year or two at least.'

'And you're not sad about that?'

'I enjoy every moment spent with her. I don't need anything else for the moment.'

'I can understand that,' he said, saddened by what he understood to be a warning off. Why should she need me? he asked himself. She had a loving mother and a close family. She lived in a comfortable home, had money enough to survive and a child of her own.

When she went inside, after running up the path anxious to see her child, he was engulfed by loneliness.

★ ★ ★

At the restaurant, Margaret was going through the accounts. Whichever way she wrote them out, there was a serious shortfall. Islwyn was right, they would have to sell. But still she fought against the obvious.

'Issy, if we take in boarders like your sister-in-law Sally did, wouldn't that bring things around?'

'It's too late for that. Too late for any last-ditch attempts. We have failed and if we don't sell now, we'll be in debt for the rest of our lives.'

'But if only you could — '

'I hate the work. I'm not like Edward. Oh, I tried to be for a while, but I hate it. I hate being subservient to people with money and no manners, people who come here and expect to treat me and talk to me as though I were stupid. I hate the mess they leave, and the stale food that we have to clear away, the dirty dishes and — oh, everything about this business.'

'Then you won't help me to fight for survival.'

'It wouldn't do any good if I did. But no, the best way I can help is to refuse to help. You must see that the only way we can survive to start again, is to sell. Immediately. Sorry, my love, but this is one of those times when taking a long step back is the only way forward.'

Edward couldn't stop thinking about his grandfather; lonely and preparing to die alone, apart from people paid to look after him. A few years previously, the old man had tried to sell the house near the pleasure beach, and move into a hotel. But although several people, including Gladys and Arfon Weston, had looked at it, no one had made an offer and there he had stayed with his housekeeper and one servant; an anachronism in a changing world.

When the phonecall came later that day to tell him the old man had died in his sleep, he felt guilt that he hadn't bothered to show more concern, and a determination that, as the oldest member of the immediate family, he would take it upon himself to deal with the funeral.

He rang Margaret to tell her, and when she put down the phone, her words to Islwyn were, 'Perhaps he'll leave enough money to straighten us out?'

Islwyn shook his head. 'I'm leaving, and I want you to come with me, but if you choose this place, then you're on your own.'

He knew that wasn't true; he would never leave her. The relationship was stormy, but Margaret made him happier than he'd ever been with Sian. Besides, he didn't want to find a job, not even cooking fish and chips. No, his future was with Margaret, but he had to persuade her that Waterside Restaurant was not the place in which to live it. A conversation with Edward, as arrangements for the funeral were made, gave him an idea.

★ ★ ★

Terrence wasn't expected to come down for the funeral. When he was told of his grandfather's death, he simply asked Edward to let him know whether his grandfather had left him any money.

'There's got to be something. There's the house,' he interrupted excitedly as Edward began to speak. 'Once that's sold — '

'There is no house. I've been told that Grandfather left it to the housekeeper who looked after him all these years — when none of us bothered.'

'But there's money?'

'Not enough to get excited about, and what money there is, will be shared with the maid.'

The funeral was a small one. As the old man had explained, there was no one left who knew him well enough to care. William Jones, looking smart and well cared for came to represent his dead father, and he had persuaded two more sons of long-dead friends to go with him. Margaret was there with Islwyn, Edward was grateful to Megan for promising to accompany him.

In the church, the dozen mourners spread themselves around the first three rows of pews but on the vicar's recommendation, gathered closer together to add strength to their voices for the single hymn.

During the brief sermon, the ancient door opened and a tall, slim, expensively dressed figure entered. Edward's heart squeezed with disappointment as Terrence walked down the aisle and sat on the other side of Megan.

★ ★ ★

Margaret went straight home after the funeral and worked out their finances once more.

'You're right, Issy. The only way out of this mess is to sell. Grandfather's money will just about pay enough of our debts to evade that summons.'

'Then we should be grateful to him. At least we don't have to face a court appearance and all the publicity that would bring.'

'I wish I was still in Montague Court, Issy.'

Islwyn looked at her thoughtfully. 'Perhaps you could go back. I understand from Edward that Annie Grant is looking for an experienced housekeeper for the hotel.'

'I couldn't!'

'Couldn't you? Is there anyone more suited?'

★ ★ ★

Only the men went to the graveside. Megan went back to the old man's house with the housekeeper and the maid, who had prepared a spread for the mourners. To Megan's surprise and irritation, Terrence joined her there.

'Aren't you supposed to be at the cemetery?' she demanded.

'I came to look around, see whether there's a keepsake or two I can find.'

'Oh no you don't!' Megan called the housekeeper, a Miss Harriet Griffiths, and told her nothing was to be touched until Edward, who was the executor, had returned. Terrence poured himself a Scotch and sat on the chaise longue and smiled at her.

'You are beautiful,' he said. 'Why don't you marry me?'

As he entered, Edward heard her reply. 'If we married, Terrence, you'd have to grow up fast.'

'I don't agree. Marriage to you might be

323

fun, except of course, the complications of your baby.'

'You'd never cope, Terrence.'

'Because of Rosemary you mean? Oh, I'd leave all that to you until she was at least fifteen. But,' he mused, smiling at her, 'Marriage does have its temptations, darling.'

As the others walked into the house, each greeted by the maid, Edward said, 'Thinking of getting married, are you Terrence? To which of your children's mothers, might I ask?'

'Don't ask, Edward, the disappointment would be hard for you to bear.'

12

Early in December, as Pendragon Island was waking up to the realisation that Christmas was fast approaching, Margaret visited the estate agent and arranged for the house, Waterside Restaurant, to be sold. There was defiance in her eyes as she answered the estate agent's questions and even more defiance as she walked into Montague Court and asked to speak to Annie.

'I understand you are looking for an expert housekeeper,' she said as Annie entered the room. Annie was dressed in a perfectly fitting brown skirt and white frilled blouse, with moderately high heels enhancing her well-shaped legs. Her figure was trim and she walked with quiet gracefulness. A long necklace of amber beads moved in rhythm with her strides, the matching earrings joining in the movement. Her jacket was gingery-brown which suited her colouring and gave her a look of confidence and dignity.

Margaret lost some of her battle when Annie quietly asked, 'And what makes you think you will suit, Miss Jenkins?'

Margaret had expected the woman to show

relief that her hotel would be in such capable hands. 'As you well know, Mrs Grant, I owned the place and ran it from the time we opened its doors to the public,' she replied.

'You don't own it any more and if you'll forgive me, you ran it until it failed.'

'No, the truth was, I depended on my brother and he let me down.'

'You were in no way to blame?'

'No.' Margaret was emphatic.

'Then you think you could come back and work here, accepting that I am in charge?' Annie's brown eyes looked at her visitor thoughtfully. 'I would have to insist on having the last word, and indeed, the first.' She stared at Margaret for a long moment and asked again. 'Could you cope with that?'

'I don't have much choice.'

'But I have,' Annie said. 'I'll think about it and I'll call you when I've seen the other applicants.'

Instead of going back to her restaurant, where the preparations for three parties of four awaited her, Margaret walked through the gardens of Montague Court, past the lake, and on to the bleak but beautiful pebbly beach. What was she thinking of, going back to her previous home as a housekeeper? Annie was right, she wouldn't be able to cope with not being in charge.

The Rose Tree Café was open and she looked in and saw Sian, Issy's wife, serving teas to a group of ladies who had bags bulging with early Christmas shopping piled on a chair near them. Ordinary people with ordinary lives; for a moment she envied them. They were laughing as they unpacked their purchases to show their friends. Margaret realised with dismay that there had been very little laughter in her own life.

Sian was sharing in their jollity as they demonstrated a toy or discussed a record, or joked about a tie. She seemed to be coping well with the near collapse of the family firm and the departure of her husband. Sian had had to settle for a lot less when the family business had got into difficulties, but her disaster wasn't as devastating as losing a house like Montague Court, a house that had been in the family for generations. Sian had chosen to sell their home and move to a tiny terrace house. Her move hadn't been forced on her by a stupid brother.

Then she admitted to herself that Sian's disaster had been caused in part by Issy. He had taken a good living from the family business, and had been negligent, lazy and uncaring. Besides not doing the job Old Man Arfon had paid him to do, he had stolen money. Then, when things went wrong and

Weston's Wallpaper and Paint was on the point of closure, he had left his wife and come to her. Sadly she faced the fact that neither she nor Islwyn were exemplary people.

When she went back to Waterside, she was surprised to see that Islwyn had finished the preparation of vegetables and fruit, and was cleaning the fish ready for the open-topped pie with creamed vegetables, which, served with duchess potatoes, was one of their more popular choices.

'Thank you, Issy. I'm late.'

'Did you see Annie?'

'I did and I have to decide whether or not I can work with her as my boss in a house that was once mine.'

'You don't have to, there are other places to work. We can surely earn enough by doing less hectic things to pay for a flat and a comfortable life?'

'I want to go back,' her voice was weak and Islwyn realised that Margaret was near to tears.

'Then we will.'

'She might not have me, I'm not the easiest person — '

'You're the only one for that position. Annie knows it. She'll take you. And I hope she'll find me something too. Ring her now.'

'I'm to wait for her to ring me.'

'Don't wait. Kick down the fences and tell her how much you want the job.'

'There isn't time, it's already six o'clock.'

'There's time for this.' He picked up the phone, dialled the number and handed it to her.

In her unusually emotional state she was more reasonable and she listened intently as Annie Grant explained her duties. When she replaced the phone she stared at Issy in disbelief.

'I've got it. The job is mine and d'you know, Issy, I think I can cope; so long as you don't leave me I can cope.'

★ ★ ★

In the small town the burglaries continued. The thief seemed to know when a place was empty, and where and if burglar alarms were set. At a house in Chestnut Road, not far from Barry's former home, Bob and Greta Jones were avid collectors of medieval weaponry.

On learning that the Joneses were out for the evening, Percy went in and began carrying the unwieldy treasures out through the garden to where he had parked the van. Pikes that were almost ten feet long were difficult to handle but he patiently carried them, wrapped them in sacks, and propped them over the passenger seat, along the length of the vehicle. There was a separate journey with some sixteenth-century rapiers, again long and awkward to handle. One had its matching dagger, which would have been held in the left hand of the swordsman, with his hand protected by his cloak. Beautifully decorated, he paused for a moment to admire the exquisite craftsmanship.

There were several display cases holding arrow heads as well as some early guns, including a wheel-lock, the precursor to the flintlock. He carried these in a bag brought for the purpose, and was making his last journey when he was interrupted.

The Joneses had gone to the New Theatre in Cardiff, but during the first act, Greta had become ill. She had a severe headache, felt hot, and her skin was burning up. Apologising to the patrons for disturbing them they left and drove home.

Percy Flemming was still in the house, and as he failed to hear the low, expensive purr of the car pulling up outside the front door, he was trapped in the upstairs room where most of their treasures were kept.

The windows were all securely locked and the only way out was via the back door which he had unlocked in readiness as soon as he had entered. He had come in via the pantry window set high above the ground outside and which had been considered too small to be a problem.

Although he had entered by the window he couldn't use it as an exit. Climbing up and coming in head first, he had fallen gently onto the work surface with his arms outstretched to help his landing. But going out the same way he would fall several more feet and risk injury. Trying to get out feet first was impossible too. The lights were now on outside the building and although it was a quiet area there was the possibility that a pair of legs dangling through the window would cause some curiosity. No, he was trapped unless he could get past them and out through the front or back door.

Bob Jones was escorting his wife up the wide staircase and Percy decided to wait until they were in a bedroom before running down the stairs and through the gardens. Unfortunately, Bob noticed a door left ajar.

'Wait,' he hissed to his wife. 'Someone's been in here!'

'Oh no. We haven't been robbed, have we?' Greta whispered back, clinging to his arm.

'Come on, let's get you up to your

bedroom. I'll lock you in, then I'll investigate. It's probably nothing; we could have simply forgotten to close it.' Although, he thought, that was unlikely. They were fastidious in their routine, and shutting all the bedroom doors was a part of it, but 'Anyone can make a mistake,' he told Greta, 'and forget a small detail.'

No longer believing there was anything wrong, he stepped back onto the landing and bumped straight into Percy Flemming.

Masked and wearing a well-cut suit, chamois gloves and shiny black shoes, Percy was unrecognisable and he pushed Bob Jones into the bedroom where he fell heavily. Greta heard the noise and opened the door, stepping out to investigate. Percy grabbed her arms and spun her several times, then ran down the stairs calling back in a hissing whisper, 'Run for it, Eddie!'

Confused, Bob and Greta — whose aching head was forgotten — went from room to room expecting to confront the second man. All they found were empty display cases, the weaponry missing. On the floor, discarded in Percy's haste lay arrow heads and coins still attached to their display boards.

Belatedly, Bob ran out into the dark garden, shouted his frustration to the night air, and rang the police. He told them one of the two men involved was called Ed or Eddie or perhaps Edward.

* * *

Two days later another burglary was interrupted; this time Percy had engineered the break-in to coincide with the owner's return. He didn't intend to steal anything. He simply used the opportunity to confuse the police. The man who 'disturbed' him swore he had heard the thief calling for 'Lew' to bring the car.

Tired of being questioned yet again about his movements, Edward went to see Lewis.

'Why are we being suspected of these thefts?' Edward demanded. 'I've never been involved in anything even slightly shady.'

'Don't look at me like that! I haven't either!' Lewis pointed a finger in the direction of the back yard where Charlie and Gwyn were bathing the dog. 'I'd put it down to being involved with him, the ex-con. But now I think we're just being used. Only one person is ever seen, and the man is stupid enough to call out the name of the other one. D'you think that's believable?'

'No, and neither do the police. I agree with you. I think they have a suspicion about the real thief and are saying nothing in the hope of making him overconfident. He's cheeky, you have to admit that.'

'I'll kill him for using my name! Causing all this aggravation,' Lewis spat out in indignation.

'I wonder who he is? Smartly dressed, tall and neat, well spoken and as nimble as a monkey.'

'That should let us out. You with a gammy leg and me almost fifty. We're hardly to be described as nimble, are we?'

* * *

William Jones had settled happily into the house of Catrin Gwilym and every afternoon he walked around the area where he had previously searched for oddments of food to steal, and marvelled at his good fortune. With three hundred pounds in the bank and a comfortable home, he counted his blessing daily.

He often called in to the shop to see Edward, sometimes fortunate enough to choose a quiet moment and share a pot of tea. A sudden surge of appreciation towards the man who had made such a difference to his life, led him to the sports shop one Saturday afternoon, where Edward and Mair were serving four brothers with football boots, jerseys and socks for their first match in the school team.

Edward invited him to sit and he waited until the boys were satisfied and went out with their father, excitedly carrying bags and boxes filled with their treasures.

'I just wanted you to know how I appreciate you finding me and helping me like you did. My life is wonderful now and it's all down to you, Mr Jenkins,' William told him in the brief lull.

'I'm pleased, really pleased,' Edward smiled. Old William never failed to thank him when they met. He wished he could make him believe that further thanks weren't necessary.

'Now if someone could solve my problem for me,' he said to change the subject, 'I'd be content too. I've just had the police here yet again. It's these burglaries. They seem determined to prove that Lewis Lewis and I are responsible. Isn't it crazy?'

'Of course it's crazy. I know who the thief is.'

'You do?'

'Until you saved me from my miserable life, I wandered around a lot at night. I saw him going into a derelict house one night and I watched. He came out dressed like a toff. I thought he was carrying on with another woman, you know how men seem to want a bit of excitement sometimes.'

'And?' Edward was impatient.

'Later, I saw him running out of a garden as if his pants were on fire, with a zipped bag banging against his legs,' the old man chuckled. 'We weren't far away from the main road and I saw him get into a tatty old van. I cut across the fields back to the derelict house and saw him coming out of there wearing his usual clothes, denim trousers and an old jacket. Percy Flemming it was. Saw him as clear as I'm seeing you now.'

★ ★ ★

Although Ernie Griffiths and his fiancée Helen Gunner had implied they had told Helen's parents of the unplanned baby, in fact they hadn't said a word.

Ernie felt embarrassed as well as ashamed. It was always the woman who took most of the blame but he knew he could have held back and didn't. Telling his family was the easiest, he'd known that and they had both hoped to gain confidence from the reaction of Janet and Hywel.

As he was leaving the Gunner's house a couple of weeks before Christmas, Ernie finally came out with it. Gloria screamed at the top of her voice. Wilfred tried to sooth her for a moment then told her to 'Shut *up!*'

'But what will people say? What about all the arrangements I've made?' Gloria wailed.

'They'll have heard worse things and the arrangements will have to be unmade,' Helen said calmly. 'Come on, Mam, d'you think I don't know why you and Dad never celebrate wedding anniversaries?'

'What d'you mean?'

'I mean that we haven't committed a criminal offence. We just loved each other too much and too soon. Now, what about a Christmas wedding?'

'A register office? Never!'

'Pity, because it's booked.'

It was midnight when Ernie finally left, after being assured by Helen that she would go straight to bed and not allow her parents to harangue her any further that night. He walked home in a gloomy mood, wishing he and Helen had been brave enough to disappear and marry in Gretna Green as Jack Weston had done. He wondered idly whether it was too late.

* ★ *

Another Griffiths was feeling miserable. Frank Griffiths hadn't given up hope of a date with Mair Gregory, even though her father was a copper. He was sitting in the kitchen of the sports shop on the following morning, having been called back to retouch some paint that had been scraped while moving a heavy display unit. Having finished the small job he was sitting drinking coffee, while Mair washed a shelf, when his attention was caught by one half of a telephone conversation taking place in the shop area.

'Yes, Mr Lewis,' Edward was saying on the telephone. 'I am almost certain that these robberies are carried out by a man called Percy Flemming. Now, shall we meet and discuss it?'

'All right, I'll come,' Mair said to Frank, having been invited to the pictures. Frank didn't reply and she poked him with a soapy finger and said, 'You deaf then? I said yes.'

'Sorry, Mair, I've got to go.' Leaving Mair staring at his retreating back with eyes filled with fury, he ran out of the shop.

He ran as fast as his long, skinny legs would allow. This message couldn't wait. Percy had to be warned they were onto him. Percy wasn't at home. He left a message with Barbara asking Percy to meet him at The Railwayman and warned her that it was something very urgent.

Back at the shop, he asked Mair again to go

338

out with him, pretending to be unaware she had agreed and had been ignored.

'Get lost!' she replied. Frank sloped off home offended, to complain to Janet about the unpredictable behaviour of women.

* * *

Edward didn't go straight to the police with William's information. He discussed it by telephone, with Lewis, the conversation overhead in part by Frank. Edward and Lewis agreed that after the inconvenience of being accused of his crimes, they deserved the pleasure of catching the man themselves. Edward smiled at the story he would have to tell Megan, and Lewis imagined how he would stretch the story out and have Dora thinking he was a hero. Like two children playing out an adventure story, they devised a plan. A plan in which Willie Jones, to his great delight, was invited to take an active part.

* * *

There was no distress involved in the selling of the restaurant. Losing Montague Court had been so traumatic Margaret thought she'd never feel anything so painfully again. Several viewers called in the first week and she carried on with the routine of the restaurant, while Islwyn showed them around, as if selling was the least important part of her life. Any questions directed at her were answered briefly, to the point of rudeness.

So they were surprised to hear that a Charles and Peggy Covington had made an offer, something below what they were asking. Islwyn wanted to accept but Margaret dug her heels in and insisted on the full asking price.

'We should have some reward for the work and effort we've put into the place,' she complained.

'I think you should accept. We could wait months for another offer and the position of housekeeper at Montague Court might be taken by someone else.'

With little interest on Margaret's part, and enthusiasm on Islwyn's, they were soon quarrelling practically daily until they decided not to discuss the transaction except when the solicitor was present. Agreement was finally reached and the contracts were drawn up for completion in January.

As there was a licence to sell alcohol involved, possession would take place on the same day as completion, with a court appearance in which the new owner would receive a protection order which at the next sitting of the Brewsters court would be confirmed. It had all happened so recently when they had sold Montague Court that the procedure revived her original sadness. Unreasonably, she was irritable with Islwyn, needing to take out her frustration and disappointment on someone.

Islwyn said nothing, he knew she was still finding it difficult to think of returning to her old home as a paid employee.

* * *

When Percy Flemming was told that Willie Jones had recognised him and had passed the information on to Lewis and Edward — his two scapegoats — he smiled.

'They haven't gone to the police yet,' Frank added. 'I think they've got some plan to catch you themselves.'

At this Percy laughed out loud. Confidence had grown over the years he had been actively stealing and he had no doubt that he could outwit a couple of amateurs like Edward Jenkins and Lewis Lewis. It might even be amusing. One more job and then he'd have his fun.

'Thanks,' was all he said after Frank had repeated carefully everything he had heard.

341

Frank, who had been hoping for a fiver for his trouble, was disappointed.

Willie Jones felt like a child again. He was shadowing Percy Flemming, hiding behind corners wearing an oversized coat and carrying a bag, as he had done for so many lonely years before Edward had found him and returned his self-esteem and his money.

'It's almost like I'm invisible,' he told Edward and Lewis. 'I wander around the streets and look in dustbins and I'm disregarded as no one of any importance.' He took out a notebook and read out what he had observed so far.

'He's walked past number sixteen Bell Lane several times. He doesn't appear to be taking a great interest, but I think he's checking on windows, alarm systems, drainpipes and all that.'

'I wonder who lives there?' Lewis frowned.

'Major and Mrs Bloom-Davies,' Edward supplied. 'They used to eat regularly at Montague Court. He's retired and I remember him telling me he was interested in Oriental china and porcelain. That must be what Percy's after.'

'I know where he hides the van he uses too,' William smiled. 'I'll take you to see it, shall I?'

Acting as though they were taking part in a

crazy amateur film, they went separately to a part of Pigog Wood where, hidden by undergrowth and overhanging trees, they saw the battered old van.

Edward called on Major Bloom-Davies with the excuse he wanted him to mention his shop at the golf club to those who hadn't yet used it. During the conversation it was easy to learn that the major and his family were going to London for the weekend.

On Friday evening, having seen the Bloom-Davieses on their way, Edward parked nearby and waited. At three in the morning, Lewis came to take over and although he waited until ten, nothing suspicious occurred.

At ten o'clock it was William's turn. In the way of many elderly people, he had no difficulty sitting still and silently waiting. He sat there all Saturday morning, hidden in the garden of the Bloom-Davies' house and watched for movement.

The postman called, a neighbour knocked and went away disappointed, but there was no sign of Percy. At intervals during the day, the three conspirators changed places and Saturday night too passed without incident.

Convinced they had been mistaken, Lewis was prepared to give up when William came to relieve him at midday.

'Sunday afternoon's a good time to choose,' William whispered. 'Let's wait a while longer.'

'Surely he'd move before this? There's a risk of them coming back early. Percy wouldn't take that chance, not when he had the whole weekend.'

'You get off,' William said. 'Sit in your car for a while, to give Percy a chance to see you, then drive off. Pass the major's house slowly as if you're checking for the final time.'

'You think he knows we're here? How can he?'

'If he's survived all this time without being caught he's got to have a sixth sense about danger.' William settled himself comfortably. 'Well, I've got a sixth sense too and it tells me we won't be disappointed. Hurry off and don't be too obvious. Then wait where we arranged, near the lane leading to the wood.'

★ ★ ★

At four o'clock on Sunday afternoon, Percy drove the van in through the gates of the Bloom-Davies' drive. The weather was icy and the headlights caught the glitter on the tarmac before they were snapped out as Percy negotiated the gateway. William watched as he stepped out, observing the man's smart suit and immaculate shoes and gloves in the fading light. Percy walked up to the door and knocked, and William's heart was racing with excitement at the prospect of catching a thief. He saw Percy don a mask and climb up the drainpipe to a small bathroom window. After slipping the catch with a thin blade, he pushed the sash window up and slid inside.

Then Willie made his move. He scuttled through the shrubbery with practised stealth, hardly disturbing the foliage, and went out through a garden gate onto the road. Signalling to where Lewis's car was parked, hidden by shadows, he hurried on to the telephone box on the next corner.

Percy went straight through the house and opened the back door, then paused a moment to take in the remarkable decor of the house. Chinese wallpaper, luxurious rugs and ornately carved cupboards filled with delicate porcelain and ancient pottery from China, Japan and Malaya, all displayed and carefully labelled. He began to fill the bags he had brought, wrapping each item swiftly but with care. With two bags filled and placed by the open door, he ran up the stairs.

Every room had items of value but he didn't try to take everything, just pieces he could easily carry. After the medieval weaponry he'd had enough of awkward shapes. The most valuable items were two Ming vases, about which the major had boasted in talks given around the area. Percy picked them up reverently. He had a dealer waiting for these.

As he was leaving the back room with the last of his load he froze, his eyes darting around, assessing his best move. Someone was opening the door. He hadn't heard the car. He must be getting careless. Definitely time to stop.

Because of a bad-weather warning, Major and Mrs Bloom-Davies had left early for home. The major was following his wife up the stairs towards where Percy was hiding, when he became aware of a draught.

'That's odd,' he said, looking towards the back of the house, 'I think we left the back door open.'

'No, we didn't!' His wife's eyes showed fear. 'I locked it and even went back to check. We've had a burglary. I always knew we would one day.'

Major Bloom-Davies had a quick look around the ground floor and realised she was right. 'I think he's still here,' he whispered. 'There are bags near the back door.'

Upstairs Percy realised with dread that his best escape was down the stairs and past them. Exiting through the bathroom window — as he had entered — would involve a slow and careful climb down the drainpipe. But the telephone was in the hall. They'd surely get the police here before he could get away. Perhaps he could tug on the telephone wire as he passed and maybe wrench it from the wall. It was worth a try.

All these years, and for it to end now, when he was leaving Pendragon Island and starting afresh somewhere else. Life could be very unfair.

To his relief, the couple didn't go for the telephone. Desperately hoping to save his treasures, the major continued up the stairs, the woman holding onto her husband's arm.

On the landing, Percy felt a surge of hope.

★　★　★

In the telephone box, after phoning the police and then Edward, William was standing waiting for the police, as they instructed. In a lay-by, Lewis was parked ready to follow Percy's dirty old van. William, that happy night wanderer, who knew the area almost as well as the Griffiths boys, had described the route, through fields and green lanes, which Percy would most likely travel to avoid being seen on the roads, and Lewis waited for his signal before setting off to intercept him.

At number sixteen Bell Lane, Percy was poised for his run for freedom. Closer and closer the two people came and Percy tensed for action. When they reached the top of the stairs, he jumped out and punched the major and pushed him into a bedroom, then he spun the woman around several times, as he had done so successfully on a previous occasion, before shoving her towards her husband inside the room and locking the door.

Grabbing all he could, including the precious vases, he ran down the stairs and out of the back door, pausing to close it after him. Laden with valuables he was loath to leave behind slowed him, but he made it to the van and, opening a five-barred gate, he drove through and again closed it after him. He didn't want his route to be easy to follow.

He drove without lights although it had been dark for some time, the clouds having brought the day to an early end. Along a track through the trees, down a rutted lane and across a field. There were only a few miles to go and he'd be safe.

At the edge of the field was a brook and although the banks were high in places, there was a spot where he could drive down and through the water and up the other side without much difficulty. Still without lights he went slowly through the muddy edge and was in the slowly moving stream when lights blinded him. Headlights.

He couldn't see a thing, his night sight completely destroyed, but he pressed the accelerator, revved furiously and tried to drive on. The bulk of another vehicle stopped him. Beside the driver's door stood Edward, and outside the passenger door stood Lewis.

'First, Percy Flemming, you'll tell us why you used our names,' Lewis said.

'I'm sorry, but I only wanted to confuse the police. Let me go, eh?' he pleaded. 'It didn't harm you, did it? No one would suspect two upright citizens like you for long.'

'You chose the wrong ones,' Lewis said. 'We got mad.'

'We've been pestered, used and embarrassed, and that's why you're sitting there now, with nowhere to go but prison,' Edward added.

'Come on, lads, you wouldn't want me to go inside and leave my two girls and a sick wife, would you? What will happen to my daughters if I'm in prison and Barbara dies? That's what'll happen. I was doing this to send her to Switzerland. She's seriously ill with TB and only the clean fresh mountain air will save her. Please, think of my children if not me.'

'Is this true?' Edward was weakening.

'No it isn't,' said a breathless voice and William appeared, panting and leaning on a convenient tree.

Behind him, torches could be seen and in the distance, the pinpoint headlights and drone of a car aproaching.

'Sound as a bell, is Barbara Wheel. Better state than me and that's for sure,' he puffed.

Percy briefly studied the three men. Edward was the weakest link, the one who wouldn't fight hard to capture him. He wasn't committed to rough stuff, he knew that. He eased the door handle down and with a sudden movement rammed the door open against Edward before jumping out and pushing him so he stumbled. Edward got in the way of Lewis before falling into the water. Carrying the vases, Percy stumbled off through the stream and climbed out into the field he had just left.

When the police arrived, Edward and Lewis were there with the spoils of the latest robbery, together with their informant.

★ ★ ★

350

Fortunately for Lewis and Edward, William's story was convincing, and later, the van showed Percy's fingerprints and none of theirs. The van was registered to Barbara Wheel but when the police went to Percy's house to talk to her they found it empty and the family long gone.

Barbara and the girls had moved on the previous week and Percy had stayed behind to do one more job before joining them in a small village not far from Carmarthen, where they were already becoming known as Freddy Jones and family.

★ ★ ★

Lewis went home after being questioned for, hopefully, the last time and called at number seven Sophie Street. To his dismay, Dora wasn't there. He went to Trellis Street and knocked on number forty-four. Sian opened the door and told him Dora and she were going through the menus to decide on the Christmas fare for the following week.

'I've been catching the burglar the police had been chasing for months — no — years,' he said proudly, when he went inside.

'You've been doing what?' Dora asked, her blue eyes staring at him in alarm. 'Wasn't that dangerous?'

'Very. Attacked we were and poor Edward Jenkins ended up in the stream. Dangerous all right, especially when the only help we had was poor old Willie Jones from the old draper's shop.'

Lewis took off his coat, drew up a chair and began to tell them about his weekend's adventure. Although enthralled, Dora's face showed concern when he reached the part where Percy had made his daring escape.

'He hit someone in a previous raid you know,' she said. 'He could have killed you if you'd stopped him getting away.'

'I was ready for him.'

'And that other break-in where a man was beaten. He could have knocked you unconscious or he might have had a gun! Really Lewis, you should have left it to the police.'

Lewis smiled his special smile and looked at Dora, 'Would you have been frightened for me if you'd known? Would you have cared, love?'

Sian made herself scarce, busying herself with tea and cakes, while Lewis put out his arms and pleaded with his beautiful eyes, sparkling with the excitement of his adventure and with love for her. She hugged him and said gruffly that she'd hate to think of him being hurt.

Megan was surprised to see Edward when she opened the door to his knock. There was such an animated look about him that she stepped back and said, 'Come in, you obviously have something to tell me.'

'Can William come in too?' he asked and from behind him stepped the old man, changed now out of his ragamuffin clothes.

'What have you two been up to?' Megan asked as she led them into the lounge where her mother sat looking through a boxful of photographs.

'Tell them, William,' Edward coaxed.

'We've caught the burglar.' He shrugged casually. 'Well, the police weren't doing anything so we thought we'd catch him for them.'

'Unfortunately he got away again,' Edward laughed. The merriment continued as the two men told their story and the two women listened. As Dora had done, Megan recognised the danger they had faced.

'Edward. You could have all been killed.'

'Percy Flemming didn't look dangerous when he realised he was cornered. In fact he was utterly dejected. Told us he needed the money for his wife who was desperately ill and needed to go to Switzerland. Begged us

353

not to send him to prison and leave his girls without anyone to look after them.'

'I'm glad you weren't soft enough to let him go,' Megan said. Then she saw an expression on his face that made her suspect he had done just that. 'Edward?'

'I didn't allow him to escape, although for a moment I did wonder whether I could cope with knowing I was responsible for sending a man to prison.'

'Edward,' Megan said again, softly, affection and love in her eyes.

'I just didn't expect him to ram me with the door and jump out like he did.'

'But you were thinking about letting him go?' she accused.

'Until William put me right,' he admitted.

'You could have been killed,' she repeated.

'Actually, it was all great fun. In fact,' he said with a smile at William, 'if the shop doesn't succeed, William and I might begin another career as private detectives!'

'Edward. You need a keeper!'

Edward looked at her and said, 'The job is yours if you want it.'

'Is that a proposal?'

William looked from one to the other wondering whether he should leave. Sally bent her head lower towards the box of photographs.

'It was, and I'll ask you again tomorrow and the day after and on and on until you say yes.'

'For how long?' she asked, smiling at him.

'I'll never give up And I might warn you now that I want a big wedding with all the trimmings and — ' with a swift glance at Sally he added, ' — and your father will be there to give you away.'

Edward took Megan's hands in his, pulled her up out of her chair and stared down into her eyes, leaving her in no doubt about how much he loved her. 'Say yes,' he whispered, oblivious of the others. Quietly, William and Sally crept out into the kitchen, leaving them to relish the kiss that sealed their promise.

13

News of Ernie Griffiths's intended marriage to Helen Gunner was met with a variety of comments. Most people guessed the reason for the hastily planned wedding, and the happy couple had to suffer remarks like 'the pudding club', or 'one up the spout' or more politely 'in the family way'. To Janet and Hywel's surprise only three fights were begun as a result of this and no one complained at the prospect of a party.

Christmas Day was on a Sunday that year and the wedding was booked for Friday the twenty-third.

'Thank goodness rationing has finished,' Helen's mother sighed. 'The wedding would be followed by a very lean Christmas if this had happened a couple of years ago.'

'No it wouldn't,' Helen replied. 'The Griffithses have never let the lack of a ration book stop them arranging a party or enjoying Christmas.'

'Black market deals and poaching you mean,' her mother said in a hissing whisper. 'Well, the less said about that, the better I'll sleep at night! Imagine you marrying one of the Griffithses. Known for their thieving ways they are and how you ever got mixed up with them after the way you've been brought up — '

'Mam, you promised,' Helen pleaded.

'I can't help it. And this wedding, what will it be except a pile of thick sandwiches and an old sweet jar full of pickled onions?'

'You might surprise yourself and enjoy it!'

'Enjoy seeing my only daughter ruin her life?'

Helen said no more. There wasn't any point with Mam in this mood.

★　★　★

Edward was redecorating his shop window. He had several times made a Christmas display but the business was so prosperous he was constantly rearranging it because of so many items being sold. It had been Megan's advice to ignore the temptation of showing the expensive skiing clothes and equipment and instead concentrate on gifts for children. That it had been a success was clearly shown by the fact he had to go yet again to the wholesalers for more stock.

Old William Jones still called regularly and tutted if the window was anything less than immaculate and one day Edward left Mair and the old man in charge while he went into Cardiff for some football jerseys that had been ordered. When he returned about an hour before closing time he was surprised and pleased to see the shop filled and Megan helping to attend to the customers.

'Megan, how lovely to see you, but where's Rosemary?' he asked.

'Upstairs and sleeping away the hours. We've been up every few minutes to check that all is well but she's content.'

Edward ran upstairs to reassure himself. Looking at the sleeping child always delighted him. The beautiful, calm face that could pucker up and complain when things were less than comfortable for her was a constant fascination. Now she was peaceful, the long eyelashes resting on rosy cheeks, her arms stretched out above her head in a way he had come to recognise as contentment. He smiled and went back down to help serve.

They were late closing but Mair and William left at the usual time and it was Edward alone who closed up and checked the till. Megan had gone to feed Rosemary in the flat above. There was nothing prepared for an evening meal so they decided to take Rosemary to Sally and eat out.

They sat for a while, nursing and playing with the little girl, listening enthralled to her

358

early attempts at communication and joining in by replying to her funny sounds as though they all understood each other.

'Is it time d'you think for us to make plans to marry?' Edward asked.

'What about in the spring? Easter is a lovely time for weddings, Edward.'

'Then Easter it will be.'

'There's been a lot of teasing about Ernie Griffiths's marriage to Helen being brought forward because of their baby. What will they say about us? I will be going to my marriage to you carrying Rosemary — another man's child — into the church.'

'Nothing they say will worry me, but I don't want anyone to upset you,' he replied.

'Upset me? One of the dreadfully bold Weston Girls? Never!' Megan laughed. 'There is some satisfaction for many, seeing one of the wild Weston Girls being brought to such a pass.' She smiled. 'The general opinion is that you are a fool to marry me and I don't deserve such an admirable husband and I think they're probably right.' She reached over and kissed him gently. 'I love you dearly, Edward. You are a wonderfully kind man and I do consider myself fortunate.'

'And so do I.'

* * *

On the outskirts of a small village a few miles outside Carmarthen, Percy Flemming, now known as Jones, was working on the plot of land he had bought alongside his new home. He was keeping well out of sight, concentrating on growing his hair and cultivating a beard, while preparing the land ready for the small market garden he planned to open the following year.

Barbara had changed her hairstyle and colour as well as the style of her dress. They both stayed away from the local shops. The children had to attend school but the private school they had chosen was a long way from the village and they would be met and brought home without any more contact with others than necessary. The family drove long distances to buy their supplies, the intention being to only gradually make themselves known to the immediate area.

Once a few months had passed and the dark days of winter had helped them to remain hidden, they would be accepted without curiosity and no one would be looking for Percy Flemming and Barbara Wheel. Any clues Percy had given in the past had been false, such as stating his intention one day of moving to Cardiff.

* * *

The closed-in evenings and the dankness, the cheerless skies and constantly wet roads of the darkest period of the year, were brightened for a few weeks by the reflections of decorated Christmas trees, coloured lights and cheerful displays emanating from every shop window. The years of blacked-out streets and the shortages of so many basic needs were long past. Yet, beside the religious festivities, Christmas was still an excuse to celebrate the end of the war, with the shortages and tragedies it had brought.

Every shop in Pendragon Island did its best to add to the town's display and even shops with no contents relevant to the season, like ironmongers and builders' suppliers, managed a few streamers or added bows of ribbons to bucket handles to cheer and amuse the passers-by.

Something of the jubilation turned sour for Dora, aware that once again she would be on her own, so when Lewis called to discuss their plans for the Christmas weekend she finally braved herself to say, 'Lewis, I think you should come home.'

'Properly home?' he asked, staring at her with a quizzical expression.

'Properly home? What d'you mean?' She knew what he meant. She knew he was thinking about sharing her bed and she wanted it so much, yet couldn't bring herself to admit it.

'What exactly are you suggesting, Dora?'

'Come home was what I meant!' she said, her voice sharp in her distress at being incapable of telling him how she really felt. Was it shyness? How could it be after all the years they had spent together? Or was it that stupid hurt pride that she couldn't shake off?

She plumped up a couple of cushions, afraid to look at him. He was standing perfectly still and the moment seemed to go on and on. He was waiting for her to speak and she was tongue-tied. Why couldn't she say it? She loved him, so why wouldn't the words come?

'I'll think about it,' he said quietly and then he left.

★ ★ ★

The day of Ernie and Helen's wedding was dry and with a very cold, easterly wind that found its way into every corner of every house. Gone was the hope of the guests dressing up in smart suits for some cheery photographs. Everyone put on their finery then added thick coats, scarves, and hats and shoes more suitable for a walk in the country than a wedding.

The ceremony was short and colourless but Helen and Ernie weren't expecting anything more. They knew that the real celebration awaited them at the Griffiths's small cottage.

No formal invitations had been sent. The cars were those owned or borrowed by the few who attended the simple ceremony. Gloria Gunner had tried to add some formality to the wedding of her only daughter but had given up and allowed the day to happen in the casual, easy manner that the Griffithses had made into an art.

Several people had helped with the food and the tables borrowed for the occasion groaned with the weight of it. Even on such a cold day, the doors were open and people came and went during the day and into the evening. Sian arrived with her son Jack and his wife, Victoria. Rhiannon and Charlie came with Gwyn. Joan and Viv Lewis arrived later than the others as they had to wait until the wallpaper and paint shop had closed.

With the weather making it impossible for people to spill out into the garden, the rooms were soon crammed with people, each one determined not to be the first to leave.

Sian looked across at her twin sister Sally who had arrived with Edward, Megan and the baby. Neither of them had their husbands with them and it saddened the occasion to realise that her husband, Islwyn, was somewhere with another woman and Sally's husband was recovering from a nervous breakdown.

'Remember how we used to look down with disapproval on these people, Sally?' Sian whispered. 'Yet they seem to have the best of it, don't they?'

'Their expectations were low and they've achieved more than they'd imagined. While ours were high and dropped like the proverbial stone,' Sally smiled. 'But at least they don't bear us any ill will. I feel very welcome here, don't you?'

Edward handed Caroline a parcel. 'It's for young Joseph-Hywel,' he told her.

Barry watched, then his face fell with disappointment as a cricket ball and child-size bat were revealed. 'I've made one for him,' he explained, 'but I thought it was a little early to give it to him.'

Seeing the disappointment on Barry's face, Janet quickly said, 'Marvellous, Barry. He'll need two when his friends come to play.'

'Don't be daft, woman,' Hywel growled. 'You only need one bat to play garden cricket; you don't have two batsmen at once! The ball will be handy though.'

'Shush!' Janet warned. 'Joseph-Hywel is clever enough to invent his own games; he's not one to follow the herd!'

'Of course he isn't. He's a Griffiths isn't he?' someone shouted. Everyone laughed, including Barry. This wasn't a day to look for reasons to complain.

Sally was the first to leave. She took baby Rosemary home in a taxi leaving Megan to enjoy the rest of the evening.

'I don't really want her to go,' Megan admitted to Edward. 'I only feel she is perfectly safe if I am with her. Is that silly? Am I turning into an overprotective mother?'

'You might not believe it but I wanted to go with her too. She's so precious I want to be with her every moment, even though that's impossible. But your mother will take the best care. We really can relax and enjoy this peculiar wedding feast.' He accepted a sandwich as a plate was pushed past his face and handed one to Megan. 'No serviette I'm afraid,' he grinned. 'What would my sister Margaret think of us!'

★ ★ ★

In Waterside Restaurant, Margaret was giving no thought to the party at the Griffiths'. But Islwyn was aware of the wedding party, knowing his wife Sian and their son, Jack would be there with his shy wife, Victoria. He had no wish to join them. The thought of spending time in that awful hovel appalled him.

Even thinking of Jack and Victoria, whom he liked, was no draw. He no longer seemed to be a part of the Weston family. That stage of his life seemed such a long time ago it was almost like a film he had once seen or a book he had read. Not real at all. This was real. He and Margaret preparing to start a new life together; not the one they had planned, but still exciting.

'Margaret, time to go, love,' he called.

'I'm ready Issy. Will I do?' she asked, turning this way and that to show him the smart, dark green swagger coat she had decided to wear, the carefully chosen amber-coloured dress and the green and amber high-heeled shoes.

'You look wonderful,' he said admiringly. Her hair shone and there was an unmistakable look of defiance in her eyes as she took his arm and went with him to the car.

At Montague Court they were met by Annie Grant who took them straight up to see the room they had been given. The furniture had all belonged to the house when Margaret had lived there and she was grateful for Annie's thoughtfulness in providing it for her.

'It's small,' Annie apologised, 'but you have a pleasant view and there are shelves and things so you can bring some of your favourite pieces with you.'

'We've brought them, can we place them now?' Margaret asked.

'Of course. Although you won't be starting work here for a few more weeks, the room is yours.'

After a cup of coffee and discussion on their various responsibilities — Islwyn being given the vague role of odd-job man — they went to the car and carried up several boxes, a couple of rugs and a small bedside chest of drawers.

Ornaments were arranged, four oil paintings and one or two family photographs were found places on the walls, and a clock was soon ticking merrily on the chest of drawers.

'We want the room to show we live here, Issy,' Margaret said. 'I couldn't bear to live with someone else's personality on show, could you?'

Putting down the set of hairbrushes Margaret had bought him, the only item he had brought, Islwyn smiled, hugged her and said, 'With you here, what more do I need?'

He watched her as she set out then rearranged the personal items. Margaret didn't reply and he sensibly remained quiet, knowing how difficult it was for her to return as a housekeeper to the place she had once owned and called home.

★ ★ ★

The bedroom extension to the Griffiths's house that had been a bedroom for Frank and Ernie, was full of people from the overspill of guests from the small cottage. Once Barry had finished taking photographs, he and Caroline put an overexcited Joseph-Hywel to bed and tried in vain to find somewhere to sit and talk.

The air was frosty and the trees and grasses were glistening. Feet and hands were painfully cold, but they stood close to the goats' pen where they could see lights flooding the ground from doors and windows and hear voices filling the air with laughter and song. They kissed and then hugged each other. It was a time for the truth, they both knew that.

'I've always felt insecure about your loving me,' Barry said. 'I'm so different from my lively, charming brother. I feel dull by comparison, and I'm big and clumsy where he was light-hearted and as agile as a monkey. I loved him dearly and I can't imagine anyone being satisfied with me after loving him.'

'I've never escaped from the thought that you married me because you felt sorry for me and it was at a time when you were in shock after Rhiannon had left you.'

'You were never second best. It was never like that with me.'

'Neither were you, Barry. There's always something special about a first love, but it's you I want to spend the rest of my life with.'

'We've been fools, haven't we?'

'Afraid of opening out and admitting how we feel.'

'And now?' he coaxed.

'Now everything is going to be all right.'

★ ★ ★

The fire was almost out and no one bothered to revive it. Janet did notice it but the thought of trying to push her way through the ever swelling throng to do something about it made her decide not to bother. Everyone was red-faced and the room was like an oven anyway.

A few guests were already dozing in their seats; the thought of going out for some reviving fresh air was tempered by the thought that they would never find a seat when they returned.

Dora was sitting on an upturned log,

leaning against the wall with Lewis on the floor beside her. She became more and more uncomfortable and he pulled her down beside him, their closeness a much needed comfort to them both.

'We don't need this if anyone wants it,' Lewis said and a pair of hands grabbed the log, sat on it experimentally, groaned and threw it on the fire.

'Hey, you! That's one of our best seats!' Hywel growled.

The flames, revived by the added fuel, began to lick their way around the log, the sound and the smell of burning wood filled the room.

'Sod it,' Hywel muttered, gesturing indifference with a waved arm, 'our Frank can make some more over the weekend.'

'I heard that!' Frank retorted. 'Happy Christmas to you an' all!'

★ ★ ★

In the room above the living room where the wedding party continued noisily, Joseph-Hywel woke and listened intently. He was unable to work out from the sounds below, whether it was morning or still late evening. He felt at the bottom of his bed for the new cricket bat and ball given to him by Edward, and smiled happily.

He looked out of the window where the yard was lit with extra lights and with the glow from windows and door. It is morning, he decided. He could get up and play.

Stopping to put on slippers and a dressing gown he tiptoed down the stairs and through the kitchen, which was momentarily empty. He knew as soon as he went down that it was still night-time but now so wide awake he couldn't resist going out and trying out the new gifts.

Joseph-Hywel tried several times to hit the ball, and each time he succeeded he was taken further away from the house and the lights as he retrieved it.

★　★　★

Caroline and Barry came in to recover from the coldness of the night, grateful for the overfilled house and its warmth. They pushed their way to the foot of the stairs where Barry released her hand while she went up to check on her son. The noise was deafening but it was stopped within the space of second by Caroline's scream.

'Barry! Mam! Joseph isn't here!'

Caroline stood with her hands over her face, her eyes huge with shock. Barry ran up to look in the bedrooms, unable to believe her. He came down with a face like a mask.

'She's right, I've looked under the beds and in every cupboard.'

Lewis climbed over the stunned guests and took charge.

'Dora, love, you stay with Janet, the rest of you come and look around. Don't rush, we don't want to frighten him. He probably isn't far away. Call his name, softly mind; we don't want him to think he's heading for a telling-off, do we?'

What had moments ago been a group of inebriated, sleepy people, now galvanised into action. In twos and threes, Hywel, Barry and Caroline having already left, Lewis sent them all in every direction. Many, facing a walk home across the fields, were armed with torches. Others were carrying nothing more than a box of matches or a cigarette lighter.

Dora held the trembling Janet and spoke reassuringly to her. 'Caroline has been up twice since he was put to bed. He's been gone no time. He can't have wandered far.'

'What if someone has taken him?'

'What a daft idea, Janet!' Dora forced herself to laugh. 'More imagination than your Frank when he's talking to the coppers you have!'

'Look at the goats,' Janet shouted to the

372

last to leave. 'We sold the young billies last week. He might have gone to look for them.'

Dora said nothing but she knew that was the first place Hywel had looked.

* * *

Joseph-Hywel searched for his ball which had vanished in the straggling grass and low bushes at the edge of the garden. He stepped out into the lane and knelt down, feeling about but failed to find the round shape for which his cold fingers were groping. He moved as he searched and when he stood up he was no longer sure which direction would take him back home. Running, aware of the chill of the night air and with fear in his heart, afraid now of the darkness, he stumbled along the icily cold, empty lane, heading towards town and away from the Griffiths's house where searchers were spreading out and calling his name. Throwing aside his bat, he tucked his hands under his arms in an attempt to keep them warm, and thought of his safe, cosy bed.

* * *

Walking through the immediate garden and onto the lane, Edward and Megan turned to walk back across the lawn of the house but Megan stopped.

'I'm frightened, Edward. With Joseph-Hywel missing I need to ring home to make sure Rosemary is all right.'

Edward didn't argue. They walked along the silent lane where the low path and high hedges brought heavy frosty air to settle. Edward put an arm around Megan to give her extra warmth. Rising up out of the lane they came to the first of the houses of the town. There on a corner was a telephone box.

Curled up inside the booth, the door propped open by an abandoned milk crate, and wrapping his dressing gown tightly around him, was Joseph-Hywel. He was shivering, his night clothing insufficient protection from the sharp winter's night air.

At the corner, just yards away, Edward handed Megan a couple of coins but she shook her head. 'I'm being silly aren't I? Rosemary is perfectly safe at home with Mummy.' She began to turn back.

Edward pressed the coins into her hand. 'We're here now. You might as well ring.' He hugged her to show he understood and added, 'If you don't, then I will.'

'Oh Edward, you shouldn't indulge me in my stupidity. Let's go back to the party.'

The search continued, with Caroline and her family becoming more and more alarmed when the small cricket bat had been found by an exploring beam from a torch.

After half an hour had passed without the child being found, Hywel ran to their nearest neighbour and telephoned for the police to come and help find him. When they knew a child was missing and that he was insufficiently dressed, they turned out at once. Off-duty men were informed and came willingly to help.

The activity increased as word passed around the nearby houses and Janet watched the clock anxiously, wondering how long the little boy could survive in such icy temperatures.

Caroline was silent, hardly hearing when someone spoke to her. Then when she and her mother found themselves alone she said quietly, 'Do you think this is a warning? Is Joseph telling me not to marry his brother?'

'What a lot of nonsense, love. Can you imagine Joseph wishing anyone harm? Can you imagine him, the dear that he was, not wanting you and Barry to be happy?'

'I keep making promises to a God I'm not

sure I really believe in, that if Joseph-Hywel returns safely, I'll devote my whole life to him.'

Out of the corner of her eye Janet saw a movement as a group carrying torches and filling the night with excited cries, came towards the house. Quickly she said, 'Don't be too hasty with that promise.' Then as she became certain she went on, 'What if your Barry is carrying him this very minute past the goat pen?'

A jubilant Barry was indeed carrying the little boy, surrounded by a happy crowd. He was cosily wrapped in Edward's overcoat and chattering excitedly about the game of cricket he had played, confident and no longer feeling so cold. Fear had been driven out of his mind in an instant when he had seen Megan and Edward standing in the doorway of the telephone box and bending to pick him up.

A loud sobbing cry left Caroline's lips as she saw the group and realised that her son was safe.

She and Barry took Joseph-Hywel up to bath him while Janet filled hot-water bottles and made a warming drink. Within an hour the party continued but with a greater enthusiasm as they celebrated the fact that a near disaster had been averted.

At three-thirty in the morning the hard-core guests were finally leaving. Helen's mother had succumbed to the atmosphere of the evening and drunk too many offerings of port. She was lifted up out of her chair and helped home, and to her husband's embarrassment, his pompous and disapproving wife was singing a well-known nursery rhyme with words by Frank Griffiths.

Outside, someone made a jocular remark about the speed at which the wedding had been arranged and Ernie took offence. He and Frank piled into the man and Lewis and Edward, who were still relatively sober, tried to separate them.

Constable Gregory who was present, having come to escort his daughter home, decided at once to misunderstand the situation. He didn't want to arrest Frank and Ernie for fighting. Not on Ernie's wedding day. Instead, he threatened Lewis and Edward with arrest if they didn't cease immediately. They turned to stare at him.

'God 'elp us, Edward,' Lewis said. 'If they can't get us one way they'll get us another!'

He turned away and the man who began the fight called him an offensive name. Edward turned back to stop him as Lewis was about to land him a blow and they collided and fell to the ground.

'I didn't see that,' the constable muttered, leading Mair away. 'I never saw a thing.'

Edward was helped up by Megan and they wandered off. Dora offered her hand to Lewis but instead of rising, he pulled his wife down and kissed her. Later, hand in hand, they walked home through the lanes and across the frosty fields. From time to time they stopped and hugged each other. Dora knew this might be her last chance. She had to say the words that were so hard for her to admit. When they paused at the edge of the fields she turned to face him but lowered her head before muttering.

'Lewis, I have something to say.'

'Then I probably don't want to hear it.'

'Perhaps not, but I'll say it anyway.'

'Get it over with, then.' He was expecting her to tell him there was no chance of a reconciliation. Her words surprised him.

'Will you say that again, love?' he whispered.

'I find it hard to say, Lewis.'

'Try'

'I love you,' she whispered. 'I want us to get back together.'

'Thank heaven for that,' he sighed. 'And about time too you cantankerous woman you.'

They were laughing as they made their way back to Sophie Street.

★ ★ ★

On New Year's Eve, Lewis and Dora stood at their bedroom window looking out at the scene below. On practically every doorstep people were standing, talking and laughing and looking up at the sky. Arthur Harvey, a plumber, who was dark haired and already very drunk, was first-footing — going into house after house to be the first visitor of the New Year; a dark-haired man to be first over the threshold was considered to bring luck for the coming year.

As the ships' hooters continued to signal the start of 1956, a few cheers were heard. Then gradually the voices faded, doors closed, lights in the doorways and windows were extinguished. Across the road, Rhiannon and Charlie leaned out of their window, Gwyn visible beside them. They waved to Dora and Lewis in the house opposite, and blew kisses. Soon the lights were out in every dwelling except theirs. There was no traffic to disturb the stillness of the night. No voices calling. The brief celebration was over and silence fell like a soft mantle on the town of Pendragon Island. The light

across the road snapped out and soon
number seven Sophie Street was also in
darkness.

THE END

Other titles in the
Ulverscroft Large Print Series:

DEAD FISH

Ruth Carrington

Dr Geoffrey Quinn arrives home to find his children missing, the charred remains of his wife's body in the boiler and Chief Superintendent Manning waiting to arrest him for her murder. Alison Hope, attractive and determined, is briefed to defend him. Quinn claims he is innocent, but Alison is not so sure. The background becomes increasingly murky as she penetrates a wealthy and ruthless circle who cannot risk their secrets — sexual perversion, drugs, blackmail, illegal arms dealing and major fraud — coming to light. Can Alison unravel the mystery in time to save Quinn?

MY FATHER'S HOUSE

Kathleen Conlon

'Your father has another woman'. Nine-year-old Anna Blake is only mildly surprised when a schoolfriend lets drop this piece of information. And when her father finally leaves home to live with Olivia in Hampstead, that place becomes, for Anna, the epitome of sinful glamour. But Hampstead, though welcoming, is not home. So Anna, now in her teens, sets out to find a place where she can really belong. At first she thinks love may be the answer, and certainly Jonathon — and Raymond — and Jake, have a devastating effect on her life. But can anyone really supply what she needs?

GHOSTLY MURDERS

P. C. Doherty

When Chaucer's Canterbury pilgrims pass a deserted village, the sight of its decaying church provokes the poor Priest to tears. When they take shelter, he tells a tale of ancient evil, greed, devilish murder and chilling hauntings . . . There was once a young man, Philip Trumpington, who was appointed parish priest of a pleasant village with an old church, built many centuries earlier. However, Philip soon discovers that the church and presbytery are haunted. A great and ancient evil pervades, which must be brought into the light, resolved and reparation made. But the price is great . . .

BLOODTIDE

Bill Knox

When the Fishery Protection cruiser MARLIN was ordered to the Port Ard area off the north-west Scottish coast, Chief Officer Webb Carrick soon discovered that an old shipmate of Captain Shannon had been killed in a strange accident before they arrived. A drowned frogman, a reticent Russian officer and a dare-devil young fisherman were only a few of the ingredients to come together as Carrick tried to discover the truth. The key to it all was as deadly as it was unexpected.

WISE VIRGIN

Manda Mcgrath

Sisters Jean and Ailsa Leslie live on a small farm in the Scottish Grampians. Andrew Esplin, the local blacksmith, keeps a brotherly eye on the girls, loving Ailsa, the younger sister, from afar. Ailsa is in love with Stewart Morrison, who is working in Greenock. Jean is engaged to Alan Drummond, who has gone to Australia, intending to send for her when his prospects are good. But Jean shocks everyone when she elopes with Dunton from the big house . . .